Imagine if we created a new species.
What if it had a soul?
What if it were more intelligent than we were?
What if it escaped?

SECOND GENESIS

JEFFREY ANDERSON, M.D.

JOVE BOOKS, NEW YORK

THE BERKLEY PUBLISHING GROUP
Published by the Penguin Group
Penguin Group (USA) Inc.
375 Hudson Street, New York, New York 10014, USA
Penguin Group (Canada), 90 Eglinton Avenue East, Suite 700, Toronto, Ontario M4P 2Y3, Canada
(a division of Pearson Penguin Canada Inc.)
Penguin Books Ltd., 80 Strand, London WC2R 0RL, England
Penguin Books Ireland, 25 St. Stephen's Green, Dublin 2, Ireland (a division of Penguin Books Ltd.)
Penguin Group (Australia), 250 Camberwell Road, Camberwell, Victoria 3124, Australia
(a division of Pearson Australia Group Pty. Ltd.)
Penguin Books India Pvt. Ltd., 11 Community Centre, Panchsheel Park, New Delhi—110 017, India
Penguin Group (NZ), Cnr. Airborne and Rosedale Roads, Albany, Auckland 1310, New Zealand
(a division of Pearson New Zealand Ltd.)
Penguin Books (South Africa) (Pty.) Ltd., 24 Sturdee Avenue, Rosebank, Johannesburg 2196,
South Africa

Penguin Books Ltd., Registered Offices: 80 Strand, London WC2R 0RL, England

This is a work of fiction. Names, characters, places, and incidents either are the product of the author's imagination or are used fictitiously, and any resemblance to actual persons, living or dead, business establishments, events, or locales is entirely coincidental. The publisher does not have any control over and does not assume any responsibility for author or third-party websites or their content.

SECOND GENESIS

A Jove Book / published by arrangement with the author.

PRINTING HISTORY
Jove mass-market edition / August 2006

Copyright © 2006 by Dr. Jeffrey Anderson.
Cover design by Rita Frangie.

ISBN: 0-515-14198-4

JOVE®
Jove Books are published by The Berkley Publishing Group,
a division of Penguin Group (USA) Inc.,
375 Hudson Street, New York, New York 10014.
JOVE is a registered trademark of Penguin Group (USA) Inc.
The "J" design is a trademark belonging to Penguin Group (USA) Inc.

PRINTED IN THE UNITED STATES OF AMERICA

10 9 8 7 6 5 4 3 2 1

For Aaron

Acknowledgments

THERE are five people who made critically important contributions to this novel, whom I gratefully recognize.

My agent, Kimberly Whalen, enthusiastically supported the book's concept from the earliest draft and guided it through a violent metamorphosis to its present state.

My editor, Natalee Rosenstein, deserves all credit for turning the manuscript into a beautiful finished product. For all my readers who love a great story but do not spend pleasant nights recapitulating the mathematics of perturbation theory in population strategy spaces for zero-sum games, Natalee is your champion.

My reader, Karen Dionne, whose talented eye reviews and improves every page before anyone else is allowed to see it, was a crucial sounding board for the ideas, strategy, and characterization in the novel.

My scientific mentor, David Ferster, PhD, taught me modern neurobiology. In late-night experiments, while wrestling to impose order on the chaos of membrane potentials firing across our oscilloscopes, our conversations about what really happens in the brain during that earliest fog of perception were among the most exhilarating ideas

I have encountered. The excitement that something new is happening in contemporary neuroscience that will change the world forever could not be more central to inspiring this novel.

My wife Keri is my confidant, lover, companion, and colleague. Every idea in this book is the result of tears, flashes of inspiration, and affectionate debate from the conversations with her that make my life immeasurably happy.

Prologue

And the earth was without form, and void; and darkness
 was upon the face of the deep. And the Spirit of God
 moved upon the face of the waters. And God said,
 Let there be light: and there was light. And God saw
 the light, that it was good: and God divided the light
 from the darkness.

Too dark. Kenji Nakamura peered into the deepness.
His stubby fingers fumbled around the stage until they
closed on the switch and light flooded the eyepiece. *Much
better.* He slowly turned the diaphragm as a circular window of light constricted in the center of his field of view, divided from the surrounding darkness by a hazy perimeter.

And God made the firmament, and divided the waters
 which were under the firmament from the waters
 which were above the firmament: and it was so.

Nakamura rotated the 4x objective into position and adjusted the focus, first coarsely, then with greater precision until the bubble of water on the slide sprang to life from the microscopic world to his own. He dialed up the objective and focused up and down through the pool, dividing the water above the focal point from the water below until he decided his position was good.

> And God said, Let the waters under the heaven be
>   gathered together unto one place, and let the dry land
>   appear: and it was so.

He panned back and forth across the watery landscape, searching, scanning. A drop of sweat rolled off his forehead, and he paused to wipe his face with a Kimwipe from the bench. *There*. He scanned backward, then forward, then centered. A perfectly round island of land emerged from the watery void. As Nakamura rotated the objective to its highest setting, the cell was textured with wavy crabgrass over its surface. *So far so good*.

> And God made two great lights; the greater light to rule
>   the day, and the lesser light to rule the night.

After checking the coordinates, Nakamura advanced the wheels on the micromanipulator toward the center of the stage. The fire-polished electrode gradually came into view above and from the side of the isolated cell. A glint reflected from the blunt tip of the electrode like a light in the firmament, descending toward the sphere until it floated just outside the cell. Nakamura raised the attached tubing to his lips and sucked gently. The cell drifted toward and sealed onto the electrode. He proceeded to lower a second, smaller electrode from the other side toward the cell, this one with an angular, crescentic tip. As the sparkling glass electrode descended toward the globe, he twisted the wheels of the micromanipulator only microns at a time until the crescent tip hovered outside the egg.

> And God said, Let the waters bring forth abundantly the moving creature that hath life, and fowl that may fly above the earth in the open firmament of heaven.

With a deft spin of the wheel, Nakamura punctured the cell with the sharp electrode and sucked the meiotic spindle containing the DNA into the pipette. He carefully removed the electrode from the manipulator, replaced it with the electrode he had just prepared, and lowered the new pipette into position as before. He watched the dancing chromosomes within the pipette sway with the motion like winged fowl. As he depressed the plunger on the tubing, the new spindle wallowed into the nuclear fluid like a great whale submerging.

> So God created man in his own image, in the image of God created he him; male and female created he them.
> And God blessed them, and God said unto them, Be fruitful, and multiply, and replenish the earth, and subdue it.

Nakamura withdrew the sharp electrode and watched the spindle to confirm it was intact within the nucleus. Enthroned majestically in the center of the globe, the spindle dominated the cell, asserting its hegemony over the world it had come to inhabit and control. Once again, Nakamura raised the tubing to his lips, and this time breathed a slight puff of air into the chamber as the cell lifted off the first electrode and drifted away free into the slippery, barren environment. He knew that soon, very soon, he would coax the cell to multiply in two, then four cells, relentlessly reproducing toward an embryo. But for now, he simply watched the cell, so similar, yet so completely unlike anything he had ever seen. *Very good.*

> And God blessed the seventh day, and sanctified it:
>> because that in it he had rested from all his work
>> which God created and made.

He would get the cell to grow and multiply. And then he would rest.

PART I
THE EIGHTH DAY

In the Judeo-Christian view, humans were created by God and endowed with knowledge of right and wrong and the ability to choose between them. . . . Neuroscience presents a challenge to the concept of free will; as we gain a deeper understanding of the brain, it seems increasingly unlikely that the circuits responsible for making decisions are different in kind from those that underlie more lowly functions. . . . Neuroscientists should recognize that their work may be construed as having deep and possibly disturbing implications, and that if they do not discuss these implications, others will do so on their behalf.

—("Does Neuroscience Threaten Human Values?" Editorial in
Nature Neuroscience 1, no. 7 [1998]: 535–36)

And the LORD God formed man of the dust of the ground, and breathed into his nostrils the breath of life; and man became a living soul.

—(Genesis 2:7 [King James Bible])

ONE

Amazonia, Brazil

LEVINE was such an ass.

An ass and a flower child. Jamie Kendrick wasn't sure which was worse. By flower child, she meant botanist. By botanist, she meant pedantic, egomaniacal, fossilized waste of a National Science Foundation grant that should have gone to someone who could actually find his computer's on switch.

"Well, I don't usually turn it off." He smiled, looking down.

"I think that's a good idea," Jamie answered over her shoulder.

She knew his computer emergency would be a waste of her time. But in an outpost populated by only eight scientists and their support staff, a little patience went a long way.

She wandered back past the supply tent and went inside her own Quonset hut, her eyes lingering on the blanket heaped up on the cot. She glanced up at the clock and rubbed her eyes as she walked around the computer in the center of the room. The whirring of the latest batch of computations sounded like gerbils on a treadmill. She had to get a faster computer.

She stepped over a pile of clothes, picked up her small pack, and stopped at the coffeemaker on a wooden crate against the wall. She grabbed a stained, brown stein off its hook and shook it out twice. She'd picked it up while speaking at a conference in Zurich several years earlier. The tub of sugar was still empty, so she poured her coffee and stepped out again into the camp.

This time she heard the familiar hum of insects and felt the humid late morning air against her skin. She turned the corner toward the makeshift commons, and peeled back the mosquito netting over the entrance.

The day was looking up already. She saw Paolo sitting alone on a stump on the far side of the kiva, whittling at a block of fresh mahogany.

"Get you some coffee, sailor?" Jamie tried not to wince after her own bad line.

"I'm all right, thanks," said Paolo. He half smiled.

Paolo Domingo wasn't a sailor at all. He was a Brazilian native who for years had run a loose consortium of visiting scientists performing field research in the Amazon Basin west of Manaus. He was also harder to crack than a Brazil nut. Even after two years, Jamie had only recently begun to make any progress chipping away at his shell of polite formality.

From the beginning she had wondered just what lay beneath that excessively polite veneer. There were stories. One of the older botanists suggested once while drunk that Paolo was ex-military, maybe special forces. Considering the source, Jamie wrote that one off as campfire gossip.

A recently departed zoology intern had told Jamie that she had heard Paolo had a history poaching exotic birds. That one made sense. He certainly knew the forest, not in the way the scholars could name 114 species of flowering yucca, but rather he seemed to have some secret omniscience about the unwritten laws governing forest life.

The intern also told Jamie that Paolo was gay. At least that was the intern's conclusion after walking by him in a string bikini. *Only one glance*, the intern had emphasized, *and sort of a brotherly look at that.*

Jamie sat down on a crate across from Paolo. She dangled her foot over the cold ashes in the fire pit and looked through the mosquito netting into the forest. A cloud of mist drifted through the giant fern leaves at the clearing's edge, like hot breath through a predator's fangs. She took a sip from the stein.

"Lazy morning?" Paolo asked. He was a head taller than Jamie, with the sort of build that comes from spending a lifetime outdoors instead of behind a computer.

She envied his peaceful brown eyes. Even after two years, she could never look as comfortable in the forest as he did. It still seemed like an exotic wilderness. Not home. For Jamie, home was where you had high-speed Internet and Cocoa Puffs and endless stacks of journals. The Amazon rain forest didn't give a damn about accommodating mathematicians, even sophisticated ones like Jamie.

"Sort of. I was running simulations late last night."

"Anything new?" Paolo asked.

"Nothing. Don't have enough data yet." *And probably never would.*

"I'm still enjoying that banana pudding you made last night."

Jamie immediately wished she could retract the comment. Why someone as clearheaded and precise as she was would start babbling the most inane nonsense the minute she was alone with Paolo was beyond her.

"Thanks, I think." Paolo's smile was more overt this time.

She leaned forward slightly, hoping to use whatever smallish cleavage she had to advantage. "Any good gossip around town?"

Paolo looked pensive for a moment. "You know that research compound downriver? The one just past the Vicioso? Sure has been busy lately."

"No. Didn't know there was anything there. Wow, that's practically next door. How did I miss that?"

"It's on the other side of the river. I see it when I make supply runs. They tend to keep a low profile, but today there was a whole army out there moving some machine."

"What kind of machine?"

"Not exactly sure. Asked the dockhands, and they thought it was some kind of medical scanner like an MRI. But the only thing they could agree on was that it was big and heavy."

"MRI? That's got to be a first. In the middle of the jungle? Probably just an earthmover or something like that."

"Probably." Paolo folded his knife and stood up.

"Going so soon?" Jamie tried to sound disappointed.

"Need some fuel for the generators—thought I'd get a jump on it."

"Oh."

"Jamie," Paolo leaned a little closer, offering a hand to help her up. "It's good to talk to you. If you ever want to drop by after dinner . . ."

Finally.

She smiled and took his hand. "Love to."

JAMIE left the commons, kicking a tree root with her boot, and walked toward her research station, built a half mile deeper into the forest. The lab had cost her only $320 plus the instruments she brought with her to set up. Half had been spent on an aluminum ladder and some nylon rope. She had built the entire structure herself 120 feet up on an emergent evergreen tree. It was a fifteen-foot platform lashed in the crook of three sturdy branches. The structure gave her excellent visibility over the lower canopy of the rain forest, including a view of the banks of the Rio Vicioso as it infiltrated the rain forest to join with the Amazon River ten miles downstream.

Jamie usually preferred to make her observations early in the morning, before sunrise, when the cacophony of the forest reached its climax. Only in the early morning and late evening could she hear the most intense, deafening shrieks of the howler monkeys or the infinitely varied songs of over ten thousand distinct species of birds. This perch amid the tapestry of sounds used to be a shrine for Jamie, a religious experience in every sense of the word, where her work was performed in solitary reverence.

Now it felt more like the prayers in Latin she had never understood as a child. Her angst had surfaced a month earlier, after a power surge in a lightning storm had fried two months of population tallies. Half a bottle of tequila later, she started philosophizing, and startled even herself when her inebriated muse asked, "What the hell am I doing here?"

Her sober mind had no answers the next morning, and she slipped into a slow, painful questioning of her research, her ambition, everything that led her to trade a world-class academic pedigree as a population biologist for years of counting bugs and moths.

What had started out as the boldest, most expansive study ever in population dynamics had become dull, even trivial. To a mathematician, trivial was the worst kind of sin. Since college, she had built her life on one unshakable premise. She would make a great discovery—a truly original idea that would earn her a place as a scientist.

She couldn't get Paolo out of her thoughts. What did he have in mind? He probably thought she was a complete dolt. *Still enjoying the pudding . . .*

There was no way she was going to work now. She dropped her backpack by her tree and started into the forest at a brisk pace. She needed exercise. Her feet bounded over the humus, the collection of dark, decaying biomaterial that covered the rain forest floor. Scrambling around trees, she coaxed her muscles faster.

When she hit the Rio Vicioso she turned downstream and broke into a jog along the makeshift path on the riverbank, forgetting her fears, her research, concentrating on the rhythm of her breathing and the welcome sensation in her feet. It had been too long. An utter failure at the bar scene in New Haven during college, she'd taken up running steeplechase, at which she was modestly more successful. Of course that was years ago. Since she had arrived in Brazil, her workouts had spaced farther and farther apart until now her primary exercise was swatting mosquitoes.

She ran along the shoreline parallel to the rapids of the river. As she hurdled a fallen liana rooted to the shore, water crashed in successive waves over a submerged rock, spewing cool mist into the humid air. Exhilarated, she ducked through the spray while the irregular thuds of the waves pounded out the fibrillating heartbeat of the river. She jumped over the buttress of a large tree and then over a fallen trunk of another. *One more mile.* She forced herself to hold her pace as the frustration dissipated from her body.

Forgetting her destination, she ran forward, ignoring the growing pain in her legs until she tripped on a jutting rock and catapulted into the muddy brown river. Gasping for breath, she lunged to grab hold of a mangrove root and pull herself out. Prostrate on the ground like a consumed pilgrim, she panted and savored the pain, drunk with endorphins.

She spit the grit out of her mouth and raised herself up on her elbows, panting until her senses began to clear. Wiping the sweat and gnats from her eyes, she saw a metallic glint in the distance.

A fence? She looked again. What was a fence doing in the middle of the Amazon Jungle?

She picked herself up and limped toward the structure. It wasn't just a fence, but a massive barrier thirty feet high with five feet of barbs at the top that looked as though they had been lifted out of San Quentin. The behemoth stood in an artificial clearing perpendicular to the river and stretched from about ten feet into the river to out of sight in the distance. This had to be the complex Paolo was talking about.

As she moved closer she could see the wall was a durable chain-link fence with reinforcing vertical and diagonal steel beams. On either side of the fence, twenty feet of forest had been cleared away, creating an island of forest inside. Why would anyone do such a stupid thing? As if the roads snaking through the Amazon Basin weren't bad enough, now the forest is being parceled off?

A collage of graphs and diagrams captured her thoughts. While someone less fond of the *Journal of Theoretical Biology* might shrug at the fence, it was a personal assault to Jamie. A team of her colleagues during her postdoc with Martin Nowak at Princeton had undertaken a massive study confirming that the number of species that could exist on a given area was directly related to the size of the area. Thus, a network of roads or fences or similar barriers could dramatically limit the number of species the rain forest could support, wiping out up to half of them.

She grabbed a fallen liana and waded into the river. The water depth was well over her head, and she held on tightly to the fence as she secured the vine around one of the steel crossbeams. Fighting against the current with one hand while grasping firmly to the vine with her other hand, she turned her body in the water to clear the barbed edge of the fence.

Swinging around with a grunt, she clasped one of the crossbeams with both hands and rested as her vine swung off and bounced against the foaming river. Climbing out of the water, she then moved hand over hand horizontally until she could jump down to the riverbank inside the fence on solid ground.

After nursing what she was sure was going to be a wicked case of shin splints from her impulsive run, she limped into the darkness of the forest at a walking pace. The trickle of light that made it through the trees was just sufficient to see her way. Her training had made the forest familiar enough that it no longer looked the same in every direction, and she had learned to mark her path as she traveled.

Surprisingly, as she ventured farther in, she couldn't find a trace of whomever had built the curious wall. Everything seemed to indicate pristine forest. She turned back, deciding she would have better luck trying an approach from the Amazon side.

As she made her way back toward the Vicioso, she stopped. *Impossible.* She continued walking, laughing at her imagination. She hadn't taken five steps before she heard it again, louder.

She walked faster. The sound came again—rustling branches followed by a distinctive bellow. This time she whirled around, looking intently. A few seconds later she heard it again and pinpointed the location. Nothing there, but she was sure that in two years of field research, she had never heard this sound before, not here. Why should she have? This was the Amazon, not West Africa.

Her eyes searched the trees and were finally rewarded with a heavy rustle about one hundred feet up in the lower canopy. She had to be mistaken. It was probably just a sloth.

She continued to watch. Slowly, gingerly, the creature emerged from the tree. She completely lost her breath. It was definitely an ape. Anything that big was an Old World primate—gorillas, chimpanzees, orangutans, bonobos, even baboons and gibbons. There was nothing that large in the New World. Her eyes grew wider as she watched the ape climb down the tree and jump onto all fours on the forest floor. Then, she heard another rustle.

She looked up in time to see a slightly smaller animal, no less an ape, shimmy down the same tree. Two of them?

The smaller ape moved more slowly, and considerably more clumsily until it too jumped onto the forest floor and scampered over to the other ape with audible chattering. The larger ape put its arm around the smaller and the smaller nestled into the larger's fur. At this distance, there was no mistaking that these were either chimpanzees or bonobos. Was this mother and child? Is someone breeding chimps here?

She looked around her. Introducing apes into the Amazon was crazy. A delicate ecosystem like the rain forest would be sorely impacted by such a dramatic change. It didn't *feel* right. Although the climate was well suited for the chimps, they would be exposed to an entirely new set of foods and pathogens. How would they know what to eat?

The smaller ape darted away from its companion and raced over to pick up a large stone from the ground. Squealing in delight, the chimp scurried on all fours to a large tree trunk not far away from Jamie near a small clearing in the trees. He took the stone and set it gently on the tree trunk. Then, the chimp searched around and grabbed another stone. He scampered back to the clearing.

Jamie rubbed her eyes as the ape carefully balanced the

second stone on top of the first. The chimp looked back at its companion and let out a bellow. Then the chimp picked up a third stone, and successfully balanced it on top of the other two. Was this normal chimp behavior?

She continued to watch the chimp, who appeared increasingly delighted. He scurried back and forth, advancing his pace, quickly building two more towers of rocks on the stump next to the first. Then he looked around inquisitively. There was something unnatural, eerie, in his face. Jamie could only watch, fascinated.

The ape's eyes darted from object to object, finally settling on a sapling tree fern. The tree had several low-lying branches with broad leaves. The chimp reached for the leaves, and with a hop could just touch them with his fingers. He paused barely a second before lumbering over to a dead tree trunk in the clearing. With visible effort, he rolled the tree trunk underneath the sapling branches.

The chimp let out another bellow to his mom. Then he leapt on top of the log and grabbed the branches, pulling them down. They refused to give. Frustrated, the chimp tugged furiously. Still unsuccessful, he hopped down off the log and stared at the ground, as though looking for something. The expression on his face indicated he had found it, and a few seconds later he reached down and picked up two stones: one round, flat stone and one wedge-shaped rock.

He ran back to the log and climbed up, grabbing the stem to his coveted branches. With one hand holding the stem against the smooth rock, he took the sharp edge of the wedge-shaped one in his other hand and began smashing the stem between the two rocks. Soon the stem became badly frayed and yielded to his vigorous efforts.

Triumphant, he threw down the rocks and grabbed the branch that had fallen to the earth. The ape set the fern leaves on top of the three towers of rocks, over which it fit perfectly to make a fragile platform.

Jamie inched closer, watching from behind a clove of ferns next to a large tree. The chimp ran to the other side of the clearing and collected four passion flowers. He plucked each off the vine, and ran back to set them on the makeshift platform. The sunlight shone through the clearing like a searchlight onto the deep purple flowers. Jamie had to admit the result was stunning.

The chimp, having completed his shrine—*what else could it be?*—shrieked for his mother. Finding her, he ran over to grab her beefy arm and led her to the shrine, beckoning with his free hand and pointing toward the platform. The mother saw the flowers, apparently realized the youngster's prize was inedible, and paid them little further interest. Undaunted, the youngster continued to admire the construction.

Jamie shuffled her feet to better peer out from behind a tree at the edge of the clearing. The young chimp started and looked directly at her.

Jamie and the chimp locked eyes. She wanted to run, but couldn't. Unable even to breathe, she could only stare at the remarkable chimp.

He looked back for a moment, seeming neither concerned nor impressed. Then he lifted one arm, and to Jamie's further surprise, the chimp simply curled his fingers and waved her toward him.

Her fear overcome by wonder, she took a careful step into the clearing, sunlight roasting her damp clothes.

The chimp made no movement to approach, but instead

reached down to pick up a broken stick. Taking one step to the side, he cleared a patch of soil with his forearm. In the well-lit dirt he began to scratch with the stick. Taking a step back, he motioned Jamie closer again. She obeyed and took a few steps closer until she could see the patch of soil.

On the ground, in large block letters facing her, upside down to the chimp, was written,

WHO AM I

TWO

Chicago

NATHAN Hall sped his smoky granite Lexus SG 430 convertible up the Fullerton onramp to Lake Shore Drive. At 5:30 in the morning, there was only sparse traffic on outer Lake Shore, and Nathan dangled his arm out the window, diverting the wind toward his face, as he accelerated in the direction of the island of skyscrapers in downtown Chicago.

Nathan considered Lake Shore Drive the only tolerable road in the whole city. It had been one of the reasons he bought his condo in Lincoln Park, which was five minutes from the Drive, and fifteen minutes any time of day from his office on Jackson and LaSalle. The miracle of Lake Shore Drive was that it was a freeway stretching north from Chicago's Loop that fizzled out fifteen miles north into residential districts, sparing it from the swarms of suburban commuters that plagued the city's other freeways.

There were other reasons to settle in Lincoln Park. Nathan couldn't think of another place in the world where someone young and driven would find himself in a neighborhood of people so completely like themselves. The only admission test was that one was young, professional, and willing to spend a few evenings a year at Ravinia Park eating Gouda cheese at outdoor concerts, but working all of the other evenings of the year. Nathan passed this test with ease.

Nathan had moved to Chicago eight years ago to take a job with Goldman-Sachs as an investment banking intern. Having just graduated in economics from Berkeley, he was elated about the offer, especially when they agreed to sponsor him at the Kellogg School of Business.

He enjoyed the work, all ninety hours a week of it, enough that he stayed on after finishing his Master of Management degree at Kellogg and became the biotechnology section head at Chicago's Goldman-Sachs office. It was a quirk of fate, really, that led him into the biotech sector. The division was understaffed at the right time, and Nathan thought the field was volatile enough to give an investment banker both challenge and opportunity.

Two years later, he began having increasing conflict with upper management about his aggressive risk-taking, and two years ago had finally quit the company altogether to become an independent biotech fund manager. Starting out with a modest biotech/pharmaceutical mutual fund, he quickly secured enough clients to manage three risk-stratified funds with total assets over three hundred million dollars.

He made out like a bandit, and although most of his

wealth was tied up in unpredictable investments, he had enough cash flow to vastly improve his lifestyle over his Goldman-Sachs days.

The change in lifestyle had made him cocky and aggressive and created an instant addiction to wealth that was both insatiable and consuming. Until now, despite his staffing problems and the constant threat of a bad trade, he had felt on top of the world. His funds had outperformed the Nasdaq Biotechnology Index by 5 percent over the last two years, and Nathan knew luck had very little to do with it. But that was changing.

As he drove past North Street Beach and looked over at the blue waters of Lake Michigan on his left, he flipped on the satellite broadcast on his dashboard radio. His attention immediately perked up.

A woman's voice on the radio intoned:

> *The recent quarter percent rise in interest rates at the last meeting of the Federal Open Market Committee may well have another unexpected consequence. Genomic Engineering, one of the few remaining companies focused on medical stem cell research, announced yesterday that it would close its doors. The interest rate hike may have been the last straw for a company whose projection of profitability has finally advanced out of sight in the future. The collapse of Genomic Engineering is a portentous omen for the entire stem cell research enterprise, and particularly for BrainStem Therapeutics, a division of Soliton Industries that also has yet to predict a profitable quarter.*
>
> *The financial difficulty encountered by the large stem cell research industries is an unexpected turn from the*

last several years, where market capitalization has been buoyed by market optimism that dramatic medical therapies will eventually arise from such research. Many in the biotech finance sector have started to question more openly whether such hopes were unrealistic and oversold to investors. One analyst, Donald Harding of Goldman-Sachs, went so far as to say, "The entire stem cell research enterprise is financed by a bubble that is ripe for bursting. Like the nineties when Internet stocks needed little more than a prayer and a half-baked idea to obtain soaring stock prices, so the biotech sector today has invested in stem cell research out of proportion to its financial promise."

Nathan grimaced and muttered "idiot" under his breath. Donald Harding had been one of the main reasons he had left Goldman-Sachs. Nathan had been unable to convince Harding that stem cell research had a financial future, and their disagreement gave him no choice but to leave.

The woman's voice continued, "Whether this will be merely a realignment of the stem cell research industry, or is a harbinger that the technology is just not ready for big business remains anyone's guess. Reporting from Saint Louis, this is Susan Archer-Bentham for Associated Press news wire."

Nathan snapped off the radio as he navigated upper Wacker Drive and drove through the early rays of the sunrise toward his customary parking lot. He felt irritable and angry. A technology he had made his mark promoting was rapidly becoming a target for doomsayers.

Nathan waited for the elevator to climb to the forty-seventh floor and cursed under his breath. Was it time to

bail? He had worked for two years to build a biotech port-
folio, and now he was running out of viable companies.
He strode across the hallway, opening the glass door to
his office with a single motion, and slumped behind his
desk. Massaging his temples, he closed his eyes. One
thing was certain. He could stay the course alone, but he
was not risking being at the puncture site of the bubble
without knowing exactly what he was sticking his neck
out for. He reached for his keyboard.

In Nathan's business, information always had a price.
The reason he was successful was that he wasn't squeamish about paying a fair price for the right kind of information. He began typing.

<ENCRYPT>
To: Carlos Escalante <cescalante@earthlink.net>
From: Nathan Hall <nh@biomf.com>
Subject: BrainStem—Brazil
Message:
Flurry of new activity on BSTX Manaus site. New
scientists on payroll. Drake visit this week. Timing
inconsistent with substantia nigra project. New development on spinal cord regrowth? Need inside
information. Please see me immediately. Will make
usual arrangements for payment. NH.
<ENCRYPT>
<SEND>

THREE

Amazonia, Brazil

A dried plantain sailed across the room, scoring a bulls-eye on Skip Jordan's bald head.

"Wake up, boss."

After a few particularly ungraceful snorts Jordan's head began to bob and eventually surfaced above the final snore that lingered like fog in the room.

"What!" Jordan looked over his shoulder. "Jorge, go give yourself a swirlie." Jordan gave a condescending look of complete aggravation like he always did when Jorge came by. It was an act. They had a relationship of perfect symbiosis, however pathological it was. Jordan was the chief of security at BrainStem Therapeutics's Brazil compound. Jorge was a former banana picker from Manaus who had been hired on as a janitor in the complex.

Their first meeting hadn't been much more dignified. Jorge had come in to sweep the floor just as Jordan was finishing off a box of Ding Dongs, of which one had somehow become flattened underneath Jordan's swivel chair. Jorge cleaned up the mess spread uncomfortably close to the room's only occupant. "About time someone came in. This room's been a mess for three days. That's something we wouldn't have tolerated on the force."

"The force, sir?"

"Twenty-five years—Chicago PD. Seen things that'd make your skinny carcass hurl."

Thus began their peculiar friendship, with Jorge stopping by sometimes for amusement, sometimes out of simple curiosity to hear about Jordan's experiences. Jordan couldn't be more pleased than to have a young disciple to talk at, and showed this to Jorge every chance he got by putting him in his place. It had also become something of a game to have a story ready for Jorge each time he visited.

In truth, the stories were mostly hearsay from other cops, with generous embellishment at that. The main reason Skip Jordan was in Brazil now was that he had long since outlived his usefulness as a police officer. The last three years before being offered retirement he was valued considerably more by the greasy spoons he frequented than by the people of Chicago.

Over the years he had added more weight than experience, and his sleep apnea was graciously proffered as a medical disability for which he might take early retirement. Accepting the offer, he moved on to the corporate security beat, for which he was eminently qualified. Three years back, his supervisor at Soliton Industries had cornered him and asked, "How would you like to double your salary working someplace it never gets below seventy degrees?"

Today, Jorge just smiled and then pointed to the bank of TV screens on the far wall. "It looks like someone is paying you a visit?" Jordan jumped up and looked closer, squinting in a way that confirmed anything left unsaid by his physique. "What the . . . ? When did you see this?" He demanded of Jorge.

"Just now when I came in, sir. She is a very good climber, no?"

The figure of a woman three feet above a river, grasping a silver link fence and moving horizontally hand over hand, was clearly visible on one of about fifty television screens on the wall. As Jordan and Jorge stared, she took a few more sideward movements and leapt onto the riverbank inside the fence.

Jordan memorized her face. Rusty or not, he had spent twenty-five years on the beat, and he had a few reflexes to show for it. He bounded over to a filing cabinet across the room and began ruffling through papers, mumbling to himself and breathing noisily.

He grinned, and turned to Jorge. "Good eye, kid. Now this is strictly confidential, you hear. You better move out while I do my work and don't say nothing about this to anyone, right?"

Jorge waved and shrugged as he exited, leaving Jordan clumsily dialing a phone number.

"Dr. Nakamura, sorry to bother you, but this is Skip Jordan and I . . . Skip Jordan, chief of security . . . fine, sir. The reason I called is that I just spotted someone breaking into the compound . . . actually not he, sir. She . . . by one of the chimps, that one with the collar . . . well, I've already done that. Her name is Jamie Kendrick, and her bio should be in your security files . . . yes, I'll send an escort right away . . . I'll do that, sir."

JAMIE'S first instinct had been to bolt. She would have, except that her mind was too busy analyzing to panic. She had unmistakably seen the chimp clear away the patch of soil. The words hadn't been there before. No, she was certain it was written by the chimp, and written upside down for that matter. That much was settled.

Was this imitative behavior? That was still too much to swallow. It was too unusual a phrase to reasonably think the chimp had merely been observing someone writing. And the symbols were too complex for even a human to remember after a brief exposure. Jamie wondered if she could reproduce a phrase in Cyrillic or Mandarin by just observing it being written. No way. The chimp had been taught to produce the phrase. There was no other answer.

But what on earth would possess anyone to spend the time teaching a chimp to write "Who am I" to travelers who stray by maybe every few years? And what about the shrine the chimp had constructed? Sure, chimps have been known to use tools, but that was supposedly cultural training, not spontaneous innovation.

The chimp stared back earnestly, as if he were waiting for applause, *or an answer.* She felt as though she was being drawn into a bizarre existentialist play.

Jamie heard the snap of twigs on the ground. Her eyes darted through the clearing toward the source. Nothing. It came again and her ears finally tracked the sound. She spun to her right in time to see a rustle in a group of ferns to one side of a massive tree trunk.

A husky figure emerged, clad in an olive shirt and shorts with an obviously visible holster and sidearm. The man stepped directly into the clearing. "Dr. Kendrick, could you follow me please?" It was not a question.

Jamie obeyed, taking a last look askance at the chimp, and then back to the reality police or whoever it was leading her off.

"Could you tell me where we're going?"

"All of your questions will be answered shortly, Dr. Kendrick."

"How do you know who I am?"

The security officer just kept walking until they came to a man-made clearing in the trees, this one perhaps a half mile in diameter. Sitting in the center of the clearing was a structure the size of a large hospital. Four stories high and sprawling in its width, the building couldn't have surprised Jamie more.

"What is this place?" She scanned across the clearing to the building's most obvious exit. A door opened and a lone figure stepped out. Jamie and the guard walked directly toward the open door. As she approached, the man's Asian features became more distinct, and his face indicated he was definitely not pleased to see her.

As they arrived at the paved entrance, the man gave a curt bow and said, "Dr. Jamie Kendrick. Please come in."

"I'm afraid I'm not exactly dressed for a social call." Most of her fieldwork was done in shorts and a tanktop, but on top of that she was still damp from the river and covered with a film of dirt and sweat. She had a purple bruise on her right thigh where she had fallen against a rock in the water.

The man waited until Jamie was walking beside him,

the security guard falling several paces behind, and explained, "We saw your most agile entry on a security camera near the outer fence. We do have a front door, you know."

Jamie shrugged. "I tend not to do things the easy way."

"Why don't we talk in my office."

They walked some distance down a carpeted corridor and turned aside into a bank of offices. He motioned her into an austere but elegant office that strangely reminded her of her research advisor's office at Princeton.

There were two obvious exceptions: a picture of the man and what appeared to be his wife and daughter at Disneyland, and a wall hanging with flowing black on white Japanese script. Otherwise, the file cabinets, the stacks of books, the Sun workstation, and the simple black Formica desk might have been found in any university office.

The man closed a back door leading to what looked like a large bench laboratory and motioned for Jamie to sit down.

"Welcome to the Lula Da Silva Wildlife Preserve and the BrainStem Therapeutics research laboratory."

Jamie looked quizzically at the small man.

"Ah, the name. Most influential in securing a suitable tract of land, along with an appropriate expression of appreciation to the late president of Brazil. I am Kenji Nakamura, lead scientist at this institution. Please make yourself comfortable."

Jamie fidgeted under his stare, then sat down after a long pause. Nakamura sat as well, and leaned back in his chair. He shifted his weight, as though he was having difficulty finding a comfortable position. *Is he nervous?*

"I didn't even know this place was here until today," Jamie said.

"Indeed. Then perhaps I can start by telling you a little about us, in the interest of being neighborly." His tone was formal, distant. "We conduct basic science research on stem cells and related technologies."

His reply made her freeze. A hunch pushed its way into her mind, shocking her by its implications. *Could it be true?* She pushed the idea aside. "Why on earth set up a laboratory here? Isn't it easier to do that sort of thing in the States?"

Nakamura's face was inscrutable. "Several reasons. There are certain U.S. regulatory issues we find . . ." His voice trailed off momentarily. "Cumbersome. Moreover, most of our expenses are for personnel. Here we have a highly trained labor force for a fraction of the cost in the United States or Europe."

Nakamura rose to his feet, stepped to the window, and gestured outside. "Most important, for our research, we require a large number of chimpanzees. As an endangered species, chimpanzees are in short supply. We have addressed this problem by establishing our laboratory on grounds suitable for a large-scale chimpanzee breeding project, of which I believe you were a witness today."

Jamie slipped into a practiced academic tone. "The rain forest is a complex and delicate ecosystem. Introducing an advanced species like chimpanzees is completely unpredictable."

"Our chimps are fully contained within our compound, and will have no effect on the outside forest."

"Until they get out."

"Impossible."

"I got in easily enough."

"You are an excellent swimmer, Dr. Kendrick. Chimpanzees are deathly afraid of water. They can't swim. Not enough body fat. I assure you our chimps will stay on this side of the fence, at least until we know it is safe."

Jamie looked at the phone on Nakamura's desk. A plan began to form in her mind. *What did she have to lose?* If she was right, then this was the opportunity she would never forgive herself for passing up.

"Dr. Nakamura, I'm actually anxious to get back to the lab. Do you mind if I phone our lab administrator, just to let them know I'm OK? It was a little impulsive of me to wander off this morning."

Nakamura nodded graciously and returned to his seat, making no offer to grant her any privacy.

Jamie concealed a smile. *Never hurts to be a little paranoid.* She reached for the phone, dialed a number at random, and waited a few rings. "Hello, Paolo? Yeah, it's me. Sorry for not telling you I was going out today . . . no, I'm fine. I'm here with Kenji Nakamura of BrainStem Therapeutics. It's the complex down past the Vicioso . . . They're taking very good care of me; I hadn't realized I was on their property. Anyway, I'll be home soon . . . Thank you." She hung up the phone, her hand over the still-ringing receiver.

Nakamura bowed slightly, "In the future I must ask that you respect our privacy here—we can't accept the liability of visitors on our compound. May we offer you an escort back to your laboratory? We certainly wouldn't want anything to . . ."

Jamie straightened up and leaned into the desk, cutting

him off. "Dr. Nakamura, please tell me about the chimp I saw."

He froze, and Jamie saw in his face a brief glimpse of uncertainty. *Bingo.*

Gathering his composure, he replied, "I have already said we are breeding chimpanzees. What do you mean?"

"Well, I've seen a few chimpanzees in the zoo now and then and they don't tend to spell out words on the ground, or make art projects, or ask existentialist questions. Don't you find that curious?" She raised her eyebrows and smiled.

Nakamura's face sunk. "Art project, you say. Writing? I'll have to ask our chimp colony director. Most unusual, indeed."

She reviewed again her train of thought: stem cell research, chimpanzee breeding, BrainStem? It was a long shot, except she had seen it with her own eyes. If she were right, this would be the project of the century, and would sure as hell beat counting insects. *Here goes nothing.*

"It's just that I'm pretty sure there's something very different about this chimp. In fact, I'm so sure about it, that I'm more than curious. You might say I'm a bit obsessed with it right now. Because if there's something that really grabs me, I'm the sort of woman that likes to know more. A lot more."

"We'll have to look into it. Thanks for bringing it to our attention."

I'm crazy. He's not biting. Probably a bogus instinct. But that chimp. "Dr. Nakamura. I know what I'm proposing is a bit of a stretch, but I'm not coming up with anything else. You see, it crossed my mind when you said stem cell research that, well, what if a few of those stem cells got over the wall, so to say? What if these chimps had been modified somehow? Sounds funny, I know." She studied his face for a hint of expression. "But you see, it's the sort of thing that I find very interesting, and if it were the case that you have some sort of a modified, maybe transgenic, animal, I'd sure love to be involved in that research."

Nakamura stared right through her eyes. "Let's just suppose that what you're saying were possible. What would a field biologist have to offer such a project?"

Jamie swallowed hard. *It's true!* "Perhaps a great deal. I bet you haven't had a lot of research take place on what the environmental impact would be for bringing these chimpanzees here? It might be helpful to have a world-class population biologist arguing on your behalf should the issue ever come up in the wrong context. You know, environmental activists wondering about it, and all."

Nakamura pursed his lips, then paused. "That's a very gracious offer. Perhaps we could consult with you if such a situation were to arise." He smiled as if to offer closure.

Time to drive it home. "Or maybe I'm not making myself clear. I'm amazed, Dr. Nakamura, at what you seem to have done. It's the sort of thing I've always wanted to be a part of. I could be a resourceful partner. And I want in. I want it so much that I'm willing to work for free. I've got plenty of grant funding and a lot of experience looking at population dynamics in the Amazon." She paused. "You might be surprised what a gracious colleague I could be." She sat back in her chair and folded her arms.

Nakamura looked down, as if weighing the options. "Why should I trust you?"

"I'm a good scientist. Look in your file. You don't get to where I am without knowing how to do good work. I care about this idea, Dr. Nakamura. And my scientific curiosity hasn't come out of its tailspin since I saw your chimp's performance. Don't get me wrong. I'm a tough woman, but I can play by the rules."

Nakamura closed his eyes and thought for a long moment. It was all Jamie could do to not press her hand further.

He finally looked her in the eyes, resolutely. "I might consider a limited partnership. I could bring you on as a consulting scientist, and if I see evidence that you can be a team player, have something to offer, your role will expand. I can offer you a small stipend, an office. But this has to be with one condition: this experiment is strictly confidential. I don't want too many people working on this project, but I can be gracious as well and you have obvious enthusiasm. And as it so happens, we are having a few problems obtaining enough chimpanzees for our research. An appropriate," he lingered on the word, "endorsement from a respected scientist may indeed be helpful in quieting some troublesome concerns."

"Deal. You tell me who's on your back and I'll handle them."

"And I want you to know that if things don't work out, this will be a very short-term arrangement. I'm taking you in only because your ambition and perceptiveness suggest you may be a valuable colleague. Is that understood?"

"Completely."

"And one more thing, Dr. Kendrick. Field biology is a very different world from genetic engineering. There are different challenges when you not only try to describe the world, but change it. Some people don't like the idea of change. They think we shouldn't 'play God,' so to speak. I can't have someone like that working on my team."

"Since when was anything truly useful ever achieved without changing the rules just a bit? I can take the heat, or I wouldn't be asking to play."

"Mr. and Mrs. Tate?"

Richard and Hiroko Tate nervously stood up from their seat on a divan against the far wall and walked up to the reception desk. As they approached, Richard slid his hand clumsily over his wife's slender forearm. He was about to speak when the receptionist, a young, motherly woman in a khaki jumper, came to his rescue. She smiled at them and said, "Would you follow me, please? Dr. Batori's office is right this way."

The elegant feel of the waiting room had surprised Richard. It seemed more like a bank lobby than a doctor's office. Even more surprising was the check-in experience. He had already pulled out his pen and insurance card expecting to be handed a clipboard with a list of irrelevant questions in fine print when the receptionist had said warmly, "You won't need that today. Please just make yourself comfortable and I'll let Dr. Batori know you're here." Only one other couple was in the waiting room, and they were studiously avoiding eye contact with the Tates after a brief initial glance. The other couple was obviously expecting, a fact not lost on Richard.

A few minutes and a few uncomfortable glances later, the receptionist had summoned them. She led them not to an austere white exam room, but to a subdued study featuring a tasteful mahogany desk and a few impressionist prints of young girls at the piano and the seashore. Dr. Batori, dressed in a green business suit, stood and smiled with an authentic, disarming expression as she walked around the desk and shook each of their hands. She motioned them to sit down in two very comfortable chairs in front of the desk, and she then joined them in a third in front of the desk as well.

Kate loathed the routine. Each new patient visit made her feel like a cheap actress doing laxative commercials for a living. But she was a supreme actress, and instinct took over. "Why don't you tell me about yourselves?"

The passive look on Hiroko's face seemed to confirm that she had no intention of speaking first, and Richard began, "We've been married three years now. We met at a costume party about eight years ago for unemployed programmers." He gave a tentative laugh that the doctor reinforced with an understanding nod. Kate studied his expression while he talked. He was a thirty-five-year-old former geek, she gathered, who had probably made a good deal of money joining a start-up Web company sometime in the late nineties. After his company had folded, he probably had taken two years to travel, spending most of his wealth thinking he could easily find a new job. He had then awakened during the following recession to find that he no longer cared about wealth and prestige, and proposed to the first woman he had seriously dated.

Richard went on to describe how they had been trying to get pregnant for a year and a half without success, had tried fertility drugs to no avail, and had worried about whether they would ever be able to have children. Kate listened patiently, although she already knew everything he told her. One of her smartest business decisions was to hire a former nurse to work from home on all new patients' medical histories. Whenever someone would schedule an initial appointment, her staff would as a matter of routine request records from previous physicians. Since her patient base was almost exclusively referrals, patients came with detailed records. Her records specialist was well trained to sift through all of these and condense the patients' history, labs, and pertinent study results in a two-page document that was waiting on her desk the morning of their appointment. The summaries were invariably complete, and Kate knew exactly how to proceed with each patient before she ever met them. The interviews and physical exams were just to build trust really, nothing more.

Kate was one of dozens of in vitro fertilization specialists in San Francisco. Even in such a crowded market, however, she was easily booked months in advance given that she was one of only five hundred physicians in the country actually board certified in reproductive endocrinology and infertility. Ironically, her private and professional lives couldn't be more dissimilar. She had never anticipated marriage, certainly never children, and she guarded her independence like a Siberian tiger. Tall, imperious, and confident, her attractive build was overshadowed only by her sense of infallibility.

Richard finished his unpolished summary of their medical care and looked at Hiroko as if to give her permission to speak. She did. "Dr. Baskin was optimistic you might have other ideas that could help us to have children." Her voice was accented, but precise and intelligent. Kate sensed in her a clear, organized mind, and a pleasant personality.

Kate explained, "I will need to examine you, Mrs. Tate, in a minute, but I wanted to discuss with you first some of the options you have. After reviewing your history and laboratory results, I am very confident that we should be able to help you to become pregnant."

Kate rehearsed her usual speech. Although her office advertised various services, Kate knew that her only function as a practical matter was in vitro fertilization.

The fact of medical economics was that she received patients from other obstetricians who invariably pursued the same course with every patient. Kate knew, though most patients did not, that obstetrics had an unwritten practice guideline: a couple trying to conceive for six months to one year unsuccessfully would have the same standard workup by any obstetrician. The woman would be screened by checking various hormone levels. The partner would have a semen analysis performed. Except in cases where an easily correctable problem with ovulation or hormonal milieu was found, the couple would begin a trial of clomiphene citrate and occasionally with gonadotropins. Several months later, if unsuccessful, they would be sent to Kate.

Although infertility had dozens of causes, the final common solution was always in vitro fertilization. That suited Kate fine, since IVF was well reimbursed. She gave the pretense that the problem was complex with dozens of issues to consider, while in fact she simply ran an IVF shop. Her practice, under her excellent business instincts, had become well organized. New patient appointments were always scheduled at the same time as six-month follow-up appointments for successful pregnancies whenever possible to give patients the impression that fertility was inevitable as soon as they walked into the waiting room. She knew her clientele, and had designed her office to cater to the taste of a highbrow population. In downtown Palo Alto, couples didn't generally enter her office who couldn't afford to pay her fees, and what was more priceless than a couple's first child?

Kate's speech was polished and had the desired effect. She discussed various medical treatments, factors that were likely responsible, and then led the discussion to the efficacy and safety of IVF in her hands. She briefly described the procedure, what would be involved, and what the Tates could expect from the process. She asked if Richard or Hiroko had any questions before starting a physical exam.

"You said that Hiroko would have to take some drugs to make her release eggs for the process. Do they have any side effects?" Richard asked in a concerned tone.

Kate uncrossed her legs and folded her hands in her lap. Her erect posture had been perfect throughout the interview. It was remarkable how at each interview the same questions seemed to be asked, often in the same order. In a reassuring tone she answered, "Most of our patients don't report any significant side effects. The drugs we use to help harvest the eggs used in the procedure can occasionally cause some nausea or flushing, but these effects are usually transient. The one thing we do watch for is something called ovarian hyperstimulation syndrome, which can be serious. This occurs in less than one percent of patients, and in the few cases where it does occur it can generally be treated successfully by stopping the drug and giving supportive care until it subsides."

Hiroko seemed very anxious to ask a question and finally voiced, "When a baby is born through in vitro fertilization, is it more likely to have genetic defects?" She appeared to feel guilty asking the question.

Kate responded promptly. "It doesn't appear from the data that IVF itself poses any risk of genetic anomalies above baseline risks predicted by a couple's age and family history." She leaned forward and appeared thoughtful. She steepled her fingertips together and continued with a more academic discussion. "For couples particularly concerned about this possibility, we have a state-of-the-art genetic diagnostics facility. During the early stage of growth for the embryo, we have the ability to isolate a single cell from prospective embryos and perform genetic testing on them. The technology is quite sophisticated. By amplifying the DNA from one cell, we can screen for over two thousand common mutations known to cause genetic diseases."

"Are there any laws about screening embryos?" Richard sounded a little defensive, and Kate took this to mean that it was something that had crossed his mind before.

"Actually, no. This technology is far too new for a legal framework. More important to us, however, is that we use the technology in an ethical way," Kate said with a smile. She continued, "It is a matter of policy in our practice that we don't use this technology to screen for gender or obvious physical characteristics of the infant. We feel it is better to avoid any question of ethical impropriety."

Hiroko and Richard nodded piously in agreement. Hiroko investigated further, "If a couple were to find that all of the embryos suffered such a defect, what would happen then?"

Kate was unfazed by the question. "We would have the technology to repair the defect and grow a normal embryo with the corrected gene. Our collaborating laboratories are the finest in the world for such delicate manipulations. We have the ability to correct in vitro single regions of DNA in a small group of living cells such as an embryo. Perhaps a more difficult ethical question is whether the parents would want to know about a genetic susceptibility that they might not even know they have, say something that increases their risk of early cancer or Alzheimer's. This is even more concerning for defects the parents can't necessarily do anything about." Kate paused for effect. "Our policy in such a situation is to determine before genetic screening is ever attempted whether the parents would like to be informed of a genetic susceptibility should one be found and corrected."

Richard shifted position anxiously. "I don't suppose you could make the baby a bit smarter while you're in there?" He laughed awkwardly.

Kate hid her surprise by looking deeper into Richard's eyes. The question had caught her attention in an unmistakable way. An instant later her composure had returned. "Perhaps someday, Mr. Tate."

The Tates had no additional questions, so Dr. Batori led them to an exam room, stating warmly, "Please get ready Mrs. Tate; I'll be back shortly."

KATE walked back to her now empty office to find the telephone ringing. She picked up.

"Dr. Batori."

"Oh hello, Kenji, how timely to hear from you." Kate twirled the cord in her fingers. "I heard on CNN last week that BrainStem is going public. You didn't tell me."

Nakamura paused on the other end. He resumed awkwardly. "A purely administrative detail that does not concern me. How's your practice?"

"Couldn't be better, Kenji. But you know perfectly well that the practice is just a diversion while life's more interesting opportunities unfold."

"You and I, Dr. Batori, find individual patients too narrow a focus for our life's work."

"Kenji, you're acting like a sophomore asking me to dance. I'm still enthusiastic about the project. Are you calling me to tell me you need more?"

"You are as perceptive as ever, Kate. Yes."

"Fine. We're destroying a batch next week. Same address?"

"Yes. Thank you, Kate. And I'll send you a set of vectors."

Kate fell silent. "What are you telling me, Kenji?" She tightened the cord around her finger.

"It is a success. Beyond anything we discussed."

When the receiver clicked several minutes later, Kathryn Batori was trembling—aroused, exhilarated, and alive with power.

FIVE

JAMIE walked across the compound with the kind of knot in her stomach she hadn't felt for a very long time. Wandering through the empty dining hut like a sleepwalker, she fumbled through the cooler for a banana. Slumping into a chair, she stared at some crates along the far wall while she mindlessly peeled the fruit.

She could feel her self-assuredness draining from her. The stunt she had pulled with Nakamura was the most impulsive thing she had done in her life. She trusted her instincts, but never to this degree. She couldn't believe she had been right. Even more unbelievable were the implications of what being right meant.

But it was exactly what she wanted, what she *needed:* a chance to really make a difference. She'd been processing what it would mean for the Amazon to have a new species of primate. It would mean changes in the food web, new territories for predators; it definitely could be destabilizing as populations shifted in response. The perfect setup for studying population dynamics, and that was totally aside from the chimp itself.

There was something more, something important just beyond her reach about the idea. It was about the chimp. She shook her head, but couldn't seem to get her mind around it. Yet she knew this was big, really big.

Maybe this was how it happened. You do your best to design good experiments, chart your course, and then something totally unexpected comes along and if you can just recognize what's landed in front of your nose, that's how big discoveries are made. Well, she wasn't about to pass this up. What else was she going to do? Start over?

Her prime was already spent. At thirty-one, she had a better chance of starting a career in fashion modeling than mathematics, where discoveries made after the age of thirty were the exception, not the rule. That couldn't be helped. She'd had a rough start.

Jamie grew up in a suburb of South Bend, Indiana. Her father was an accountant. Her mother was crazy—not take off your clothes and dance in the street crazy, but depressed, hopeless crazy. She'd also suffered from endometriosis. At least that was how her mom had explained her lack of children to the women in the neighborhood.

Life in South Bend was about football, basketball, and religion. Since her father knew no more about basketball than he did football, Jamie's family was defined by the only thing left in her community, the church.

Being an only child in a devout Catholic suburb was like being overweight in Beverly Hills. Girls in school would sometimes invite her to go camping so she could experience what it was like to have a real family. Even worse, it seemed clear that her mother had one child more than she was ready for, so Jamie dutifully accepted the responsibility of entertaining herself.

Desperate for hard-earned smiles from her mother, she was the first one of her peers to recite the catechism, the only one to read the entire Bible, and the last to drink beer. Approving smiles were no more frequent in high school, so Jamie immersed herself in academics.

Her gift for science was matched only by her persistence. Honors accumulated faster than she could absorb them, her father happily taking credit for her aptitude in mathematics. By the time she had entered college, she had acquired the self-confidence to shatter her father's dream of her attending Notre Dame, and she took the bus to New Haven and Yale.

Her entire foundation crumpled like a house of cards in college. Every moral fiber she had absorbed under the pious tutelage of her parents was plucked out by fellow students, who took great pleasure in corrupting her any way they could. She ultimately pushed nagging doubts about her faith into her subconscious where they slowly festered, and she withdrew again into her studies.

Unable to make sense of the universe, she made it her quest to seek enlightenment by discovering something wonderful that would push back the veil just far enough to make her life mean something more than the perfunctory lives led by her parents.

Maybe at last she had found just such a discovery.

She snapped out of her daydream. She had been so preoccupied with the chimp that she completely forgot Paolo's invitation. She got a sick feeling in her stomach as the realization set in that she had received not one, but *two* big breaks today. And they seemed to be leading in very different directions.

Would chasing after this chimp mean leaving the outpost, leaving Paolo? For two years she had respected him, unlike most everyone else who had come and gone at the research station. She hadn't needed anything from him. She just liked watching him from a distance, liked the stories he told over dinner, liked the way he didn't complain about the mosquitoes.

Only, it seemed that she had been thinking about him more and more. At least, she had been making more and more a fool of herself in front of him. Leaving half a banana on the table, she walked out the door and headed toward his cabin. The knot in her stomach began to tighten, and she knocked on his door, half believing she would just turn around and walk back.

The door opened. "Hello, Jamie." Paolo's too-perfect English, the main hint that he was not a native speaker, sounded surprisingly loud in the evening stillness. He offered a crooked smile as he rubbed his eyes with his fist.

"I hope I'm not bothering you."

"No, not at all," he answered hastily. "Why don't you come in? Can I get you some coffee?"

Sailor? She completed in her mind, cringing at the thought. "Sure." She stepped inside, closing the door behind her. "You sure you're not too busy?"

"Nothing much. Just going over some inventory."

" 'Cause I can come back . . ."

Paolo looked over his shoulder and said, "Sit down. I'll be just a minute." He motioned to a chair over by the desk—the sole chair in the room. He disappeared into one of the two other doorways in the sparse dwelling.

"Take your time." Jamie slowly walked toward the far wall. She fixed her gaze on the wall.

She studied a collection of wood carvings just above eye level. Several grotesque figurines stared at her. *Probably Yanomamo Indian.* The artwork was unsettling and captivating, alien and primal. Juxtaposed next to the figures was a large mahogany cross of expert craftsmanship. When she lost interest in the artifacts, Jamie wandered to the opposite wall and sat on the floor, curling her elbows on her knees.

Paolo noiselessly reemerged with two tin cups. He handed her one, then sat cross-legged in the middle of the floor opposite her. He sipped his drink, saying nothing, just watching her. After a moment he asked, "What's up, Jamie? Do I finally get to know why you've been acting so withdrawn for weeks?"

"You noticed."

"Chalk it up to my subtle powers of observation. Not exactly like you to spend hours a day doodling on a napkin after breakfast." He smiled with a genuineness that was utterly disarming. Although of large stature, Paolo never seemed the least bit imposing. He came across even to strangers like an older brother, someone you felt safe with, comfortable with. He was the sort of person you felt understood you completely whenever you spoke with him, but who left you with the sense that you hadn't scratched the surface of what he felt, believed, or loved.

Perhaps what mystified Jamie most about Paolo was the uncertainty whether he was just remarkably simple and pure, or rather incredibly complex and deep. Few people felt any doubt, however, that he was one of the most attractive people they had ever met, with huge eyes that were impossible to look at once and then forget.

"I guess my work just hasn't been going too well. I can't seem to make sense of all the data. I had always assumed once I had the numbers, the answers would just fall out . . ."

"You're just beginning. I'm sure you'll make sense of it soon."

She swallowed. "I don't know quite how to say this, Paolo, but I'm going away for a while, maybe for good."

"You're kidding."

She shook her head. *Was he disappointed, or just surprised?* "I went inside that compound you mentioned to me by the Vicioso and the Amazon."

Paolo seemed genuinely surprised. "Really. What did you find?"

"It's a research laboratory. Stem cell research."

"Interesting. Why so secretive? Did you talk to anyone there?"

What could she say? She promised to keep it a secret. "I really don't know all of the details. I suppose that's just how corporate labs operate." Paolo's skeptical expression made it very clear he knew there was more to the story. She continued. "Actually I did speak with their lead scientist there. Someone named Nakamura. He seemed to know who I was already, and offered me a job studying a population of primates they're working on."

"Seriously?"

Definitely disappointed.

"I'm going back tomorrow for an orientation into the project. They supposedly want someone to look at the environmental impact of introducing new species to the rain forest."

"And you're going to do it? What about your research?"

Jamie looked into his eyes, searching, questioning, longing. She nodded. "It'll have to wait. I need a break anyway; the project hasn't been going very well."

Paolo's eyes were trancelike. The five feet between them felt like five inches. There was a long pause. Paolo took a sip of coffee and looked back at her. "Tell me about their project."

"It's cool. I'm under contract not to say anything about it yet. It's just . . ." *Should she tell him anyway?*

"Just what?"

"I just can't bring myself to think of leaving. I've grown to like it so much here."

"What will you miss?"

She looked away. "The camp, I guess. My treehouse. Your stories over dinner . . ."

"Jamie, I'm not sure if this job is right for you, but if you decide to take it, of course you would always be welcome to come by." He paused for a moment. "You'll be missed. I will miss you." The warmth in his voice added to the confusion in Jamie's head. After daydreaming about conversations like this for months, she could hardly believe it was happening. And that it was too late.

"What keeps you here?"

"I've spent fifteen years more in the jungle than out. This is home to me. What else could I ask for than to be where I love, have interesting people to talk to. There's something very spiritual about life in the jungle, you know."

"Yes, I know." She stood up and turned to the side, taking a few steps toward the darkened window. "Sometimes I wonder what I really want from life. I love what I do, but it's a lonely job. You seem so sure of what you want."

He stood up and followed her to the window, putting his arm around her shoulder. "I want everything, Jamie." He looked down at her and stroked her cheek once with his other hand. His look was kind. *Wistful?*

Jamie turned to face him, her mouth only a few inches from his face. She felt herself drawn to him, moving closer, unable to think over the pounding of her pulse in her throat. She closed her eyes.

He slid his arm from her shoulder as he whispered, "Jamie, you know what the best part of being in the rain forest has been?" Her eyes snapped back open. "God is here—nowhere else more than here."

Jamie wrinkled her forehead at his statement. "What do you mean?" She whispered the question.

"Every day when I wake up, I feel like the forest showers light on me. Every day someone is trying to send me a message, trying to tell me that somewhere, close, in this forest is the answer to life. It's as if something is about to happen here that will make everything else in life trivial: something primal, something beautiful, something transcendent."

"I've felt that too, only I suppose I wouldn't call it God."

"Do you think this is where life began? Where humanity began?"

"In the rain forest?"

He nodded.

Jamie thought for a moment. "Yes, I think it must have, or someplace like it."

Paolo returned his full attention to her face. "I hope

you stay Jamie, but if you go, I hope you don't forget the forest—what it's like."

She stared out the window and then up at him. Her breath on his face, she said, "Thank you. I'll let you know what happens tomorrow." She stood for a minute with their arms touching, and then slowly turned to leave, unsure what else to do.

"Jamie," he called back to her. She stopped. "Please be careful, and come back."

"Goodnight," she turned to say, and then silently slid out the door into the night. After a few steps, she leaned against a cluster of trees, and bit her lower lip. Then she started to cry.

SIX

THE next day Jamie met the transport at sunrise as arranged on the bank of the Amazon. Though five miles farther than the Vicioso, the broad stable waters of the Amazon were infinitely more maneuverable than the fast flow of the Vicioso, so Jamie met the ferry where it had dropped her off along the well-marked path to the research station.

They traveled downstream in solitude for about an hour until the boat pulled into an alcove in the river leading to a large, paved road. An empty jeep stood waiting for them. A few minutes later, they were driving through the dense jungle when they emerged into a clearing with the laboratory complex looming suddenly in front of them. She was escorted inside to a bland conference room.

Inside the conference room were seated three individuals. Kenji Nakamura looked much the same as the last time she had seen him. In addition, she saw a middle-aged man wearing tailored shorts and a checkered shirt with a braided belt, and a young man dressed in khaki shorts, a blue sport shirt, and canvas shoes.

The third man, clearly of Indian or Pakistani descent, peered out through pop-bottle glasses that mitigated his very large eyes. His moustache was slight, as though it had been shaven sometime in the last two weeks. Excitement was the pervasive feature on his otherwise academic face. Before Nakamura could gracefully stand to introduce them, the third man was already on his feet and offering his hand to Jamie with a sing-song accent. "It is a pleasure to meet you, Dr. Kendrick. Welcome to our little jungle."

By that time Nakamura was standing, and with an imperceptible bow of his head spoke to Jamie. "Welcome back, Dr. Kendrick. As we discussed, this is Dr. Sameer Gupta, our staff primatologist and director of the chimpanzee project. And this," Nakamura pointed to the other man, "is David Mercer, the CFO for Brain-Stem Therapeutics."

"Welcome," Mercer said warmly.

Jamie smiled at each of the two men, and shook Mercer's hand as well when she managed to escape Sameer's enthusiastic grip. "A pleasure to see you both."

Nakamura continued, "I have taken the liberty of arranging a tour this morning of our facilities. Dr. Gupta will show you around. I am sure he will be most effective in answering your questions. Several of the senior staff will join you for lunch. I shall look forward to speaking with you again this afternoon. After your tour, Mr. Mercer will take care of some paperwork and help you get settled in."

"That all sounds very efficient," Jamie replied with a hint of rebuke.

"If you don't mind, there are some experiments that require my attention this morning and I shall need to be excused." Not waiting for a response, Nakamura bowed and exited the room.

"Don't mind him," said Mercer. "Not much for protocol, but a damn good scientist."

Jamie nodded.

"I do wish he'd tell me when new staff arrive. I'd rather you had a more organized welcome. Just found out myself, but don't let that stop you from making yourself at home. I'm sure Sameer will give you a nice tour."

He struck Jamie as a political animal to the core; something about him was too perfect, too well-groomed, too Disneyified. "Thanks," she said.

"I'll look forward to talking a bit later, then." He said good-bye and left Jamie with Sameer.

Not in the least put out, Sameer quickly restarted conversation. "Well, Jamie. May I call you Jamie? Dr. Nakamura has told me a great deal about you and your work. Most impressive, I must say. I am glad to have a new colleague, as I admit to being completely at a loss for what step to take next in our project. You see, so far everything has been very successful, but I do not know at all what the ramifications would be should we expand our little chimpanzee village beyond the compound. But I am getting ahead of myself. Shall we go for a walk?"

Jamie nodded assent, pleased that Sameer was talkative.

Hopefully he would be more informative than Nakamura. She still felt like he hadn't given her half the story. Then again, why should he?

Before long they had emerged again from the laboratory building in view of the rain forest at the edge of the clearing. Jamie asked him about how he came to be involved with the project, and found that he was approached by BrainStem seven years ago when he was working as a postdoc in Old World primatology at UC San Diego.

It was his second postdoc, and he was studying evolution of primate mandibles. In reality, he was trying to seem busy while he looked for a job, something rarer than the specimens he was studying. It was clear to him after a year of searching that the field was flooded with tenured professors, with very little funding for departments to hire new faculty. Having trained in India made his search that much more difficult.

His break came when a friend who was a great ape exhibit manager at the San Diego Zoo called to tell him a corporate laboratory was looking to establish a large-scale chimpanzee colony, and that he had suggested Sameer's name to them. When the human resource manager from Soliton Industries finally called, Sameer jumped at the chance to interview and quickly left his postdoc to take a position that was hardly what he had trained for but paid significantly better than anything else he would be likely to find.

The first years on the project had been intense. To this day, Sameer had no idea how it was possible to acquire so many chimpanzees so fast. Not only were chimps expensive, but they were in very short supply. Most incredible of all was that someone, somehow, had managed to obtain fifty sexually mature female chimps as part of the total.

However they were assembled, Sameer saw the magnitude of his problem as soon as they began to arrive and the facilities were constructed. First, the chimpanzees were wholly incompatible, coming from entirely different regions of Africa and various zoo colonies. Not only was there no intrinsic social structure to the new colony, but the traditions and cultures of the chimps were so strikingly different one from another as to make integration a supreme challenge.

Second, the executives who had dreamed up the project had no concept of how difficult it would be to adapt the chimps to a new environment. The chimps were mystified about what to eat, where to sleep, and more often than not withdrew into despondency or became extremely aggressive, charging every other chimp, or human, they contacted.

Sameer had begun by simply supplying the chimps with bananas, plantains, and various indigenous Amazonian fruits with a protected, remotely operated feeding station. Although most of the chimps caught on fairly quickly, some never did, wandering around aimlessly looking for familiar food sources. Several of the chimps died during the initial transition.

To Sameer's frustration, the laboratory executives had insisted on keeping a segment of the population housed in the laboratory out of his control, including more than two dozen of the healthiest breeding females, for reasons they could or would not disclose. After several months, the chimpanzees showed no semblance of forming a cohesive population. With the exception of a few familial units who arrived together, the chimps formed no partnerships, showed no interest in mating, and displayed not even the minimal grooming and partnering with zoo chimpanzees.

Things finally changed when Sameer began to limit the food supplies. Forced to compete for available food, the chimpanzees turned murderously competitive. Although such behavior had been seen before in the wild, Sameer was appalled at the extent to which the male chimpanzees would go to claim superiority among their peers.

Whereas in the wild, a dominant male need face only a limited number of aggressive challengers to maintain station, the lack of a social hierarchy made the competition brutal. On three occasions, Sameer was forced to watch as closed circuit cameras showed an aspiring chimp killed in a charging display by another chimp. Two more were found dead out of the vicinity of the feeding stations.

Several months later, however, a particularly aggressive male that Sameer had named Rambo began to dominate. Other chimps quit attempting to feed before Rambo had finished, and offered him the deference expected in chimpanzee society to a social superior. Once this critical transition had been made, other males seemed to line up nicely along the social ladder, and some semblance of society emerged.

Within a year and a half, the chimps were displaying many of the typical fusion/fission characteristics of previously observed chimpanzee colonies in the wild. Small groups of chimpanzees would roam together, with splinter groups joining and leaving the main body. Pairings began to form as the social order became more defined, and a frenzy of mating ensued. Females coming into estrus would mate aggressively with nearly every male in the colony daily, roughly in order of their social status.

The problem had remained for Sameer to teach the chimpanzees to subsist on new food sources. At first, even before the social ladder had emerged, Sameer had tried moving feeding stations close to fruit-bearing trees. This had literally no effect, the chimps not at all noticing the difference, nor recognizing the trees. The chimps similarly ignored ant and termite colonies and made no effort to hunt small animals.

When food became scarcer, some of the chimps did begin to climb more trees, exploring as though looking for familiar terrain or foods. Finally, Sameer found the trick. He obtained a ladder at night and tied fruit from the feeding station up to a fruit-bearing tree of the same type, making a virtual "fruit trail" to the upper branches.

He told Jamie how exhilarated he had felt when he finally saw chimps through his field glasses in the trees eating natural fruit. For the next month he did the same each night into a dozen different types of fruit-bearing tree. After nearly two years into the project, the chimpanzees independently sought out indigenous fruit trees and were no longer dependent on the feeding stations. By this time, his presence had become familiar to the chimps, who no longer threatened nor retreated when he was spotted. The chimps had still no propensity for eating insects or other animals, but had more or less formed a stable colony and adapted to subsist in the Amazon.

Two years into the project, another disaster struck when seven of the adult males and four of the females died of an illness that swept through the colony. Sameer for a time was overcome with the possibility that the wasting illness could decimate the entire colony. A few weeks later, however, the disease passed and the colony was intact.

That same year, one of the females that had been kept inside the lab reemerged with a male offspring. Sameer was told only that one of the laboratory females had become pregnant, and they wished the youngster to be raised in a natural environment. The mother slowly adapted to the new environment, and the youngster thrived. Frequently at first, and then more rarely, the infant was taken back into the laboratory for observations, but then returned.

On one occasion, the infant was fitted with a radiofrequency collar for tracking, and then sent back. The infant had been peculiar in the sense that it seemed much less agile and more dependent than the other young chimpanzees born in the colony, but it survived and began to grow.

By the time three years had come and gone, with new chimps continually added to the colony until the total population reached nearly one hundred, Sameer found his job had become much less stressful and much more enjoyable. Able to observe the colony more closely, he had few demands on his time besides observing, studying, and some administration, which was exactly how he liked it. He concluded his summary to Jamie by remarking in his characteristic accent, "Those were wonderful years, having no responsibility but to watch the chimpanzees grow like family. But I began to get bored. So I set up the nursery. And everything changed."

"The nursery?" Jamie questioned.

"Yes, we're almost there now. I thought we might start the tour there," Sameer continued. "The idea was that I had failed miserably in teaching the chimps to do so many things that chimpanzees did in the wild. They would not fish for termites with a stick, use tools to open difficult fruits, or make cups from leaves for drinking. I thought that if I could teach some of the younger chimpanzees in a sort of nursery school, I could have better success in letting them teach others these skills."

"I see." She was still waiting to hear about the genetically altered chimp.

"I selected a chimpanzee that was approaching an age of weaning and could spend short periods of time away from its mother and started my lessons. Ah, here we are. Please tell me Jamie if this is boring you. I understand my work of late may not be relevant to the questions you want answered."

"Not at all. I'm very curious about the chimpanzees' behavior and how you taught them to adapt to a new rain forest. It's all quite remarkable, really. A terrific piece of work." Sameer led Jamie around the corner of the far edge of the building into a fenced alcove on the far side.

Sameer opened the door to the fenced area. As they entered, Jamie noticed a hinged door near the ground, a little too small for a person to enter, that she assumed was the entry for the young chimps. Inside the alcove was a swing set, complete with tire swing, a slide, and climbing bars. Next to the swing was a huge collection of picture books strewn across the floor. On the opposite side was a small television set. A chalkboard was set up on the far side of the room across from the door. A pile of drums, cymbals, trains, dolls, blocks, spaceships, puzzles, and assorted toys were littered across the room like in a toddler's playroom.

Jamie laughed out loud. "Sameer, what a good little daddy you are! But I thought you were teaching them to fish termites?" She chided him with a teasing look one might give to a man at a bridal shower.

Sameer's expression showed no amusement, just excitement and earnestness. "Jamie, what has happened in this nursery I cannot explain. It baffles me still. Nakamura tightly restricted with whom I may discuss it after I told him. That is one of the reasons I am so anxious to have someone else who can help me understand what has happened here. You see, the lessons didn't go at all as planned. The termite lesson was my first project. I had an anthill in the corner, and tried to teach the chimp to poke a stick in to fish out ants."

Understanding dawned on Jamie as she sensed they were coming to the point. "The chimp you chose to train. Was it the one with the collar?"

"Yes, how did you know?"

"Let me guess. The lessons went better than planned."

"The termite lesson took all of ten minutes. I was dumbfounded after spending six years trying to teach the adult chimps the same thing. I thought I was a genius— all the credit to the teacher."

"And then you moved on?"

"Exactly. Within the first week, the chimpanzee could use every tool documented in wild chimpanzee colonies and more. I started to think I was dealing with Washoe's brainy cousin or something."

"Washoe?"

"The chimp who was the prototype for teaching sign language to apes. Sorry, an inside reference."

"Oh. So what exactly have you taught this chimp?"

"Jamie, the chimp seems to learn more quickly than I would have thought possible. At first, I attempted very short lessons that taught only practical skills. I thought surely the chimp would quickly lose interest without constant prodding and food. Just the opposite. I couldn't keep him out of the nursery. I brought in more and more supplies. He seemed to love to look at the books in particular. He would bring books to me and sit on my lap and point to the pictures until I would read them aloud. He spontaneously began drawing some of the pictures in the book on the chalkboard. All that would have been merely quaint, had I not pressed further." Sameer's accent became almost unintelligible as he boiled over with excitement.

"Sameer, are you telling me a five-year-old chimp can process symbols?"

"Jamie, the chimp can read. I swear it. I still cannot believe it possible, but the last two months I have become convinced. I have on several occasions been reading to the chimp where he cannot even see the page, and he will walk over to the chalkboard and write the words for items in the story. This last month, the chimp can write the numbers from one to twenty on the chalkboard in sequence, and has even been able to memorize some simple arithmetic. I feel like I am losing my mind, not being able to tell anyone about this."

"Sameer, I have met this chimp before." Jamie told him of her encounter in the forest.

"Remarkable! Perhaps that is why Nakamura was so eager to have you part of the project." Sameer quickly recanted. "Not to say that your scientific contribution would not be invaluable . . ."

"Sameer, who knows about this chimp?"

"As far as I know, only Nakamura, you, Mercer, a few of my staff in some vague detail, and Roger and his partner."

"Roger?"

"He has only been here a few weeks now. Roger Stiles, a neurophysiologist of some repute whom Nakamura has hired to come investigate the chimp."

"Can we talk with him?"

"I think he was planning on lunch today. I believe he had even planned on starting some experiments today you can ask him about. I have not had much opportunity to meet him myself beyond simple greetings."

"Sameer, what has Nakamura told you about this chimp?"

"He has stated that the chimp is the product of a small genetic manipulation, two or three small genetic alterations is all. Hardly a possibility for explaining such fantastic behavior."

"Something about him is nagging at me. Something incredibly important that I just can't . . ." Jamie appeared thoughtful for a moment, and then changed the subject. "I guess I'm still absorbing the whole idea. It seems we still have some time before lunch. I would love to see some of the chimpanzees in the wild."

Sameer smiled back and answered, "I assure you that you will not be disappointed."

* * *

A small plane uneventfully touched down on the landing strip at Manaus Airport. After taxiing to a stop outside the terminal, the plane popped open its door while a staircase was wheeled up to the opening. Soon passengers began filing off the plane onto the paved runway below and into the neighboring terminal.

As the passengers entered the terminal, a few veered off to waiting family members or relatives. Others passed directly through to the baggage terminal or various airport counters. A group of tourists with matching T-shirts began gathering in the center of the terminal, chattering among themselves.

A man in a checkered sport shirt and slacks stepped out of the sunlight into the terminal and removed his sunglasses. The man was well built, about five feet ten, with an angular jaw and short, curly dark hair. His eyes effortlessly scanned across his new environment. Pressing ahead of the crowd, he found an information counter where he asked in English, "Where could I find transportation about one hundred miles upriver to a scientific outpost?"

"On the Negro or the Amazon?" the clerk asked back in a thick accent.

"Amazon."

She pulled out a faded, worn paper and scratched a few notes onto another blank slip of paper, which she promptly handed to the man. He strode over to the far end of the terminal where two employees were loading bags off a cart onto the floor. Recognizing a garment bag and a black suitcase, the man stepped across the floor and retrieved his bags. He flashed his claim checks at the two employees, who appeared as though they couldn't care

SEVEN

"**YOU'LL** feel a little stick, dude," Jeremy Evans cautioned as he deftly slid the tip of a 25-gauge needle into the left buttock of the chimpanzee. His arm covered in a sleeve-length monkey glove, he quickly withdrew his hand from the caged enclosure and latched the door shut. "All right, Rog. He's got 300 of ketamine on board now. We should be ready to intubate in a couple minutes." The chimpanzee let out a bellow as Jeremy walked over to the anesthesia cart and began assembling equipment.

After a brief pause, Roger Stiles looked up from his workstation terminal and replied, "That's great, Jeremy. I'm reviewing the pulse sequences, and the magnet's ready to go. How was your walk?" Stiles's British accent was a sharp contrast to Jeremy's lazy West Coast speak.

Jeremy threw his arms apart for emphasis. "This place is wild. You scored some gig." He enjoyed how Stiles never quite seemed to know how to respond when he slipped into his raspy waistoid voice. He enjoyed it even more because Stiles was otherwise never at a loss for a response. Ever since Jeremy interviewed for a postdoc position with Stiles at King's College in London, Stiles had earned his reputation as a pit viper. A very pleasant, funny pit viper, but with a tongue no less forked.

Stiles's lab was an obvious choice for Jeremy. Having just finished his PhD in neurophysiology with Kamil Ugurbil in Minnesota, Jeremy was ready to move someplace that wasn't winter nine months a year. More importantly, Jeremy wanted to do no holds barred research on the cerebral cortex, and the only investigator he knew who could run the whole spectrum from intracellular brain electrodes to functional imaging was Roger Stiles. Although Stiles was relatively young, he had managed to publish an impressive collection of papers before landing a faculty position at King's College.

Jeremy was really only well trained in functional imaging, and was hoping to branch out. When Stiles had received the offer from Nakamura to come "check out a genetically modified chimp in a Brazilian lab," Stiles took the offer at once. He had mentioned to Jeremy in passing a few days later, "Hey, Jeremy. I'm going to collaborate for a month or two down in the Amazon with some molecular types. They need someone to run some experiments on a genetically modified chimpanzee. You want to come or stay and finish the attention paper?"

"Whatever, dude. The bananas here suck." Jeremy had joined Stiles on the plane the following week, and they found themselves in the middle of a tropical rain forest, something more exotic than either had imagined after spending years in a sterile laboratory.

The chimpanzee had slumped down to all fours for a minute and now lay on his side motionless. "C'mon, Rog. Let's tube this guy before he wakes up in some kind of a bad trip," Jeremy called over.

Stiles and Jeremy worked quickly to lift the monkey onto the sliding table on the MRI machine, start an IV, and begin a fluid drip. There was an intensity about neurophysiology that Jeremy's molecular neuroscience colleagues would never understand. Being able to listen in on a live subject to the brainstorm of electrical activity at the animal's core was like listening to radiation from the edge of infinity or smashing particles to see what was inside. It was the great question of life they were answering.

A blood pressure cuff, ECG leads, and a pulse oximeter were placed on the chimp's arm, chest, and ear, and a patient monitor on the far wall lit up with data showing the animal's heart rate, blood pressure, and oxygen saturation. As Stiles pushed the syringe with paralytic into the IV, Jeremy intubated the animal with a fiber optic scope and connected a plastic tube from the anesthetic gas pump to the monkey's paralyzed body. The chest wall rose and fell rhythmically with the click of the respirator.

Stiles, meanwhile, was busy placing a dozen fiber optic electrodes on the monkey's arms, legs, hands, and torso. Each of these was clamped into a long cable that led into an anteroom housing a National Instruments board on the back of the main computer. The computer terminal showed the complicated circuit diagram of the homemade Lab-View program running the experiment until Stiles hit a few keys and the elegant user interface appeared. The net result was impressive. Over fifty wires or cables emerged from the monkey's still body into a shielded collecting tube along the side of the table and into various slots on the apparatus computer.

At that moment, the door to the main room opened, and two figures stepped in talking. Their conversation was immediately cut short when Jeremy shouted violently across the room. "Stop right there! Don't take another step!" He extricated himself from various cables and bounded across the room to stare at the startled faces of Jamie Kendrick and Sameer Gupta.

"I'm very sorry. We didn't mean to interrupt. We were just looking for Dr. Stiles . . ." Sameer's voice stammered.

"Come outside with me." Jeremy ushered them outside the door like a bouncer. Once outside, he calmed down instantly. "Sorry about that, guys. I just need to check that you don't have any pens, hair clips, or any other metal objects before you come in. We haven't got all of our warning signs up on the door, but there's an 8-Tesla magnet in there and I don't want any bullets flying across the room."

JAMIE relaxed once she understood the reason for the attack. She searched through her pockets and dropped a few coins and her keychain outside the door. When they walked back inside, Jeremy returned to work without another word. She looked at Sameer. He shrugged.

"Be right there," Stiles called over. It was a minute or two before he stopped fussing with the chimp and washed his hands. He strode to Sameer and Jamie and said, "Sorry for the delay. Setup is taxing. Difficult to break away sometimes. Let's go inside the control room . . ." A nauseous wave of recognition crept over his face. "Oh, no. I totally forgot we were to lunch today. Please forgive me, Sameer. And this must be?"

"Jamie Kendrick." She smiled and reached out to shake Stiles's hand.

"Ah, Ms. Kendrick. A pleasure, indeed. Kenji tells me you do some wonderful things with population biology."

"Yes, that's right."

"Fascinating stuff. I'd love to talk about it some time. A real mathematician is always welcome in my lab. Jeremy, quit being such an ogre. Come talk to the nice people."

Jeremy ducked into the control room and finished tightening a few dials on the ventilator, glancing over his shoulder at the patient data monitor as he worked.

"Hey there, good to meet you," Jeremy added as the group moved into the anteroom.

Stiles gestured to his partner. "This is my postdoc, Jeremy Evans. A first-rate scientist who plays an MRI like a violin. Come to think of it, he actually plays the violin very badly. This is Sameer Gupta, who I think you've met once, and Jamie Kendrick."

"Cool. D'you come to see the fireworks?" Jeremy called out.

Jamie answered, "I'd love to watch. Is that the chimp—the transgenic? Seems very peaceful now, wired up like a porcupine." She pointed through the glass window to the huge, doughnut-shaped MRI scanner.

Stiles nodded. "Our basic setup for an initial screening. Today we're just trying to get some mapping data, nothing fancy. The idea is to map out the parts of the brain that process vision, hearing, touch, and so forth."

"How does it work?" Sameer asked.

"It's like this. We present carefully calibrated visual stimuli through those goggles and measure exactly what area of the brain is used to process vision. Then we do the same for sound and touch with the earphones and electrical stimulators. By using such a big magnet, we can get spatial resolution of a tenth of a millimeter."

"Is that good? I have no idea," Jamie admitted. She had a good feeling about Stiles. *That was important. She needed allies if she was going to earn her place.*

"It's spectacular. The best medical images available now use a resolution of ten times that much. Our technique lets us see things ten times faster as well, by using what's called initial dip imaging, which is critical if you want to do the mapping quickly. We've also developed a way to boost the signal in our images even above normal BOLD contrast by infusing magnetic nanoparticles."

"I'm totally lost," admitted Sameer.

Stiles looked apologetically at Jamie and Sameer. "Oh, sorry. BOLD stands for blood oxygen level dependent contrast. It's quite an amazing discovery, really. It turns out that the MRI signal has a built-in sensitivity to oxygen in blood. When the brain gets all excited about something, the brain cells start using a lot of oxygen from nearby vessels. The difference in oxygen level in the blood is enough that you can actually see a difference in the MRI signal. This fact has turned MRI from just photography to a technique that can show you brain activity at any tiny speck anywhere in the brain."

"So you not only see the brain, but can see what it's doing?" Sameer concluded.

"Not exactly, but you can see how vigorously the brain is doing whatever it's doing. The catch is that this oxygen signal is so tiny that the noise in the signal drowns it out. That's why we use such huge magnets, and contrast agents like we're injecting to enhance the small signal to something we can detect more reliably. We've done a few chimps before and have some good control data. This is our maiden voyage on this new scanner."

"Hey! What about yesterday?" Jeremy pretended to be hurt as he walked into the control room.

"Oh, sure. Yesterday we had Jeremy in the rig—not anesthetized unfortunately. Sometimes half the battle is getting the patient to shut up. Everything worked beautifully until he started thinking dirty thoughts and his brain clouded up right in the machine."

"Very funny," Jeremy responded. He grabbed a felt-tip marker off the desk and walked back into the magnet room.

"This is some setup." Jamie leaned against the table housing the computers, where she studied the interface Stiles had been using.

"I sure apologize about missing lunch. By the way, I assume Jamie has somehow managed to clear Kenny's draconian security clearance about all this?"

"Oh, Nakamura. Yes." Sameer dismissed the concern. "I'm very excited to figure out what is really going on with this chimp. Jamie and I had an excellent discussion earlier. It appears she too has learned some incredible new abilities of our furry friend."

"Don't mind Sameer," said Stiles to Jamie. "He's a bit excitable. I say a chimp's a chimp, however they open their banana. Clever little guys, I agree, and this one's probably just a bit of a fast learner. We really have underestimated chimps. Their brains are remarkably similar to

ours. A bit more parietal cortex and a little more bulk up-
stairs and that chimp would be the one giving the trave-
logue with me on the table. So what do you call this
chimp anyway, Sameer?"

"I guess I haven't yet given him a name. Perhaps
Roger would be nice."

"Easy, kid." Stiles gave a half smile back as he began
typing commands on the keyboard. While he typed he
looked at the chimp. "Seems like the resemblance is better to Kenji. Who's your daddy, eh?"

Jeremy strolled over and shut out the lights, darkening
the room except for the dim lights from the three computer terminals in the room.

Sameer rubbed his eyes. "It doesn't work in the light?"

Stiles shrugged. "We're neurophysiologists. We always
work in the dark." His answer implied no further explanation was necessary.

Sameer asked, "What's that loud clanking sound?"

"Oh, that's the gradient coils reversing in the magnet.
Annoying as hell. Be glad you're on the outside." Stiles
pushed a few buttons on the touchscreen monitor. "I've
programmed an initial T1 scan to look at the anatomy before we move on to the functional images. We should be
able to see something soon." Stiles looked back at the
chimp. "All right, little monkey, put your head in the big
loud machine for the nice man."

As Stiles spoke, a grayscale image of a cross-section
of the monkey's brain popped instantly onto the screen.
Stiles blinked a couple of times, and stared at the image
for what seemed a very long time. He finally spoke into
the microphone projecting into the magnet room. "Jeremy,

we must be getting some motion artifact. Can you check the paralytic?"

"Infusing nicely, no muscle tone, and no artifact in the CO_2 tracing. He's paralyzed all right, Rog."

"It must be an artifact. Could this be motion from respiratory or cardiac pulsations?" Stiles queried.

"Naw. Motion sensors look clean to me. What are you seeing that I'm not?" Jeremy asked.

Stiles snapped back, "Then let's repeat the T1 sagittal." Jeremy walked to the far side of the room where the patient monitor controls were housed. He hit a few keys on a touchscreen keyboard, and the clicking resumed. A few moments later the image was replaced by another, almost identical image on the screen.

"Jeremy, is this some kind of joke? Are you feeding me yesterday's file?"

"Gee, thanks Rog. I may have animal strength and courage, but I would think you could tell the difference."

Stiles seemed not to hear him at all. "Come over here, Jeremy, and tell me what you see." Beads of sweat formed on Stiles's forehead. Jeremy opened the door and walked in.

Jeremy strolled over and peered above Stiles's shoulder with Jamie and Sameer. After an initial glance, he muscled in and stared at the screen. His face changed instantly. "Jimminy Christmas, you're right. The images are real, Rog." Jeremy quickly stepped back to the far terminal and began typing in commands.

Stiles ordered, "I want maximal quality images—what can you get from 8-Tesla? Give me a volumetric acquisition with quarter millimeter cuts in all three planes down to C3. Try a shorter echo train and increase your number of excitations. Make some surface reconstructions of the cortex, too."

"Already working on it. This'll take a few minutes, Rog."

Jamie's curiosity finally got the best of her. "What's going on, Roger? What is so urgent? The chimp's not going anywhere."

"Look at this image and tell me what you see," Stiles said.

"I don't know—a cross-section of the brain up and down."

"Look at the foldings of the brain here. The part of the brain responsible for most of the higher functions is called the cortex, and it's spread over the surface of the brain like a thin film about two millimeters thick. Most of what's inside the brain is really just wiring between spots on the surface. The real important stuff is all on the outside. Evolution has allowed us to cram a very large surface area into our brains by folding it, kind of like wadding up a piece of paper to shrink it down."

"So what is so unusual about that?" Sameer asked.

"The way a brain is folded is species-specific. Any human will have, with only minor variations, folds in roughly the same places. The folds in the brain even have specific names. The same thing holds for animals. There are differences between a macaque and a chimp and a gorilla, for instance, but any two chimp brains should be, to a first approximation, carbon copies of each other."

"Are you telling us the folds are in the wrong places?" Sameer asked.

"I'm telling you the folds are so different that there is not the slightest resemblance to a chimpanzee brain."

"Are there more folds than there should be?" Jamie pressed.

"About four times as many, and that's not all." Stiles pointed to the image. "This distance from here to here should be roughly half of what it is. The entire skull has been remodeled in this animal to accommodate a larger brain. The cortex and the cerebellum, here and here, have been disproportionately increased. The brain is so tightly folded it looks like a giant walnut. I've never seen anything like this."

Sameer added, "Now that you mention it, that chimp does have an oddly shaped head compared to the other young chimps. So what you're seeing is that the brain resembles a human brain more closely than a chimp's?"

"Not at all. If anything, there is perhaps more cortex than in a human. The rest of the brain is about the same size as in a human child of similar proportions. The topography is entirely unique, however. I haven't a clue how such a thing could occur."

Jeremy was typing furiously. "Boss, I think you are going to want to see this. I'm sending the reconstructions over now. I've superimposed my own brain in red."

The other three watched on the monitor as a gridwork picture emerged showing the three-dimensional configuration of the cortex. The green meshwork figure was shown of slightly larger size and increased folding to a red meshwork image superimposed.

Stiles spoke first. "Jeremy, I never thought I'd get the chance to prove you had the brains of a monkey."

Jamie closed her eyes. Things were happening so fast. She could hardly believe that just a few days ago she had known nothing about the chimp, the lab, the discovery that had already changed her life.

Jeremy said, "Say what you want, Rog. But that picture is going to be on the cover of *Nature*."

"No," Jamie said. Her heart was in her throat as her mind furiously made connections. The picture that emerged was so staggering, so overwhelming in its scope that she could scarcely imagine it was all real. "You don't get it. This isn't about a *Nature* paper."

"Well, *Science* then. I don't care," Jeremy answered.

"What do you mean, Jamie?" asked Stiles, ignoring Jeremy's comment.

Jamie took a deep breath. "No, this isn't about business as usual. This is about the most fundamental question modern science has ever answered. It's about God."

"Keep your pants on, Jamie. We're all excited, but . . ."

"It's about the human soul, spirit, essence, whatever you want to call it."

"Slow down, Jamie. You're waxing philosophical," Stiles said.

"No. Philosophy is over. As of today, the last great debate of philosophy has just entered the domain of science."

"How so?"

"What separates that chimp from you or me?"

"His body odor, for one."

"Well, I've got a theory. What if the observations we're making about this chimp are all correct? Sameer says he has language and problem solving; I've seen artwork and self-awareness; you're telling me he's got the potential for thought as complex as man's. What if I can show you he has creativity, jealousy, symbolic manipulation? What if I can teach him to write poetry or music? Cheat on his wife? What if I teach him to pray?"

Jamie paused as her words sunk in. "The only question is—who does he pray to? Is Nakamura God? 'Cause that's who created him. If that chimp is all he's cracked up to be, you can no more say he's lacking a soul than any of us. And if you can create an immortal soul by twiddling a couple of genes, I say there's no such thing. If the chimp is fully sentient, God is dead, and we can prove it."

Sameer frowned. "Wow, Jamie. That's heavy."

Stiles shook his head. "People won't buy it. He's still an animal, however smart he is. He's not human."

"Why not? That's exactly what this is all about," Jamie answered. "Ninety percent of people on this planet believe in some kind of spirit or soul. They believe there is something inside each of us that is more than electrical shocks in a protein soup. They believe in something that lives on after we die. Something that makes us different from animals, that has free will and emotion and creativity and memory. Well, what about him?"

Nobody spoke.

"Scientists have claimed before that the illusion of a soul is all smoke and mirrors. People will say the same thing about this discovery—unless we're willing to make this project so complete, so exhaustive, so convincing that when we're done, this chimp can stand in

EIGHT

JAMIE sat across an oak desk from David Mercer. The desk was empty except for the freshly signed contract and a designer fountain pen. The plush carpeting still smelled new. Venetian blinds gave Jamie a glimpse of the forest through the open window screen. The juxtaposition of the jungle and the modern business office made her uncomfortable; the office felt unnaturally modern in the sacrosanct forest.

"That should about take care of it, Jamie. Welcome aboard."

"Thanks for your time. I was expecting this to take a lot longer."

"I just wish I'd have known you were coming earlier. Nakamura doesn't exactly keep in touch with the business end of the lab."

"Not surprised."

"You've met Dr. Stiles, I understand?"

"Yes. We were just there in the MRI suite."

"I'm curious why Nakamura is putting so many re-sources into this chimp project lately. From a financial perspective, our dopamine research seems so much more likely to turn a profit in our lifetimes." He shot Jamie an insincere smile. "I'd, er, actually be interested in your thoughts on why this chimp business is so important. I never quite feel like I've gotten the low-down from Kenji or the other two scientists who work on the project."

"What do you know about it?"

"Well, supposedly they're breeding them. There's one transgenic animal, has some strange behavioral traits." He stopped. "Look, Jamie. I think I can confide in you. I'm a representative of Soliton. It's my job to make this business profitable, and I'm taking a lot of heat from Tyler Drake back at headquarters. I just want to know if there's any-thing in this chimp project that can actually help our valua-tion. You know, I'm sure it's a great thing, but if there's no company to *do* the research . . ." He chuckled.

Jamie watched him closely. *Why ask me?* She didn't trust him, but she certainly wasn't going to give this pa-per pusher any excuse for pulling the plug on the most important project of her life. She squared her shoulders and answered, "It could be one of the most profitable dis-coveries in modern science." *What could she tell him?* "I wouldn't be a bit surprised if it leads to drugs that could fight dementia. Maybe a cure for Alzheimer's disease." She crossed her fingers behind her back.

He smiled broadly. "Thanks, Jamie. I'm sure we'll talk more later. But there's one other thing I wanted to dis-cuss, something a little more delicate."

"Yes."

"It's about Nakamura. I get the sense that there is some friction between you and . . . well, maybe things didn't get off to such a great start."

"I didn't think so. It was Kenji who signed me on. Is there something I should know?"

"Well, you're not the only one who doesn't necessarily mesh with Dr. Nakamura. I've never managed to hit it off with him and . . ." He seemed to search for the right words. "Sometimes people think that he has more authority than he does. The way it really works is I control the purse strings. I thought maybe we could help each other."

"How so?"

"Well, you're new here—I guess I just thought we could watch out for each other."

"I thought you were in charge."

"I mean watch Nakamura. I'd like to know more about this chimp project, for instance. I just feel like I'm not getting the whole story. If you have extra information, it would be a big help. I mean for the good of the company and all."

"You want me to spy on Nakamura?"

"No, no. Not like that at all. I just would appreciate someone involved in the project who has better communication skills who could keep me informed of how things are going."

"I think I can do that."

"Good. Good. I hope I can be of some help to you as well. Don't hesitate to come to me with any trouble, not that I'm expecting any." He spoke slowly and deliberately at the end.

He shook her hand vigorously.

* * *

"**PLEASE** come in, Dr. Kendrick." Nakamura bowed slightly.

As Jamie moved inside his office again and sat down, she mused how different she must look this time from her ragged, wet entrance a week earlier. She certainly felt differently. Her suspicious, demanding, confrontational bearing had been replaced by humility and eagerness to earn her place in the laboratory.

"How did you like your tour?"

"It was remarkable. Sameer had some great stories to tell. It seems the chimp project has been very successful so far." Jamie was reserved, her formality matching Nakamura's.

"Indeed it has. All the more reason for us to carefully analyze the impact our project could have before we pursue it further. Do you have any initial thoughts?"

"How long do you have? I'm rather surprised how quickly the chimps became self-sufficient on indigenous fruits, but I remain skeptical that the adaptation is over. From what I could gather from Sameer, the chimps have yet to hunt or eat meat, do not eat insects, and have been exposed to only the tiniest part of the pathogens, parasites, and predators of a totally new continent. They have a long way to go before I would consider them a stable population."

"I see." Nakamura looked pensive, but made no motion to direct her.

"Aside from dangers to the chimps themselves, here's a first look at the environmental impact. Half the species on the planet live in the rain forest. In the Amazon Basin there may be over three hundred species of large trees over a region the size of your compound. More important, trees here are grouped sporadically, isolated in patches across the rain forest. Most of these trees survive by co-evolving with other species. For most of the fruit trees relied upon by your monkeys, that means intricate webs of dependence with pollinators such as bees, butterflies, and especially fruit bats. There are probably over a hundred species of fruit bat alone in the Amazon, thousands of birds, and thousands of moths, and many of these have evolved specifically to feed on and pollinate a specific type of tree."

She saw his eyes glaze over, and decided to give an example. "For instance, the euglossine orchid emits an odor that attracts one specific bee that has evolved brushes on its feet to collect the flower's pollen. The bee gets no food from the flower, but the fragrance turns out to be an essential part of the bee's mating ritual. That's how interconnected things are."

"How is this related to the chimps?"

"Look at it this way. If the monkeys start eating all of the fruit on a given type of tree when it ripens, the tree may lose the ability to attract the fruit bat it relies on to scatter its seeds over a much wider area. The tree may then not have the ability to reproduce itself in an appropriate patch of soil and within a generation could lead to extinction of that species and the insects, birds, bats, and moths that rely on it. It is entirely possible that the change in who eats the fruit could mean life or death for many species of trees. There can often be something of a chain reaction as well when habitats become disturbed. The effect on other types of monkey populations would also be concerning."

Nakamura squinted at her. "These weren't the conclusions we talked about."

Jamie leaned back in her chair. "The point is, there's an exquisitely complicated web that if altered could either lead to massive deforestation or have virtually no effect. It's totally unpredictable, and that's exactly the sort of problem I like to solve. What people have long suspected is that massively complicated systems like rain forests are not wild, random hotspots of unchecked growth. They probably have significant order to them. The fact that rain forests in Africa, South America, and Southeast Asia are so similar almost requires that there are forces that shape the nature of what can grow there that probably boil down to a few simple rules of rainfall, temperature, and altitude. I suspect you can prove that your chimps are unlikely to hurt the rain forest one bit."

Nakamura leaned forward. "So you think that the rain forests aren't so fragile after all?"

Jamie stared back. "They are precariously fragile—when it comes to mahogany lumberjacks and bulldozers for cattle grazing. When it comes to species fluctuations, my hunch is they may be rock solid ecosystems not in the least danger of disappearing. Your chimps would fall under the latter category, and I think I can prove it given enough time and computer power."

Nakamura smiled warily. "And if you're wrong?"

"Then I can promise you I'll bury anyone with data who tries to claim otherwise."

"Perfect. You are proving helpful already."

"I want to know more about the chimp. Dr. Stiles was running some experiments today, and it makes me more curious about exactly what kind of changes you've . . ."

"You were there?" Nakamura interrupted.

"Just now."

"Who have you talked to about the chimp?" Nakamura demanded, stiffening in his chair.

"Relax, just Sameer and Dr. Stiles and his postdoc." Jamie didn't feel the need to mention Mercer.

"What did Dr. Stiles see?" Nakamura asked, his expression bordering on desperate.

"The brain is remarkable. It is three times too large for a chimpanzee; it has fold patterns in the cortex unlike any other primate, and comparable to a human."

Nakamura appeared exultant, jubilant. "That is good news."

"So how about some more information? I've got some theories about the chimp, and want to see if I can't contribute a little more."

After a long pause Nakamura began again with all of the composure Jamie was used to seeing in him. "Very well. I will call a meeting with those who know of the project to review what we know. I'll set up a briefing for Thursday at which time everything should become clear. Until then, I must insist you do not discuss that chimpanzee with anyone besides Drs. Gupta, Stiles, and Evans." A finality in Nakamura's eyes said the discussion was over.

Jamie nodded her agreement.

Nakamura immediately changed the subject. "Our human resources director would like to see you to arrange for appropriate office space, staff, and budget for your work. You may contact our CIO, Mr. Fowles, at any time should you wish more computer support. Welcome to BrainStem Therapeutics, Dr. Kendrick."

"One more question. May I call you Kenji?"

"If you insist."

*   *   *

HIROKO Tate sat on the exam table with a sterile drape still over her knees. Her feet rested on the floor and she held her hands in her lap. To either side of the table, stirrups covered with colorful oven mitts were still positioned upright.

Kate Batori finished speaking with her assistant, and then turned back to Hiroko. "Everything went just fine, Hiroko. We were able to harvest a number of eggs that hopefully will be more than enough to generate a set of embryos. Why don't you get dressed and we can review the procedure from here." A warm smile set Hiroko and her husband Richard at ease.

At least Hiroko appeared to be at ease. Richard was still looking a bit squeamish after submitting a semen sample an hour earlier. Perhaps he envied the passive, sterile role his wife had played in the procedure after some difficulty in fulfilling his part of the enterprise.

Richard cleared his throat and asked, "Dr. Batori. We have been talking and wanted you to know that we do want to go ahead with the genetic screening once the embryos are fertilized . . ." He paused for a moment. "Including the genetic therapy if something is found."

"That was my understanding, Mr. Tate. We will certainly do that."

"Is there any paperwork or anything we need to sign for that?"

"No. I'll take care of ordering the appropriate tests. We should have results by the time the embryos are ready to implant in a couple weeks. Any other questions?"

Richard reached over and squeezed his wife's hand. She looked happy, and gave a timid smile back.

                    *   *   *

A few moments later in her office, Kate Batori pulled her
flatscreen terminal away from the open door. Reading an
email with growing interest, she thought for a moment
and began typing:

> To: Kenji Nakamura <Nakamura@BrainStem.com>
> From: Kathryn Batori <Batori@NewConcept.com>
> Subject: Phase II
> Message:
> Kenji,
> Read your account with great interest. Agree with
> proceeding to phase II. Have identified appropriate
> couple and am ready to commence. Are vectors you
> sent most recent batch? Please advise, Kate.
> <SEND>

CARLOS Escalante picked up his cell phone and dialed
Nathan's back office number.

"Hall."

"Hi Nathan, I think I've got some information."

"I was hoping you would. What's going down?"

"I found a tech that works in the lab. He's a student at
the university here."

"And?"

"And he seems to think that some of the big shots
there are acting differently."

"For example?"

"I guess Nakamura is starting to get on a lot of people's nerves. He's restricting access to information. He
had everyone at the lab fingerprinted."

"Why?"

"Not sure yet. I also hear that he and the CFO, Mercer, are a little frosty. Sounds like they're under a lot of pressure."

"Carlos, what's going on in the lab? Pressure as in a new discovery? Or pressure as in they're out of money?"

"I can't tell."

"Look Carlos, I need to know whether to buy or not in this IPO, and that only gives us a few days. I want you to get inside."

"You mean break in?"

"I didn't say how—I just want real, credible information. That's what I'm paying you for."

"Not enough."

"Then double it. But get inside that compound, and find out once and for all what this company has under its skirt."

"Consider it done."

NINE

Washington DC

SUSAN Archer-Bentham stood by her friend's desk. Janet Davies, a fellow reporter at AP's Washington Bureau, had recently returned from maternity leave, and had been catching up with Susan on what she had missed. What that had really meant for Susan was that Janet had been barraging her with baby pictures until her friend was satisfied that Susan had been sufficiently effusive in her praise of the baby's chin, eyes, and ears.

At that point, the conversation shifted to work. Janet started out, "You know, while I've been away, I've hardly been able to think about anything else except that you just have to do this story."

Somehow Susan already doubted the point.

Janet continued. "You see, like you know, we had to use in vitro fertilization for this baby, and my eyes were opened as a result. Somebody needs to figure out exactly what is allowed and what isn't allowed." Janet covered the society beat, and Susan had always thought she was a perfect fit for it.

"What do you mean?"

"It's like this." Janet continued with a dramatic wave of her hand. "When we met with the doctor, it seemed pretty straightforward. You plunk the embryo in and out comes the baby, hopefully. But when I was in the hospital, I met two other mothers who also did IVF, and you won't believe what they told me. They said their doctor had told them that it was okay to choose the sex of the baby. I thought that was illegal, or something." Susan suspected Janet had probably talked to every mother in the hospital that hadn't used IVF as well.

"Which doctor?" Susan's instinct took over.

"I don't know. It's not like I go around asking nosy questions in the hospital! Anyway, I asked them whether they chose beforehand, and they both said, 'No way! We would never do anything like that. Blah, blah, blah.' Can you believe that, though? Do they do that now? You'd think I would have heard more about it."

"Maybe those doctors don't want to draw attention to it."

"Well, I think you should look into it. People should know, don't you think?"

"Thanks, Janet. Maybe I'll run it by Cindy."

"Well, I already did, and she said she'd think about it." Janet smiled sweetly. "Just so you know."

Susan was walking back to her own desk when a passing messenger grabbed her arm. "O'Reilly wants you in her office. Don't know why." He hurried on without another word.

Susan diverted her course and stopped by her editor's office. Cynthia O'Reilly was an opinionated woman whose gender alone had more than once saved her from being called an SOB. Nevertheless, Susan got along well with her, and had managed to forge a productive working relationship with her as well. She opened the glass door to the office.

"Oh hi, Susan, I was just looking for you."

"So I've heard."

"There's this idea for a story that Janet brought to my attention."

"About choosing your baby's sex?"

"How did you know?"

"Since when did Janet keep an idea to herself?"

"Good point. Well, anyway, I think it might be worth doing. Only thing is, I'm getting so much lip about running negative stories lately. Every day half of the letters we get seem to be griping about how the news is always so gloomy and so forth. So I have an idea."

"Why am I thinking I won't like it?"

"It's simple. Why don't we balance the story with a happy feel-good story? Something that makes you cheer about moms and babies and so forth."

"What's the story, Cindy?" Susan sighed.

"There's this family in St. Louis that just had a litter of babies. Five, I think. See what you can do with it, and we can go after this IVF thing next."

"Do I have a choice?"

"Not really."

NAKAMURA sat rigidly behind his desk. After a handshake and a bow, he had welcomed Tyler Drake to a chair he had brought in specifically for that purpose, and waited for Drake to begin.

"Good to see you again, Kenji." Drake was professional, courteous, and immaculately dressed.

"It is always a pleasure." Nakamura lied. Their conversations had become somewhat more strained over the last year since Drake had taken over as COO of Soliton Industries.

"I'm looking forward to the tour and being able to chat with the other scientists, but first I want to talk a little business, as they say."

"Go on."

"I've just been visiting with David." Drake paused, as though to let the implications sink in. "We've talked before about the financial issue, and I've just had my staff do a full accounting assessment of BrainStem. We're running out of time, Kenji."

"What do you mean?"

"Like we talked about before, the startup capital is pretty well spent and Soliton can float BrainStem for a while, but not indefinitely. After the IPO, BrainStem has got to support itself. You know I fully support this venture; I helped get it off the ground personally. All I need is something that I can show investors."

"The Parkinson's project is coming along nicely. We just need a little more time."

"How much time?"

"I don't know—perhaps a couple years."

Drake shook his head crisply. "Won't fly. I didn't think I needed to spell it out, but the board is giving a lot of pressure. They want us to wash our hands of Brain-Stem. It's getting a lot harder to justify more capital. I need something else. Biotech firms are folding like card sharks in Vegas. How about the spinal cord regrowth stuff?"

Nakamura thought for a moment. "I suppose I could put together a summary of our accomplishments in that regard. We have had a few promising experiments."

"That's more like it," Drake said approvingly. "Is there anything else? Any other new lines of research besides those two that are new or interesting or hot?"

"None at all," Nakamura said. "Our attention is focused on the substantia nigra and spinal cord projects. Of course, we are constantly looking for new ideas to exploit."

Drake asked pointedly, "What about those new scientists you hired: that guy Stiles from England and this new population biologist? Kendrick, is it?"

"Support staff. They really haven't even gotten off the ground yet. I was hoping to try some imaging to see if we can follow spinal cord regrowth that way without going through so many animals. The girl is to help with the chimp colony." Nakamura began to sweat behind his desk.

"Why don't you bring me up to speed on the dopamine stuff?" Drake pressed on.

"With pleasure," Nakamura said with relief.

TEN

JAMIE sat in her office moving icons around the screen of her new workstation. The rest of her office was utterly bare, excepting a file cabinet, a marker board, and a large oak desk. It was not that Jamie had no inclination of making her office more personable. Rather, it was simply a matter of priorities that her computer came first, and when that was satisfactorily explored and organized, she could move on to other issues. And making her machine more lived-in would take a good long time, especially when she couldn't take her mind off the chimp.

Her new apartment in the south wing of the complex would have to wait as well, and her clothes, equipment, and belongings had been piled along one wall until she could get to it. Most of the scientists without families chose to live in housing within the lab complex for convenience.

Others who wanted the stability of living in Manaus often chose to sleep in the lab on weeknights. Even with a fast speedboat, the commute was nearly two hours, which was prohibitively long for many scientists accustomed to work-ing long hours. Even some of the families with children ac-tually lived on-site, and a playground had been erected adjacent to the complex for children who lived in the build-ing. This was carefully fenced off from the "chimp play-ground" that was close by. Many observers had wondered whether the children or the chimps enjoyed and learned more from watching the play of the other group.

That morning, Jamie had been timing some simulations run in MatLab on her computer as well as through her re-mote link to the supercomputers in the basement. Geomet-rical patterns flashed on the screen with breakneck speed as the timing diagnostics ran through computations and displayed complex visuals. When the visual fireworks fin-ished, Jamie looked over a stream of numbers and smiled inside at the speed she had harnessed. The phone rang.

"Hello, Jamie."

"Hi Sameer, what's up?"

"I got it. It's perfect. I had it faxed over from a friend at Berkeley and this is exactly what we talked about. Come on over to the nursery and watch."

"Wait. Slow down, Sameer. What are you talking about?"

"I found some materials to do some formal psycholog-ical testing on the little chimp. I want to start this morn-ing. So, are you coming?"

"Sure. I'll be right there." She hung up and started a few simulations running in the background on her monitor. Then she left her office as it was and walked outside to the footpath around to the nursery.

Before long, she pressed the code she had seen Sameer type yesterday on the wire door frame. The door swung open. Inside she saw the chimp with the collar playing with some blocks next to Sameer. Two towers stood on a small, flat platform. The towers were both hexagonal in shape, sharing one common wall. In the interior of each tower, multicolor supports spiraled outward from the center like spokes on a wheel. A camera was positioned on a tripod to film the chimp's playstation, and a small closed-circuit television was broadcasting the field of view for the camera nearby.

The chimp, just finishing a top layer of blocks, bounded over on all fours to a couple lawn chairs set up a few feet away where Jeremy Evans and Roger Stiles sat watching. Jeremy had a bag of microwave popcorn in his hand, which he was lazily eating. The chimp tugged at Jeremy's sleeve, and pointed to the tower.

Jeremy responded, "Nice job, but where are the windows?" The chimp gave him a puzzled look, and then deftly reached a hand into the bag and emerged with a handful of popcorn, which he popped into his mouth. The chimp then grabbed the bag with the other hand and jumped away back to the blocks eating his prize. "Hey!" Jeremy exclaimed as Sameer laughed to one side.

Stiles, watching with amusement, remarked, "It looks like the whole tower was just a ploy to distract you, Jeremy. You can't keep letting little Ken Jr. outsmart you or before you know it he'll have you in the scanner."

Jamie walked up to the group and nodded to Jeremy. "So much for breakfast, I guess."

Jeremy shrugged. "The little creep."

Stiles said, "I'd be careful what you say or you'll read about it when Ken Jr. writes his memoirs." He turned to Jamie. "You come to see the show?"

"Wouldn't miss it."

"So what have we got planned for little Kenny today?" Stiles asked Sameer.

"I have wanted for some time to assess more formally how he would do on a standardized test, but most of the usual intelligence tests like the Binet or the Wechsler are so vocabulary-based that they didn't seem valid. After we talked yesterday I got excited about the idea and called a friend in clinical psychology at Berkeley.

"He suggested a test that looks at general intelligence but requires no speech, and he even faxed me a copy. It's called the Comprehensive Test of Nonverbal Intelligence, or CTONI. I'm not sure how this will work, but I've been looking it over this morning and I think it's worth a try," Sameer explained. "I made an extra copy for you to follow along." He pointed to a stack of pages on the ground, which Jamie promptly scooped up.

Jamie pulled a chair over next to Stiles and Jeremy and sat down while Sameer motioned to the chimp, who had just finished the bag of popcorn. Stiles pulled out a stack of papers that Sameer had given him, and Jamie and Jeremy looked over the questions as Sameer coaxed the chimp to pay attention.

The first section of the test involved pictorial analogies and Sameer tried to explain an example problem to the chimp. The first problem showed a picture of a bird in a tree next to a picture of the same bird in flight. Underneath those images was a picture of a dog lying down next to a blank frame. Below were five choices showing a dog walking, a dog sitting, a dog sleeping, a bird in a nest, and a bird in a birdbath.

The chimp stared at the pictures on Sameer's clipboard, and after a moment pointed to the dog walking. Sameer made a note in his notebook and flipped to the next page in the stack. Jamie moved to the next page as well, with Stiles and Jeremy alternating glances over her shoulder and at the closed-circuit TV screen.

The next page went much more quickly, as the chimp pointed to one of the bottom choices almost instantly after the page was turned. One by one, the pages flipped and the chimp selected an answer, sometimes very quickly and other times with more of a pause. After about two dozen pages, Sameer patted the chimp and gave him a juice box with a straw. The chimp beamed at receiving the drink.

The next subtest was similar, but involved geometrical figures. The first example showed a hollow oval with a spike pointing down next to a filled oval with a spike pointing up. Below was an image of a two-spired, hollow figure pointing down, next to a blank frame. The chimp looked over the pictures and pointed to the frame below in the center showing a filled, two-spired figure pointing up.

Again Sameer began turning pages and noting the chimp's answers in his booklet. He gave the chimp a small cookie after the subtest was done. The chimp wolfed it down and walked around Sameer, apparently trying to inspect the duffel bag from which Sameer had produced the treats. Sameer clamped the bag shut just in time, and the chimp loped back in front of Sameer and folded his hands in his lap.

The final two tests showed pictorial and geometric sequences. The first example showed three pictures of a man painting a fence at various stages of completion next to a blank frame. A geometrical example showed a sequence of polygons with progressively more sides. The

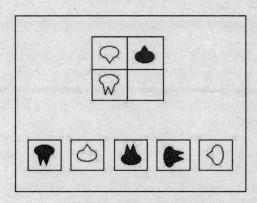

chimp likewise made selections through twenty-five examples of each subtest, and waited for the expected reward from Sameer's bag of goodies.

When the test had finished, Sameer huddled over the notebook and began scratching various marks on the answer sheet. A minute later he finished writing and flipped pages in his notebook to a table of numbers. After that, Sameer began browsing through the questions again, pausing at various questions.

Stiles mimicked Sameer's gestures. "Let's see. Would I have got that one? That's probably a mistake. At least two answers are just as good here . . ."

Finally, Sameer looked back to the others and smiled. "The chimp obtained perfect scores on all three geometrical subtests, and missed only four items from the other three tests combined. In every case, the missed items were pictures of things the chimp could not have seen before or recognized. This puts his IQ score in the very superior range for a twelve-year-old child, and

likely underestimates his score substantially. It's remarkable."

Stiles pointed to Jamie's copy of the test. "Maybe it
has something to do with the big arrows under the correct answer choices in your version?" Sameer reflexively
flipped open the questions again before giving Stiles an
agitated look.

Stiles continued in a more thoughtful tone. "Seriously,
nothing would surprise me after what I've seen. I'd say
we may as well start saving up to put Algernon here
through college. That is, if he has time for college between late-night talk show appearances."

Sameer put the test on his lap. "I have been thinking a
lot about our discussion yesterday. Jamie seems to have a
very good point. The chimp's symbolic logic is well within
the human range, maybe at the upper end."

Jamie turned to Stiles. "What happened with your experiment after we left?"

"We still have a lot of data analysis to do, but a crude
first look showed basically normal sensory processing. The
visual, auditory, and sensory cortex areas of the brain are
normal size for a chimp, or a human for that matter, and in
roughly the same positions. The activation patterns were
pretty unremarkable. The baffling thing is the acres of cortex between the sensory areas. That part of the brain is usually called association cortex, and this guy's got a lot of it.
We've got a lot more experiments to run, but first we'll
have to train little Kenny to lie in the scanner awake."

"Awake?"

"Sure, it's not too hard even for normal chimps after a
few weeks' training," Jeremy added. "It's going to be critical because to figure out what the rest of the brain is do-

ing we'll need to have the chimp doing cognitive tasks in the scanner. That way we can look at how he processes decision making, emotion, language, and so forth. Those areas can't be tested while he's anesthetized. What I'd really love to have is a brain biopsy. It would be fascinating to see if the cellular anatomy is changed in any way, look at the density of the neurons, and do some tracer studies. All we'd need is a small bit of tissue. He'd never miss it, and it could answer a lot of questions."

"Biopsy? You're going to cut him open? I don't need to tell you how valuable this chimp is." Jamie lingered on the visual image of opening the chimp's skull.

"Sure. We even do it in people for difficult diagnoses. It's really quite safe. With microsurgery, you can do everything through a tiny burr hole with very little risk to the subject."

Jamie glanced at the chimp, who had since lost interest in the group's discussion and begun thumbing through some books. He returned her gaze. *Does he understand what we're saying?* She decided to change the subject.

"What else were you planning on doing?" Jamie asked.

"The whole enchilada," Stiles said. "We want to see how he responds to music, language, pain, fear, and pleasure. With a subject this easily teachable and this intelligent, we could collect some of the most useful data neuroscience has ever known."

"Pain?" questioned Sameer.

"Well, just some simple experiments to see whether an electric shock is processed more in the primitive brain or in the cortex. Nothing harmful to the chimp," Stiles added. "You realize this is one of the most important scientific discoveries in the history of science. We are witnessing the creation of a new type of mind, and how that mind behaves could be one of the most provocative pieces of information we have ever had in terms of how our own minds work. Questions like mind–brain duality or the seat of consciousness that have only been asked by philosophers in the past all of a sudden are fair game. Like Jamie said, we have to be thorough and meticulous. It's just too important."

And someone will be analyzing every misstep when we're done, Jamie thought. "I wonder if something like an IQ test is simply not adequate in this case. What people want to know is whether the chimp is sentient. More than being able to recognize patterns . . . Does he feel empathy? Does he think? Does he dream? What we really need is a genuine Turing test."

"A what?" asked Sameer.

"A Turing test. Alan Turing was a philosopher/scientist who proposed the classic experiment for an artificial intelligence. The basic setup is like this. Suppose you had an intelligent machine. The only way to verify its intelligence is by head-to-head competition with another intelligent being. The test he proposed was to ask both the machine and a real person questions, and to have a third party try to determine who is the machine, and who is real. If a third party can't tell the difference, then the machine is intelligent."

"Sure," Jeremy echoed. "That's exactly the right test. The question is, how do you apply it in this case? The chimp doesn't have enough language yet to do a verbal test. Maybe with some language or mathematics training you could input equations or questions into a computer and do a head-to-head test, but that will take some time."

"I don't know how to do it yet either. But I'm working on it."

"In the meantime," Stiles began, "I certainly hope old Ken can give us some answers tomorrow about just what makes Ken Jr. here tick. I'm not going to sleep until I at least have some plausible explanation for all this."

"Roger, is it really ethical to do what you're proposing with the chimp?" Sameer inquired. "From what we've seen, the chimp certainly seems to be sentient. Doesn't he have rights? Not human rights, I guess, but intelligent being rights?"

"I'm not going to blow the single most important chance science has had to learn how the brain really works. To me, he's a genetically modified monkey, and monkeys are fair game for experiments. I'm in this for the human race, and I'm not about to let the animal rights community get wind of this until I have my answers. They can debate all they want about it afterward. Fact is, even normal apes are to some extent sentient and that hasn't stopped anyone before."

"Rog, that sounds a little extreme. Important or not, we can't do anything really dangerous to the chimp. And he deserves respect," Jeremy countered.

"Fair enough. You can tell them in Stockholm about how respectful we were," Stiles answered with a wry smile. He stood and walked toward the gate.

The chimp remained motionless, staring absently at a picture book of Curious George in a firefighter's hat. As Jamie got up to leave, she waved to the chimp. This time, the chimp just watched her closely, and didn't wave back.

ELEVEN

STILLNESS spread across the small conference room as Kenji Nakamura walked inside. Jamie had been talking with Stiles and Jeremy about the experiment they were in the process of planning. Sameer sat next to Jamie. Two other scientists Jamie had not met before sat together on the far side of the table.

One of the two was male, the other female, and beyond greetings neither was very talkative in the minutes before Nakamura entered the room. In the center of the table was a platter with fresh fruit aside a small stack of plates and a cup with toothpicks. Next to the fruit plate, the soft hum of a video projector was now the loudest sound in the room.

Nakamura unceremoniously sat down next to the projector and began to plug the video cable into the port on his laptop computer. Unfolding the computer, he punched a few buttons and a black screen showed up on the white wall on one side of the room. He then stood up, flipped out most of the room lights, and sat back down, clearing his throat. "Welcome, colleagues," he began.

"As most of you know, the last several years have been good to our research at BrainStem Therapeutics. We have successfully grown dopamine-producing neurons from neural stem cells, and are nearing completion of safety trials for implanting these cells in a mouse model of Parkinson's disease. We have had favorable preliminary data on using nerve growth factors to stimulate spinal cord regrowth in vitro. But perhaps the most promising development so far has been something completely unexpected. Some early experimentation five years ago investigating cortical development has only recently been found to be not a failure, but a striking success."

Nakamura motioned to the two strangers in the room. "Let me introduce my colleagues Dr. Patrick Michaels and Dr. Michelle Simons. They have worked with me from the outset on the creation of the chimpanzee. Each is an accomplished molecular biologist and a credit to our laboratory. Dr. Simons will begin by explaining the problem that we were working on at the time."

Nakamura then tilted the screen of the laptop toward the female scientist at his left. She took the mouse and projected onto the wall a schematic model of the developing brain.

"Thank you, Dr. Nakamura. It is nice to see some new faces. After so many years in the molecular wing, I'm afraid I haven't kept up with the staff in other departments."

She looks uncomfortable, Jamie thought. *What's she hiding?*

Dr. Simons continued, "We set out early in the company's history to determine exactly what proteins are involved in the early development of the cerebral cortex. The idea was that if we could determine how cortical neurons are grown naturally, we might be able to replicate this sequence of events in stem cells. The ultimate hope was that we could regrow areas of the cortex damaged in strokes, for instance. I will first give a brief summary of what we know about this process."

Simons launched into a lecture on neural development, filled with graphs and diagrams of the developing embryo.* Dr. Michaels then took the pointer and explained how they had modified a key pathway in brain development to increase the size of the developing brain. Nakamura finished by relating how the experiment was initially thought to be a failure, but that the recent observations of Dr. Gupta had radically changed that assessment.

Stiles gave a long, slow whistle. "You did it, didn't you? You actually made a monkey that may well be as or more intelligent than a human being."

Nakamura responded matter-of-factly. "That is what we want you to answer. Your role in determining the chimp's abilities is critical, and that is why I have agreed to this briefing. You must know where the chimp came from to make a proper assessment of him."

Jamie asked intently, "What are you going to do with him?"

Nakamura closed his eyes. "Study him. This is a great advance in the study of the brain. We want to understand completely the effects of our enhancement. We will likely

---

* Details of this discussion can be found at www.sciencethriller.com.

begin constructing more similar embryos and alter the intervention in various ways."

A gnawing thought surfaced in Jamie's mind. *Should she ask?* She decided she had to. "Kenji, could this same genetic alteration produce a similar change in a human embryo?"

Nakamura cast his eyes downward. "We have much more work yet to do. Such speculation is grossly premature."

Stiles gave Nakamura a suspicious look. "What more do you have in mind?" Nakamura returned his question with a silent glare.

Stiles again cleared his throat. "One thing's for sure. Once we publish the results, you're going to have a very easy time raising capital."

Nakamura immediately stood again. "There is to be no talk of publication. Not yet. I want this discovery fully fleshed out before the world learns of it. Even if it takes us several years. Then, only then, will I allow the full story to be told. As an added security precaution, I should let you know, I have decided to prohibit any communication outside this compound. I have cut off our telephone and intranet from outside."

Stiles erupted, "Kenji, that's ridiculous! I can't be cut off from my lab like that. We're professionals. That's no way to treat a consultant."

"I'm sorry, but I cannot afford any risk of a security breach. My mind is made up. Any outside communication will have to be approved by me."

Jamie watched as Stiles's face reddened, sensing an opportunity. She lifted her hand off the table as a restraining gesture. "Kenji, we understand the significance of this project, and why you're so worried about security. But if you're going to cut us off from outside, we need assurances that you're going to let us do our jobs in studying this chimp's abilities. What you've done is no longer genetic engineering. It's genome engineering. You are creating new species. A lot of people may find it a shock to wake up one morning and find they're no longer the only intelligent beings on the planet. This could alter human society in ways that are completely unpredictable. Are you prepared to accept that risk?" She looked at Stiles and Sameer, hoping they would stand behind her position. Stiles sat back in his chair and gave her an imperceptible nod.

Nakamura shot her a penetrating stare, with an uncharacteristic hint of emotion. "Are you suggesting we should stop the project?"

Jamie thought during a long, intense pause. "No. We're on board. I just want to make sure you understand what you've set in motion."

"Perfectly."

TWELVE

DR. Kate Batori opened the door to her office and smiled warmly at Richard and Hiroko Tate. She sat down and clasped both of Hiroko's hands in her own. "Do you feel ready?" she asked.

Hiroko became tearful and withdrew one hand to brush a tear from her damp mascara. Her smile was innocent and genuine. "Yes. We are very excited." She gave a shy look to Richard, who returned her glance.

Kate continued. "The procedure today is really quite simple. Everything went very well during the fertilization process, and we have plenty of viable embryos. Usually we implant three or four embryos a cycle in hopes that at least one will result in a successful pregnancy. Sometimes we are fortunate, and other times not. On average, most couples in your position become pregnant within three or four cycles. No guarantees, though."

Richard fidgeted in his chair. "What if more than one of the embryos attaches?"

Kate smiled teasingly. "Then you have twins—or triplets. You have to remember that with in vitro fertilization, multiples are more common than with the old-fashioned way."

Hiroko said softly, "Twins would be nice. Triplets . . . I don't know."

Kate asked, "Any other questions?"

Richard thought and questioned, "How soon will we know?"

Kate responded to Hiroko, "If you haven't had your period within about two and a half weeks, you can take a pregnancy test. Sometimes it takes a little longer with in vitro fertilization for the pregnancy test to become positive, but they are quite accurate. Now why don't you go into the exam room, and I'll give Hiroko a minute to get changed. I'll go thaw the embryos and will be in shortly."

KATE slipped out the door and went down the hallway to the laboratory. She reached into the minus-eighty-degree freezer and pulled out a sliding rack with numerous boxes of tubes. In one box, two sets of tubes were segregated on either side of the box. One side was labeled "transgenic," and the other "native."

Kate stared at the tubes. Slowly she reached down and selected four small tubes from the transgenic side of the box. She slipped the tubes between her fingers to warm them up and began slowly tipping the contents back and forth as she shut the freezer door.

She proceeded to a desk against the wall and sorted

through some paperwork on the desk. She looked one last time at the photograph of the gel on top of the stack. Seven columns of fuzzy, black horizontal lines streaked down the page like bad roller marks from an old copy machine. But this was anything but an artifact.

Kate put the paperwork down and looked through each clear plastic tube, flicking each with an index finger. Then she opened a drawer at the bench and pulled out a blue micropipette and a container of translucent blue tips. She set the four flasks into a tube rack, and attached a tip onto the pipette. Expertly, she siphoned up the contents of each tube and injected it into the barrel of an open 5-milliliter syringe.

When all four tubes had been emptied, she took a larger pipette and siphoned off some sterile solution from a rubber-topped vial, emptying the contents into the syringe and replacing the plunger. She then gingerly laid the capped syringe onto a tray with a package of thin plastic tubing, a stopcock, and a second syringe into which she drew up more of the sterile solution.

She gingerly fingered the tubing, looking down at the syringe on the tray with the embryos. *It's risky, but worth it.* A genetic alteration was completely untraceable, she assured herself one last time. Unless someone knew exactly what he or she was looking for, finding a mutation in a single subject was literally impossible. What could be done—sequence the whole genome?

She knew it would not come to that, not quickly enough to . . . Unusual children were born every day, and no one blamed the obstetricians. Well, some people would blame anyone. She had spent too long waiting for the chance. It was easy to make a buck in the world, but to make a difference, a real difference—that was worth a little risk.

She pulled out a pair of size 6 sterile gloves and set it on the tray. Finally, she picked up the tray and with a final glance back at the lab, exited into the hallway. She knocked briefly on the door to the exam room, and then entered the room. Hiroko sat on the exam table with a drape over her knees with Richard seated in a chair by the head of the table, holding Hiroko's left hand.

"Shall we start?" Kate asked rhetorically, and began washing her hands. She then moved over to a stool at the foot of the bed. "If you could lie back for me please and scoot down to the end of the table." Kate adjusted her light, spread a sterile towel over a stand at the end of the table and opened the packaging for the tubing and stopcock, placing them on the towel. She opened her gloves and carefully put each glove on her slender hands. She attached the tubing onto the syringes, removing each cap and fixing them onto the stopcock. Finally, she withdrew a speculum from the open drawer at the foot of the bed and announced to Hiroko that she was going to look at the cervix before implanting the embryos.

HIROKO felt Richard squeeze her hand, his gaze intermittently broken as he glanced back at the white sheet over her legs, then back at her. She saw Kate reach for a long Q-tip on the towel and a moment later heard it drop into a bucket at the foot of the bed. Kate announced that she was going to insert the thin tubing into the cervix, and that Hiroko might feel a little pinch.

She stared up at the impenetrable drape and waited.

The stirrups were shackles, pressing against her ankles. Her heart pounded against her chest wall like a fish on a hook. Her thoughts raced. *Was this right? Did she even want this?* A sense of doom crept into her intuition. Suddenly, her left calf tightened up and a shot of pain exploded up her leg. "Wait!" she screamed breathlessly. Kate flinched back with a start.

Hiroko lifted her leg off of the stirrup and rested it onto the table. Her eyes darted helplessly across the sterile white walls of the exam room, finally settling on Richard. He looked uncomfortable, awkward. *For Richard?* That was the reason. For him she would do it. *It was too late now anyway, wasn't it?* Hiroko replaced her leg and offered a feeble smile. "Sorry, just had a charlie horse."

"Cross your fingers." Kate smiled back, and within seconds she depressed the plunger on each of the two syringes in turn. She withdrew the tubing and dropped it into the bucket at her feet. Hiroko heard a clink of metal and saw Kate wheel back on her chair, drop the speculum into the sink, and remove her gloves. She reached over to press down on the drape and help Hiroko replace her feet onto the floor and sit up.

"That's it?" Richard asked.

"I told you it was a simple procedure today. You can go ahead and get dressed, Hiroko. Call me right away if you have any good news. Otherwise, I'll see you back same time next month." Kate cleaned up her tray and stood, motioning to leave.

Richard cleared his throat and interrupted, "You know, doc, we were talking, and if it's a girl we want to name her Kate."

Kate shot a glance over her shoulder. "That's very sweet. Let's hope it's a girl." She left the room.

KATE leaned back in her office chair and walked to the small refrigerator in her office. Procedures always made her hungry. The long hours in residency and fellowship had taught her to eat when she could, and that usually meant snacking after deliveries. She reached in and pulled out an apple, then closed the fridge. She sat down at her desk, stared at the apple, and polished it with her sleeve. She took a bite.

With her other hand, she picked up the phone. A short time later she heard a click at the other end. "Well Kenji, it's done. Thought you'd like to know."

After a brief pause, Nakamura replied, "Excellent. You are sure this couple meets our agreed criteria?"

"Kenji, of course they do. I already told you that. What's new with the chimps?" Kate snapped.

"I should fax you the results of alpha's MRI. He is remarkable, indeed. The team is working on describing his abilities and making good progress."

"Well, you keep them busy for a good long time. I don't want to hear anything about any of this on CNN until we know if it will work or not. No abstracts, no meetings, nothing until we have an answer. Otherwise people get nosy. It could blow up on us before we know. Don't underestimate how suspicious people will be about all of this."

"There is plenty of work to do before the next phase. I will see to it that nothing goes public. I've cut off the consultants from any outside communication," Nakamura replied.

"What happened with that woman? Is she cooperating?"

"She is fitting in nicely, and may turn out to be a great asset after all."

"That was fast thinking. I give you credit for keeping her where you have an eye on her," Kate complimented. "And they think there's only one chimp?"

"Only Michaels and Simons know about the others."

"That was a stroke of luck that you made so many up front."

"We thought they were only going to be useful as breeding stock after the initial disappointment in the alpha. It is wonderful to know that the enhancement is so robust in the population. Michaels is going to look at the others more formally. So far, they look just as promising."

"What about Drake? Did he catch wind of anything when he showed up?"

"It was a routine oversight visit. We talked about nothing except the Parkinson's project. Everything went fine."

"What about Michaels and Simons?"

"They were perfect in the briefing. We all agree. We can't get the information we need without letting the neuroscientists know how the chimp was created. Greed and ambition will keep them in our pocket until they've finished their work. Michaels and Simons are as committed as I am to the project. We'll finish the analysis on the alpha chimp, and then we can take it on our own. I give you my word. One tragic accident, then no more consultants. Just the four of us."

"The four of us and billions of children. What do you think they'll be like, Kenji?"

"An improvement. The world has been butchered by

random evolution long enough. It's about time someone took control of evolution."

"We'll know soon enough."

"And if they don't work, we'll make better."

"You make it sound so easy. Are you sure we're doing the right thing?"

"There is no other way."

Kate smiled as she spoke. "Very true. Something this big deserves a little risk."

"It deserves ultimate risk. You and I are above the petty ethical concerns humanity squabbles over. For our project, all things are permitted, because we alone have the capability and vision to change humanity. We can accomplish more for the future of intelligent life in one generation than millions of years of blind evolution."

"I'll call you when I know more."

"Thanks, Kate."

The receiver clicked and Kate closed her eyes, letting the tension slip away with a long, slow breath. Somewhere inside, a visceral disquiet rose as the impact of the conversation sunk in. She squelched it. *All things are permitted* . . .

She took another bite of the apple, and laughed. *Wasn't that how all this supposedly started anyway? An apple?*

THIRTEEN

JAMIE pulled up her baseball cap and rested back on her elbows. She squinted in the bright sunlight as she watched the chimp playing on the tire swing in the nursery. Sameer had planned on reading to the chimp, and Jamie had wanted to watch.

She wondered when the lesson would start, and glanced at Sameer. He shrugged. "He likes to play for a while first. Then he meanders over when he's good and ready. Everything has to be his idea."

Jamie smiled and commented, "I bet you're getting pretty attached to the little guy."

Sameer stared over Jamie's head. "Yes and no. Sometimes he sits on my lap and it's like I'm his daddy. But he can be very strange. It's harder to get close to him than the other chimps."

"How do you mean?"

"He doesn't seem as affectionate. It's almost like he thinks

I'm his servant. One minute he'll be very cute and childlike, but the next aggressive, destructive, and indifferent."

"Maybe he's just a toddler," Jamie suggested.

"But he's not vulnerable like a toddler. He never looks at me like he needs my approval. I guess he's emotionally more like a teenager than a toddler."

Jamie shifted to lie on her right side. "It's funny how I expect his emotional development to be human. I expect him to learn the same way a human child would, even in the same order. But there's no reason to think that. He's unique, and the way humans develop may be completely different."

"I've thought that too. After some of the tests we've run, I've begun to wonder what his *emotional* makeup and behavior will be. How does having a more evolved brain change what emotions he feels?"

"That's a huge question. I've been thinking really hard, ever since the MRI experiment, what is it that makes a human soul? When you strip away the mystery and fear we have for our minds, what is the core? You know what, I always seem to end up with the same answer—it's about our emotions."

"How so?"

"There's nothing so personal, so priceless to a human being as the way we feel. It's how we differentiate ourselves from animals and computers, by the depth of our emotions and the personal sense of identity they give us. It's about how we feel when we see a field of tulips in bloom, or hear a baby giggle, or feel wet sand between our toes. It's about empathizing with the mother of a kidnapped girl, or feeling embarrassed when we try on swimsuits."

"Of course, Jamie. Why is that so surprising?"

"It's just that we're not going about this right. If we want to prove this chimp has a soul, we need to be looking for a way to measure his failings more than his intelligence. Instead of proving he can succeed at problems where some humans might fail, we should show that he absolutely flubs up something when he should know better."

"Now I'm not so sure I follow you."

Jamie looked over as the chimp jumped out of the swing, then slid over to a pile of blocks. "Think of it this way. Most of the things we associate with our deepest core are really maladaptive. How often does a bruised ego, or a jealous obsession, or even a pleasant daydream turn out to be efficient or helpful? And often, we humans try to do the absolute wrong thing, just to be obstinate—just to prove we have the right or ability to do it."

"You mean like smoking?"

"Sure. We have a defiant streak in us a mile wide. Every stupid thing will be tried over and over again, especially once it's been proven to be stupid."

"But not all emotions or impulses are bad, Jamie. We owe most of our civilization to them."

"Don't you find it odd that every major religion in its quest to develop our souls tells us to bridle our passions? Religion is all about self-control, mastery over emotions. The height of spirituality is about self-denial, in spite of the fact that it's exactly those passions that define us as human, spiritual beings."

"I guess I've never been very religious."

"I think some of the most religious people are those who profess no religion. I grew up not being able to tie my shoe without being convinced God would strike me down if I did it wrong. The church was everywhere in my life. It's a powerful feeling, Sameer, to believe that your life is dictated by a higher power. It's a feeling I've never been able to lose, or wanted to. But when I went off to Yale, I never found such superstition as when I got to college. Instead of God deciding whether they were rewarded or punished, how students performed on a test was about which pencil they used, where they studied, how their date went the week before. No matter how bright, how educated, people never lose their superstition. You ever been to Las Vegas?"

Sameer nodded. "Once."

"Hard to find a more godless group of people on the planet. And yet, you walk in any casino you choose, and you'll see an old woman with yellow teeth and a peeling bucket of coins walk from slot machine to slot machine putting one quarter in each one, as if one is any different from the next. You watch closer and you'll see an even older man may play a slot three times, shake his bucket of coins, then move two to the right and three rows back. He'll wait for the crummy machine if he has to, just so he doesn't break his routine. He knows this routine is the one that will get him the jackpot."

"It's a crazy place."

"Just like everywhere else people live. You see, Las Vegas stands for everything that is human and spiritual about a person. It's the height of emotion and passion, but above everything else, it's about escape."

"You lost me again."

"Escape. It's the one common thread in all human society. We hate what we're doing, and our spiritual life, religious or not, is planning for our escape to some better world. Once we lose the drive to escape, we lose our sanity. It's engrained into our psyche. And I think I'm finally starting to understand why."

Sameer said nothing.

"Emotions, for better or worse, are engineered into our brains. They're primal, given ultimate control over our behavior. It's a part of a system that goes much deeper. Novelty detection. Think about any kind of stimulus you want. A sound that you hear frequently. A picture on your wall. After you hear it or walk by it a few times, it becomes invisible. We often can't remember the simplest details about the furnishings in our homes. Emotions work the same way—they constantly fight for control, and we keep experiencing whatever is new, exciting, and different. No matter what your occupation, you get quickly bored of 95 percent of what you do, and come to associate happiness with the 5 percent of your life that is novel. You dig wells for a living and yearn to sit on a beach and rest. You win the lottery, move to a beach house, and find yourself miserable because your life has no purpose and you yearn for the days when you dug wells."

"And that is what you expect to find in the chimp?"

"Why not? He's wired the same way, presumably. And he has the brain to drive complex emotions. To prove he's human, that he's got what we would call a soul, we need to be looking for stupid, brave, inexplicable, or confusing things he does that prove he's driven by a wide range of emotions, none of which can ever stay with him for any length of time. If we're going to find a real Turing test, something that could tell a being with a soul from one without, mistakes driven by emotion will have to be wrapped up in it."

Sameer looked pensive, pausing before responding, "That's incredible. I never thought of it before, but it seems true. But for the chimp, sometimes he acts out, but most of the time I can't read him like I can a human," Sameer concluded. "Do you think that general intelligence and emotional intelligence go together?"

Jamie thought back on a college boyfriend. *Hell no!* More diplomatically, she said, "Seems like the stereotype is more of the opposite. Often humans with more logical prowess seem to struggle with social interactions. You know, like the empathy circuit gets borrowed as a spare memory bank. Of course, that's just a stereotype. You know, there's no reason for us to believe that his having a bigger brain would make him more compassionate or magnanimous. It may be that it makes him more ruthless, self-centered, and conniving. There's no way to know."

Sameer's voice drifted off. "Sometimes he scares me, Jamie."

"Scares you?"

"I don't worry about the other chimps, once they get to know me, but I don't feel completely safe with this one. It's this look in his eye that never lets me know quite where I stand with him." Sameer reached over to a nearby bookshelf and rested his hand on a pile of children's books as he spoke.

The chimp suddenly leapt off the swing and bounded over in a few jumps to leap onto Sameer's lap. The chimp looked askance at Jamie, and then pulled Sameer's hands into position with a book in front of the chimp.

Sameer repositioned the chimp to a more comfortable spot, and the chimp turned slowly to look into Sameer's eyes. Sameer started reading, "In the great green room . . ."

Jamie crawled to look over Sameer's shoulder. She asked the chimp, "Can you show me where the telephone is?"

The chimp pointed to the telephone on the nightstand in the book. Sameer continued to read.

After finishing *Goodnight Moon,* the chimp scampered over to a pile of toys on the ground. He picked up a toy telephone and held the receiver to his ear.

"Hello?" Jamie motioned playfully with her fingers as though speaking into her own telephone. The chimp listened for a moment, and then stared at the telephone. In one motion, he grabbed the receiver and yanked the rope that attached it out of the phone. He stared at the receiver in his hand, and then hurled it against the fence.

"Apparently, he's not very impressed with the phone," Sameer observed.

The chimp then leapt back onto Sameer's lap. With his oversized fingers, the chimp grabbed Sameer's T-shirt and began to feel the material. The ape's thumb and forefinger rubbed back and forth over the fabric on Sameer's sleeve until the chimp finally lost interest.

"He likes to feel things. I think it's comforting to him," Sameer commented.

Jamie was about to ask a question when the chimp jerked its head to one side. Immediately, he darted off Sameer's lap and scurried out of the small swinging door that allowed him entrance into the nursery.

Using hands and feet he lumbered around the cage and stood outside the fence, stopping just outside of where Jamie and Sameer were sitting.

Jamie was the first to spot what had interested him. "Sameer, he's looking at that little bird." It had a broken wing, struggling limply to fly against the weight of its body.

The chimp watched the bird for a moment, studying its clumsy movements. Without warning, the chimp jumped forward and grabbed the bird in its hands. The bird's wings fluttered against the chimp's grasp, then became still.

With one finger, the chimp began stroking the bird's head, straightening the feathers on its neck. The bird chirped a call, and bobbed its head under the chimp's caressing finger. Exploring its new environment, the bird pecked against the chimp's hand.

The chimp immediately seized the bird in one hand, and with two fingers of its other hand, grasped the bird's head and yanked it from its attachment to the body. The chimp mused over the mutilated head, rubbing it back and forth between his fingers. After a moment, he discarded the lifeless body and head of the bird, and scooted off on his hands and feet into the forest.

"Lesson over for today," Sameer said.

FOURTEEN

SKIP Jordan slung his holster around his generous mid-section, visually inspecting his pistol as he had done half a dozen times in the last decade. It was not that he expected to find anything wrong; his cursory inspection would barely have been able to distinguish that he was not holding a water pistol.

It was simply a matter of routine that he checked it out before a "real job." He glanced again at the wall of television images in the BrainStem Therapeutics security office. The problem had not required the janitor's assistance to spot this time. On at least five cameras, the intruders were all too visible.

He picked up the telephone and dialed a number. Momentarily, a Brazilian voice responded, "Diego."

"Listen, Diego. We have a disturbance at the south entrance. Suit up and meet me in the atrium in five minutes. Got that?"

Diego's quick "Five minutes, boss" came across just as the receiver clicked.

Jordan downed the last of his coffee and swaggered out the door with one last glance at the monitors. "We'll see about that," he muttered under his breath.

After navigating a series of corridors, he converged upon the front entrance where he peered out through glass windows in the front doors. He saw about a dozen young men and women carelessly dressed in shorts and sandals carrying large placards, posters, and signs. One held a portable camcorder at a distance, filming the scene. Another was dressed as an ape with a rope around its neck coiled into a noose.

The one dressed as an ape looked particularly uncomfortable even in the cooler evening temperature. Through the door, Jordan heard the voice of one of the protesters speaking into a megaphone in perfect English: "No more chimps! No more chimps!"

The posters cleverly portrayed scenes of apes in tiny cages or medical beds with various tubes and lines protruding from them like patients in an ICU. Slogans of "They think too," "How many more?" or "Who's next?" garnished other posters showing colorful images of apes hunted in the wild. Most striking of all was a bright red digital display mounted beneath the words "Chimpanzees Left." The digital readout was steadily ticking down from about 250,000.

Jordan turned around at the sound of footsteps to see Diego walking briskly his way. He called out, "All right, Diego. Let's take care of 'em." Diego nodded his agreement and the two stepped outside. The cameraman immediately shifted his focus to the two security guards, and the chant gained focus and intensity.

The guards strode toward the crowd, somewhat at a loss of what to do. Jordan marched up to the man in the ape suit and asked, "Who's in charge here?" To this the ape gave a shrug and pointed to the noose around its neck. Jordan gave his best disgusted look at the ape and walked over to the woman carrying the megaphone. "What is it you folks want?"

The woman with the megaphone seemed delighted at the question and motioned the cameraman over. She began in American English, "What we want is the treatment of chimpanzees with respect. What we want is an end to the pillaging of their homes, the criminal assassination of mothers to steal their children, the unconscionable . . ."

She was cut off by Jordan's boisterous voice, "Now look, I don't care what you think." The woman nodded toward the camera and pointed toward Skip. Jordan continued, "What I care about is that you are trespassing on a private laboratory, one that has as a major goal to breed and protect chimpanzees. If you don't immediately leave, I'll be forced to call in police to see to your arrest."

"Oh, sure. Why don't you go ahead? We're doing nothing illegal. We just came to visit the Da Silva Wildlife Preserve," she said distastefully. "Owned in trust by the people of Brazil, which we represent. In fact, I expect we'll be here for quite some time." She promptly sat down, crossed her legs, and smiled at Jordan. The other members of the group followed suit, save the cameraman who shot a close-up of Skip Jordan's exasperated face.

As Jordan confronted the woman, Carlos Escalante

stealthily crept from behind Jordan and Diego to enter the laboratory compound. He signaled to the woman with the megaphone and let the door close quietly behind him.

He watched through the glass of the door and noticed that several of the protestors who had been watching his entrance refocused their attention on the confrontation between Jordan and their spokeswoman so as not to divert attention. The woman with the megaphone sat down, followed by the rest of the crowd. Carlos turned and walked farther inside.

He strode purposefully through the corridors of the compound. It had been a simple matter to arrange the demonstration. Foreign students at the University of Amazonas were plentiful, and most of them were there on a crusade to study the rain forest. Within two days he had located a dozen individuals, some Brazilian, some American, and a couple European, who were pleased to help him undertake his "demonstration." He had come prepared with logistics and materials, and had chartered a boat for the expedition.

Finding inside information had proved much more difficult. He began asking molecular biology students if any knew the layout of the complex. Most just gave him a blank stare. Others recognized the compound and had seen advertisements for employment, but did not know anyone who had worked there. Through brute force he found a few technicians who held low-level jobs, including the one who initially suggested that Nakamura and Mercer were at odds.

On the second day of questioning, he got a phone number from someone who had worked there a summer and then quit. He got lucky. He called asking about employment options, and whether this former technician might know someone he could hit up for a job. After a lengthy conversation about what type of work went on there, who the important people were, and where their offices were, he asked about Nakamura. The tech had little interaction with Nakamura, and could offer only that he was the first one there in the morning, rarely talked to anyone in passing, and as gossip went, would go home in the evening to be with his family, who stayed in an apartment on the compound. Carlos thanked the tech and hung up satisfied.

The information paid off. He quickly found his way through the mostly empty corridors to the genetics wing. He nodded to the few passersby he encountered, who returned the nod with somewhat puzzled looks.

After navigating in what seemed like circles, he stumbled across a hallway that looked familiar. The carpeted corridor had three doors on the left side and he approached the last door and stopped. On the doorframe was inscribed "Kenji Nakamura, Chief Technical Officer." He looked over his shoulder to verify he was alone.

He rapped three times softly on the door and stood back. There was no answer. He tried the door. Locked.

He removed a lockpick from his pocket and quickly opened the door and peered inside. With a furtive glance down the hallway, he stepped inside and softly closed the door. He heard a low whir of machinery from a slightly ajar back door to the office. The light was dim, but sufficient to see where he was going. He lost no time in opening the filing cabinets.

Pulling the top drawer of one of the three cabinets open, he ran his fingers along the labeled tabs. Cursing under his breath, he found that all of the labels were in Japanese. He began looking in each of the folders. He quickly found the drawer was full of multiple reprints of scientific papers. Most were written in English, and Carlos discovered that Nakamura's name was on all of the papers in the drawer. He went on to the next.

Each of the drawers in the first cabinet was filled with clipped journal articles, apparently organized topically. Carlos quickly moved on to find the second cabinet also was full of scientific papers. The first two drawers of the third cabinet appeared to be empty.

In the third drawer, Carlos found a few sparse folders that looked distinctive. He rifled through the folders. Inside were financial documents, organized by year, including the company's financial statement, cash flow reports, shareholder prospectus, and correspondence. He fingered through the correspondence, which was mostly useless information from Soliton's executive board about strategic plans, requests for updates, and the like.

Nothing appeared particularly helpful, and Carlos went on to the final drawer, only to find office supplies and paper. As he rummaged through the drawer, he heard voices and footsteps in the hallway outside Nakamura's door.

The final drawer closed with a loud snap, and Carlos reflexively crouched down. One of the voices outside became audible. "Hey, it sounds like Kenji's still here. Why don't we ask him?"

The other voice responded, "No, he works early—he's never here this late."

"I'm sure I heard something."

Carlos heard the door handle rattle, and he slid down under the desk as quietly as he could.

"Kenji, you in there?" the voice probed. "It's all dark, I guess you were right."

The voices grew quieter, and Carlos waited until the footsteps had faded before wiping the sweat from his face. He stealthily walked to the door and turned the lock.

Next, he moved to the bookshelf, looking over the many titles lining the shelves. Most were textbooks or scientific works, which he passed over quickly. Finding nothing of interest, he moved to the desk.

On top of the desk were neatly stacked piles of paper. He looked through these carefully, but recognized nothing of value. Most were raw data—lists of sequences, diagrams of genes, and photographs of gels. Although he trusted there was an organization and purpose to the papers, it was clearly over his head, and he moved on.

Seeing the desktop computer, he grabbed the mouse and clicked on the screen. A password box came up, and Carlos abandoned his efforts. Finally, he began opening drawers in the desk. The first was full of paper, pens, paper clips, and the like. The second contained a host of medallions, awards, certificates, and photographs. A nametag with Nakamura's name lay on top attached to a braided neck strap.

Carlos pulled the bottom desk drawer and heard only "click." He fumbled through his pockets and produced the lockpick device. Within a few seconds of tinkering with the lock, he slid the door open. Inside were several file folders, labeled in Japanese. Underneath the folders was a black plastic case. Carlos quickly opened the case to see a dart gun inside. He closed it and turned his attention to the file folders.

He opened them one at a time. The first contained

correspondence about one of the company's projects involved with dopamine-producing neurons. He sat down to begin reading the papers, but thought the better of it and simply pulled out a small camera and began photographing the contents, replacing them back into the drawer. He then examined the contents of the other folders.

The second folder grabbed his attention. He turned to the first page. It was a technical report filled with what looked like cross-sectional radiographic pictures of the brain. He flipped through to the end of the report.

He stopped on a phrase in the conclusion, "It is still far too early to access the functionality of the chimpanzee's brain. Anatomically, the chimpanzee has a brain comparable to a human in size and complexity. It would not be implausible, given recent behavioral observations, for the subject to be capable of behavioral complexity on the level of or exceeding that of a human adolescent."

Carlos grinned broadly, and quickly photographed and replaced the remaining contents of the folder. He then reached in his pocket and removed a small device. He scrutinized it and flipped a tiny switch with his fingernail. He slid the device into a tiny crevice on the underside of Nakamura's desk. Confident he had found his target, he closed the drawer and began to make an exit when he heard an inhuman shriek from the back door. He slowly walked to the door, minimizing the quiet sound of his footsteps.

The door was locked. By the side of the door, a card swipe hummed softly with a red LED lit up on its front console. Carlos couldn't help the smile. *Easier to teach particle physics to a politician than security to a scientist.* It was one of the memorable quips of his CIA mentor early in his career. Carlos slid back to the desk, retrieved

Nakamura's name badge, and swiped through the card reader. The door clicked, and the LED glowed green. Carlos opened it, slid the tag in his pocket, and peered inside.

The room was huge, dimly lit, and relatively empty. Inside were long black tables above which cabinets were filled with small jars and glassware. On the far side of the room were rows upon rows of animal cages, each housing a chimpanzee. Carlos stepped into the room.

He swallowed hard as he walked toward the cages, struck by the large, powerful arms of the chimpanzees. A first row of chimps against the far wall paid almost no attention to his entrance. The two other rows became immediately more animated as he came into the room, moving to the front of the cages and watching him.

Carlos looked more closely at the first row. Something was not right about the way they were acting. None of them were moving. They all looked as though they were dazed. He looked over at the chimps again, searching for identifying features. Every one was female. He looked closer. From the shoulder of each chimp, he saw a small blue cap that looked like the port to an IV.

His curiosity growing, he strode over to a cabinet to the side of the cages. Inside the cabinet were two large padded gloves, two dart guns, and a large collection of pill bottles. A sheet of paper was taped to the wall above the cabinet. On the paper was written "Dosages: Prednisone 60 mg in AM, Levofloxacin 500 mg in AM, Diflucan 200 mg in AM, Folate 1 g in AM, mycophenylate 1 g in AM and PM—please do not give to cage 5." A small refrigerator stood next to the cabinet. Inside were large bags of fruit. A small logbook lay on the desk next to a telephone and a ring of keys.

Carlos thumbed through the pages of the logbook. Each page was labeled by a cage number and a series of dated entries. He looked at the last entries on the first page. "Nov. 15 23 weeks 3 days: Fetal Heart Tones 160. Meds given in banana. Afebrile." A realization dawned on him and he looked back at the chimps. *How could he have missed it? Nearly half of the chimps looked obviously pregnant.*

Carlos thumbed through the rest of the book. The last page of the book contained a list of phone numbers:

Nakamura	5317
O.R.	4173
~~Batori~~	~~2315~~
Lab	4175
Tech	2781

He closed the book and replaced it on the table. Next, he turned his attention to the other two rows of chimps, standing only a few feet from one of the rows of cages when another uneasy feeling crept over him. Then he understood. The sounds they were making were not random noise he had heard from chimps in the zoo.

He listened.

From a cage in the middle row, Carlos heard a faint throaty noise. A moment later, the two dozen or so other chimps in the two rows repeated the sound. Several of the chimps then turned, grouped in fours, uttering low gutteral tones barely audible to Carlos.

He moved along the wall to a series of large freezers. He opened one to find it stuffed with racks of small vials, bottles, and tubes, each meticulously labeled with alphanumeric codes. He tried to open another. It wouldn't budge. He found the lock and quickly set to picking it. In a moment, he opened the door and saw a column of four drawers.

Carlos opened the first. Inside were boxes labeled 203d, 214d, 225d. He removed the 203d box from the freezer and placed it on a nearby table. His fingers stung from the bitter cold. He slid off the lid of the box and stared at the contents. An upper tray contained several rows of microscope slides, each with blue, red, and green outlines of tissue samples. Next to the slides in the tray were several containers of formaldehyde containing pink tissue specimens.

Carlos gently removed the tray and gasped at what he saw inside. He took two steps back and dropped the tray onto the floor, hearing a crash as microscope slides shattered into pieces along the floor. The chimps began to shriek at the noise and one by one erupted into activity, banging against their cages.

On the floor next to the box was the unmistakable form of a human fetus with the head surgically removed. A miniature skull rocked back and forth next to the tiny, well-preserved body until coming to rest on a circular hole cut into the bone on the back side. Carlos heard a brisk knock at the far door to Nakamura's office. A voice shouted through the door. "Hey, is everything OK in there?"

Carlos panicked, looking to either side. He quickly began shoveling the slides back into the box, cutting his fingers in the process. He slammed the tray on top, closed the box and replaced it in the freezer, closing the freezer door. The voice came again, this time knocking louder.

"Is someone in there?" He heard the door lock to Naka-mura's office click open.

Carlos quickly ran to the cabinet, grabbed the keyring off its hook, and fumbled with the lock at the first chimp cage in the middle row, the chimp banging the bars near where he was working. The first key failed to fit the lock. So did the second. Carlos heard the beat of footsteps approaching the laboratory.

His fingers were trembling. The third key slid into the lock, and he thrust open the cage door with a bang. The startled monkey took one puzzled look at freedom, and then clamored into the laboratory. Carlos dove behind the freezer as the door to the lab opened. He held his breath and waited.

The footsteps continued a few paces and then stopped abruptly as the door opened. "Oh shit!" he heard a voice exclaim. "You stay right there!" The footsteps retreated rapidly with the slam of the door. Carlos exhaled.

The chimps from the latter two rows then did something utterly unexpected. They began vocalizing all at once, not randomly, but in an organized, chilling fashion. It sounded like each chimp was making the same sound. Carlos could make out repeated syllables coming over and over in synchrony from two of the rows of chimps. Then the chimp that was loose in the laboratory began moving slowly toward Carlos.

Carlos made to flank the chimp, moving toward the door, but the chimp was too fast, anticipating his path. The chimp cornered him against the wall, holding one arm poised while snarling a menacing growl. With the other hand, he held his palm out as though asking for something. Carlos couldn't move. The chimp beckoned with its opened hand, pointing toward Carlos's fist. *The key. It wanted the key.*

Carlos tossed the key behind the animal, and as it stooped to pick it up, he sprinted toward the door. He threw open the door and slammed it shut, reemerging into Nakamura's office. He jumped to the front door and listened again carefully. There was a faint sound of metal and the vocalizations of the chimps, louder and now synchronous—coming to resemble a chant.

Carlos ran across the room, literally throwing Nakamura's nametag back in the desk drawer, stepped outside, and briskly walked down the corridor when he heard approaching footsteps, lots of them. He slipped into an adjacent door and stared into the face of Dr. Michaels, typing at his desk. The muffled footsteps ran past. "Who are you? What do you want?" Michaels asked.

Carlos faked a thick Brazilian accent. "I'm sorry. I am lost. Which way is the cafeteria?"

Michaels relaxed. "Oh, sorry. You *are* lost. It's down that hallway to the end, then left, then left again. That will take you to a staircase. Go down two flights and ask for help. Someone should be around to point you in the right direction."

"Thank you very much," Carlos managed.

"Say, you look a little pale. You feeling all right?"

The footsteps clamored past the door outside as several individuals ran by talking as they walked. "He was loose?!" Carlos overheard.

"Just need a little dinner. Been working too long."

"Know how that is. Good luck." Michaels stood from his desk. "Say, is something going on out there?"

Carlos peered out and shrugged innocently.

Michaels took two steps toward the half-open door, and called out, "Is everything all right out there?"

Carlos heard the response. "Chimp's loose in Naka-mura's office!"

Michaels sprang into action. "I want that door locked. Everyone stay out of there. I'll handle this. Page Dr. Simons and Dr. Nakamura now!"

"Yes sir!"

Michaels turned back toward Carlos. "You better be going. We have a problem here."

Carlos didn't have to fake a queasy look of concern. "Thank you. I'll do that." He walked briskly into the hall-way in the opposite direction from Nakamura's office.

Carlos opened the door fully to the empty hallway. He heard voices from next door and a bellow of a chim-panzee as he quickly retraced his path down the corridor. He turned left, walked down the connected corridor and turned right.

He took a deep breath, and began walking calmly until he arrived at the atrium. He looked out the front door, then opened it and stealthily moved behind some trees to the far side. Jordan was still there arguing with the crowd. His loud voice intoned, "My crew will be here with tear gas in two minutes." He tapped his intercom. "If you want to file a protest, go ahead, but I am authorized to use force on vandals. I suggest you go peacefully."

The woman with a megaphone in her lap shot a glance to Carlos's figure in the trees and stood up. "All right," she said calmly. "We'll go. But you'll see it all on the evening news. And we'll be back." She turned to leave, and the others joined her. Jordan and Diego watched as they began collecting their equipment. The woman turned to one side and motioned for Jordan and Diego. They turned their bodies to face her.

"One more thing," she said. "I don't know how you can do what you do and still sleep at night." As she spoke, Carlos slipped through the trees and joined the group. One of the protestors quickly handed him a sign with a wink.

The group turned to leave when they stopped abruptly. In their path was a chimpanzee standing on the road, looking at them quizzically. The protestors stopped uneasily. For all of their good intentions, none had ever seen a chimpanzee so close. In the chimpanzee's hand was a folded up palm frond shaped like a megaphone. The chimp put the funnel to its mouth and hooted into the mouthpiece, imitating what he had seen the protestors doing.

Jordan let out a guffaw. "Now you see how caged in our chimpanzees are. You poor saps just picked the wrong place to pull your stunt. Have any of you ever seen a chimpanzee in the wild?"

As he spoke, the chimpanzee began to tremble. The makeshift megaphone fell to the ground. His arm began to shake with increasing force until he toppled over and his whole body began to convulse in rhythmic contractions.

Pulsating in a frightening display, the chimp elicited a scream from one of the group members. The group broke into a run and passed the chimpanzee toward their waiting boat. Jordan looked at the chimpanzee in horror as he heard a voice shout through the megaphone, "We'll be back!"

As the group slowed their pace into the distance, the

security guards watched as the chimp stopped convulsing and lay motionless on the ground. Diego turned to Jordan and asked, "That is the one with the collar, no? Why is everyone so uptight about that one?"

Jordan put his arm around Diego and answered, "Can't tell you, son. Just be grateful he helped us get rid of those hippies tonight. What a bunch of losers."

NAKAMURA ran to the office door, where Michaels and Simons were already gathered. "What happened!" he hissed. He looked over his shoulder to make sure no one else was around.

"One of the animals got out of its cage."

"Is it back in?"

"Not yet. We didn't have a tranquilizer."

Simons spoke to both Michaels and Nakamura. "I told you we shouldn't let the techs take care of the chimerics. They must have left a door loose. Those chimps are too smart and too pissed for us to be making mistakes like that. What if he'd escaped? This one hasn't exactly had a lot of positive human interaction like the alpha."

Michaels snapped back, "What choice do we have? Do you want a full-time job cleaning monkey shit?"

Nakamura raised his hands. "I have a dart gun in my office. Let's go in and get this chimp back in its cage. Then we can talk."

The other two nodded. Nakamura opened the door.

They walked into his office, and Nakamura unlocked the drawer on his desk, pulling out the dart gun. He grabbed his nametag from the desk drawer and swiped it

on the card reader on the laboratory door. The others followed him inside.

As soon as they stepped in, their eyes jumped to an
open cage in the middle row.

"I thought you said one was loose, not gone! Where is
he?" Nakamura said angrily.

"That's what I was told!"

The three began walking toward the cage.

They heard a dull thud from behind them and whirled
around. A single chimp was positioned at the open door
to the office. *Where did he come from?* Michaels looked
up at the network of pipes and ducts along the vaulted
ceiling. The chimp made a long slow whistling sound.

Nakamura shouldered the dart gun immediately and
took aim. As he steadied to fire, the sound of clanking
metal came from behind. He whirled around. The entire
two rows of chimeric chimps, several dozen, were now
out of their wide-open cages and scrambling directly toward them, *toward him.*

Simons screamed.

PART II
LONE AND DREARY WORLD

The forest interior is a magical and mercurial place—an enchanted realm where anything is possible. . . . Grass in the form of bamboo grows 100 feet high, at the rate of 36 inches in twenty-four hours. . . . There are "roses" with 145-foot trunks; daisies and violets as big as apple trees; 60-foot tree ferns . . . , and lily pads over 5 feet in diameter . . . , flowers 38 inches across, weighing 38 pounds, and holding several gallons of liquid in its nectaries. . . . bats with 5.5-foot wingspans, vining rattan palms with 785-foot trunks; 18-foot cobras . . . , frogs so big they eat rats, and rodents themselves weighing over 100 pounds.

　　—(Arnold Newman, *Tropical Rainforest* [New York: Facts on File,
　　　1990])

And the LORD God commanded the man, saying, Of every tree of the garden thou mayest freely eat:
But of the tree of the knowledge of good and evil, thou shalt not eat of it: for in the day that thou eatest thereof thou shalt surely die.

　　—(Genesis 2:16-17 [King James Bible])

FIFTEEN

"**WHY** don't we try one more time Mrs. Thompson?" Susan Archer-Bentham turned on her recorder with a click, then folded her hands on her burgundy pantsuit. Touching as little of the threadbare couch as possible, she sat up straight and began speaking. "I am here in the St. Louis home of Christa and Jerry Thompson who are the proud and exhausted parents of quintuplets just six weeks old. How is it, Mrs. Thompson, to finally have the last of your babies home with . . ."

Her last word was obscured by a loud crash from an adjoining room. Two infants on a blanket a few feet away erupted into hysterics, "Laaa, Laaa, Laaa!"

Jerry lurched to his feet, exclaiming, "That's it! Taylor, what in the Sam Hill are you doing?"

Christa Thompson, an infant on each arm, awkwardly pointed to the tape recorder, hissing "Jerry! It's OK."

Jerry, paying no attention, stomped into the kitchen.

"Aw, Taylor. The whole can of rice?! Now clean that up! Hey! Where's your shirt?" From the kitchen the patter of very fast footsteps preceded only momentarily the scene of a small child darting through the living room into the bathroom on the far side, slamming the door behind him.

An embarrassed Jerry walked over to open the bathroom door. No sooner had he opened the door than the child sprinted out, carrying behind him a trail of rapidly unfolding toilet paper. He darted around the couch where he dropped the free edge of the toilet paper, and ran to an open staircase on the far side of the room.

He reached down and deftly stripped off his diaper, incanting, "Hate! Hate! Hate!" in a tiny voice, then hurtled up the stairs as fast as his little naked body could go, stumbling every few steps.

Christa turned bright red and said softly, "Sorry, that's the naughtiest word he knows. He tries to get our attention . . . you know how it is with two-year-olds." Turning to her overweight husband, she said, "Jerry, the doctor said to just ignore his tantrums."

Jerry, completely exasperated, turned to sit down on a chair that looked a poor match for its occupant. Christa, in the meantime, had stood up to exchange the two babies in her arms for the two crying infants on the blanket, with a nervous glance over to a sleeping child in a vibrating chair a few feet away.

Susan stood up as if to help, then thought the better of it and switched off the recorder. "Well, Mr. and Mrs. Thompson, I think we have plenty of tape to cut and paste a short segment together. Thank you so much for your hospitality." Jerry's face looked crestfallen.

Christa muttered something like "anytime" as she

gingerly rocked two babies out of sync, while she lifted each one in turn for a whiff of their diapers.

At that moment a shrill ring came from inside Susan's handbag. She reached in and pulled out a small cell phone. She motioned that she was going to slip outside, grabbed her tape recorder, and stepped out the front door with a sigh. "I'll call you when we have the clip ready to air," she said, waving good-bye and shaking their hands hurriedly.

She took a few brisk steps down the walk, unfolded the phone, and snapped, "Susan."

"Ms. Archer-Bentham?" The male voice on the other end was completely unfamiliar.

She responded, somewhat less irritated, "This is she."

"Ms. Archer-Bentham, I have a story for you."

"I'm listening, but it had better top an interview with screaming quintuplets."

The voice ignored her attempt at humor. "How would you like the first exclusive interview with an intelligent, alien being in the history of broadcast journalism?"

"Oh, for crying out loud, Jack. Is that you? I don't need this right now."

"How about a story about the first human child conceived in nonhuman parents?"

"Listen, I don't have time for jokes right now. Who is this?"

"I understand your skepticism, Ms. Archer-Bentham, but this isn't a joke, and I'm completely serious. Can you guarantee anonymity of your sources?"

"Of course I can. Even the crackpots. Now are you going to tell me what this is all about?"

"I need your assurance that my identity will be kept in

complete confidence in exchange for a tip on the story of
the century."

Susan became more businesslike. "Unless you're going to tell me you or someone else is about to kill someone, commit suicide, or endanger national security, you
have my word."

"When could you be in Chicago?"

"I'm flying through O'Hare tonight."

"What time?"

"Five twenty. United from St. Louis."

"I'll be there."

"Listen, I don't have time for games. I have an hour
layover for you to make your case—no more."

The receiver clicked.

Susan took a deep breath. He was a nut. It wouldn't be
the first time some or other psychotic had hounded a reporter to cover his pet conspiracy theory. They were
mostly harmless, she had learned, and usually turned else-
where when refused. Still, he had sounded remarkably articulate, and the exchange was different. How did he get
her cell number?

What she hadn't told him was that she was so frustrated with the mindless, uninspiring stories she had been
covering that she was ready to quit. It seemed she had
fallen to a new low with this latest story. As a health and
science correspondent for the Associated Press, she had
expected to spend each week dissecting the intellectual
high country of string theory or the newest cure for breast
cancer. She had not intended to spend her time being
drooled on by a gaggle of infants or sifting through piles
of press releases on hypnotism, magnets, and health.

The truth was she was desperate. Her job was not

threatened, only her ego. With a husband who was CEO of one of the fastest growing Fortune 500 companies, she was tired of being known as "Bentham's wife, the reporter." When she was honest with herself, she knew that the only reason she had gotten the job with AP was because of her husband's reputation. She had thought covering the hard sciences would earn her a little respect of her own, but her husband treated her job as a nice way to keep her busy while he was gone, which was basically all day.

And now she was taking seriously a tip on alien visitors. She got into her rental car and started laughing out loud. She laughed until her mascara started to run and her chest hurt from laughing and the rest of her hurt from feeling so useless and unhappy.

"**MS.** Archer-Bentham?" The voice woke her from a daze.

"Yes." She had all but forgotten the strange conversation from earlier in the day, but she recognized the voice instantly. Attached to the voice was an immaculately dressed businessman with a smile and an intelligent, charismatic expression.

"I thought it might be you. Free to talk?"

"Sure. You hungry?" Her curiosity instantly sparked as she sidestepped to move away from the stream of passengers exiting the gangway. How did he get in there anyway? Had he bought a ticket just to talk with her?

"Not at the moment. I was actually hoping to talk in private, if such a condition exists in this airport." He gave her a determined smile. Whatever he was, he was serious. She followed his lead out of the terminal, through the security gate, and down a packed corridor. They descended on an escalator and came upon a large hallway full of New Age music with brightly colored neon tubes tracking across the ceiling. A ubiquitous voice sounded instructions about the moving walkway.

"Come this way," he said, moving away from the crowds pressing in either direction to stand alone against the far wall. She joined him.

"My name is Nathan Hall, and I'm an investment banker specializing in valuations and investment management of biopharmaceutical firms. I run a midsized mutual fund and investment consulting business. I'm afraid I've done something a bit unethical."

"Nobody's perfect," Susan encouraged him on.

"In my business, information is king. I find that information, however I can get it. Where you come in is in relation to some information I've uncovered about a major pharmaceutical research company, BrainStem Therapeutics."

"I know the company."

"Yes, I know. I heard your story on the radio a couple weeks ago."

Susan smiled in spite of herself. It was the perfect way to get her attention.

Nathan continued. "I recently decided something big was breaking at BrainStem's lab in Brazil."

"How did you know that?" Susan's weight shifted from one foot to the other as her feet began to hurt.

"When you track financial data, it's easy to tell when someone begins to throw money around like it's going out of style. You know something is going on. Anyway, I sent a fellow I do business with on occasion to find out what exactly was causing the increased activity."

"Some kind of a corporate spy?"

"You might say that."

"So where do the aliens come in?" she said with a raised eyebrow.

"Let me show you some photographs." He opened his briefcase and pulled out a manila folder. Inside was a large stack of papers, from which Nathan removed a few. "What do you see?"

Susan fingered a faxed image showing a photograph. "It's an ape." She wondered if he expected more.

"Chimpanzee, actually. BrainStem Therapeutics is establishing a breeding facility at their Amazon Basin laboratory complex. What I've found out, though, is that there is something extraordinary going on in their breeding project. They've created a genetically modified chimpanzee that is fully sentient."

"Sentient?"

"Conscious, intelligent, however you want to say it. Somehow, they found a way to make a chimp with a vastly enlarged brain, with smarts to rival human beings. They've created a new species."

Susan furrowed her forehead. "Who did this?"

"Chief scientist's name is Nakamura. He's a brilliant developmental geneticist, and has a talented staff of senior molecular biologists. If there's anyone capable of such a thing, he would be the one."

"How old is this chimp?" He had her complete interest now.

"Five years old. It's only in the last few months, for whatever reason, that they've realized the chimp's potential, however."

"How do they know it's intelligent?"

"Brain scans, intelligence testing, behavioral studies. I have everything documented from the company's own records. They're even teaching the thing to read."

"So why me? What's in it for you, and what's the angle?"

Nathan ignored the questions. "There's more. My, er, friend found something else while he was inside. He sort of stumbled across one of their laboratories where they are breeding chimpanzees and found something very disturbing." He was practically whispering. "All of the documents that I have are very secretive about how the necessary genetic enhancement was discovered. I think I know how, and I can't sleep at night knowing."

She leaned forward and asked hypnotically, "Tell me."

"My source was looking in the lab and saw a row of cages with pregnant chimpanzees. He found an elaborate regimen of immunosuppressant drugs that were apparently being given to the chimpanzees. In a locked freezer by the cages, he found the remains of dozens of human fetuses, carefully dated with tissue samples from the fetuses' brains."

"Do you have photographs?" She held her breath.

"No. He was forced to leave before he could snap a picture. But he got a good look at one of them, and the fetus was in perfect condition, with the head severed by a competent surgeon. The specimens were very carefully prepared."

"So couldn't a laboratory have access to a reference set of aborted fetuses?"

"No way. First, it's been patently illegal, at least in the U.S., for years to use aborted fetuses for research. Second, some of the boxes he saw were dated into the third trimester, beyond the point that the babies are technically able to live outside the mother's uterus, and beyond the point that abortion would be legal."

"So where's he getting the fetuses?"

"He's growing them. That's why he needs the immuno-suppressants. He's growing human fetuses in chimpanzee wombs to get the information on brain development he needs. Lack of information about which proteins are turned on in the brain when in development is the key scientific hurdle to understanding how the brain is constructed. It looks as though he's found a shortcut."

"Nathan, I can't publish any of this. The information was illegally obtained. There's no conclusive proof that you're right. Do you have any idea what the liability would be if we're wrong?"

"If it's over your head, I can ask someone else." Nathan's comment stung deeply.

"Can I talk to your source?"

"Absolutely. In fact, he's agreed to be part of a factfinding team should you want to go investigate."

Susan froze. The thought of a trip to Brazil, chasing after one of the most important stories in recent history, made her ache with anticipation and fear.

She looked at him coldly. "I have to know why you want this public."

Nathan's face looked innocent as a young soldier leaving to battle. "This has gone way beyond business. I couldn't live with myself if I let this continue. Listen, this has Pulitzer Prize written all over it and you know it. I need to know if you'll chase it." He offered the manila folder to her like a carrot.

"Where can I call you?"

"Don't . . . unless you fail." Nathan handed her the

folder. "His name's Carlos, and his hotel number is inside." He started walking away down the corridor. Susan stood frozen in place until long after he was out of sight.

Nathan Hall picked up his cell phone and dialed a number. "Hi, it's Nate. I want you to sell everything we own in BrainStem Therapeutics and Soliton Industries over the next week. Sell short as far as our margin safely covers on both. And I don't want this getting public for at least a month. No, I want it to go completely unnoticed. Take the hit if you have to."

SIXTEEN

JAMIE hunched over a small laptop computer, attaching a cable to a port on the back of the machine. The cable connected to a small device with two large buttons on a metal box barely held together with duct tape. Above the buttons were two light panels and a speaker. "That should do it, Sameer. Come have a look."

Sameer had been playing a game with the chimpanzee in the far corner of the nursery. Jamie had wandered over a while earlier out of curiosity, and found the game involved a dozen cardboard shapes that if arranged correctly could form a perfect square. The chimp had been avidly puzzling out different permutations of the shapes. Next to Sameer was a box with a scrambled Rubik's Cube, a stack of interconnected rings, and an assortment of jigsaw puzzles.

At Jamie's invitation, Sameer hopped over to the small table on which Jamie's computer was now displayed. He looked at the box and laughed. "Where did you get this piece of junk?"

Jamie grinned at him. "Made it myself by ravishing an old mouse and using some spare parts in the shop. It felt good to get my hands on a soldering iron."

"What does it do?"

"It plays the Prisoner's Dilemma. Stayed up half the night writing the software for the simulations."

"The Prisoner's Dilemma?"

"It's a game, Sameer. If we're going to show this chimp thinks like a human does, the best way is to watch him play games. Humans show some of their most revealing behavior in games. And the Prisoner's Dilemma is one of the key games scientists use to demonstrate unusual, uniquely human behavior."

"How does it work?"

"The story goes something like this. Suppose two criminals are accused of and imprisoned for a serious crime. While waiting for their trial, they get wind that the prosecutor has shaky evidence against them. Their attorney advises them that if they both keep quiet and don't confess, they'll probably get something like one year in the slammer and then go free. If they rat on each other, they'll probably both get at least two years for confessing but cooperating."

"How do they know what they'll get?"

Jamie sighed. "Let's just say they have a very smart lawyer."

"All right."

"So one of the prisoners asks, 'What if I stay quiet, but he rats on me?' The attorney answers that the one who keeps quiet will probably get three years while the one who sings will go free. The dilemma is as follows: should the prisoners cooperate and settle for one year each, or try and outsmart each other and go free?"

Sameer looked frustrated. "I didn't quite follow you."

Jamie pulled out her notebook from her pocket and began to sketch a small diagram. "Maybe this will help. Think of it this way. Each player has two choices and has to make a choice without knowing what their partner will choose. Let's call the prisoners Bugsy and Yard Dog. This grid shows what sentence each prisoner gets for each of the possible combinations of choices."

THE PRISONER'S DILEMMA

	Yard Dog Cooperates (Keeps quiet)	Yard Dog Defects (Tells on Bugsy)
Bugsy Cooperates (Keeps quiet)	Bugsy: 1 year Yard Dog: 1 year	Bugsy: 3 years Yard Dog: Free!
Bugsy Defects (Tells on Yard Dog)	Bugsy: Free! Yard Dog: 3 years	Bugsy: 2 years Yard Dog: 2 years

Sameer stared at the table for a minute. "Easy. They should keep their mouths shut and cut their losses at one year. That's what I would do."

Jamie grinned. "That's why you lose, Sameer. Since you have explained why it's so beneficial to us both to cooperate,

I would figure that's what you would do and put you away for three years while I went home to count my money."

"But what if I thought the same way? If we both tell on each other, we both get two years. Isn't it smarter to cooperate, and cut our sentence in half?" Sameer looked upset at having lost.

"I agree, if you think there is so much honor among thieves."

"But it's not about honor; it's simple self-interest. You do better if you both cooperate."

"That's why I want to test the chimp on this game. It's a great way to see what kind of a strategist he is. Humans always blow it on a game like this. Truth is, the game has a simple solution."

"You cooperate."

"No, you rat on your partner. Think of it this way. If you tell on me, the best thing I can do is tell on you too. That way I get two years instead of three. If you don't tell on me, the best thing I can do is tell on you. That way I get off free. No matter what you do, I come out smelling better if I sell you out."

"I see." Sameer admitted defeat. "But it's still ironic that if both people follow that strategy, they both lose compared to what they'd have gotten if they both cooperated."

Jamie shrugged.

"How do you explain all this to the chimp?"

"I don't have to. I have the computer set up to select one choice or the other as soon as the chimp presses a button. His reward will be based on how his choice compares to the computer's choice. I've changed the rewards slightly to a point system: one point for each year you stay out of jail. If he pushes the cooperate button and the computer turns on the cooperate light, he gets two points, and the speaker beeps twice. If the computer turns on the defect light, the chimp gets nothing. If the chimp pushes the defect button, he gets either one or three points depending on which light the computer chooses. For each beep you hear, please give the chimp a piece of candy. Call him over." Jamie tossed a bag of Skittles to Sameer.

Sameer beckoned for the chimp to come over. When he arrived, Jamie pointed to the two buttons. The chimp pressed the one on the left. Shortly thereafter, the light on the left turned on and the speaker beeped twice. The chimp appeared pleased, and expressed his pleasure with a bellow when Sameer handed him two pieces of candy. The chimp then pressed the button on the right. The light on the right went on and the speaker beeped once.

The chimp alternated pressing the left and right buttons four more times, each time collecting his appropriate reward. After that, the chimp depressed the right button, and continued pressing the right button time after time. Eventually, he tried to press it faster and faster with one hand, while he held out his other hand to Sameer to collect the candy that accumulated as fast as the chimp could make the device beep.

Jamie laughed. "He solved it, Sameer. This is wonderful!" Jamie felt as pleased as the chimp looked. She punched a key and the game stopped.

"So what does that mean?" asked Sameer.

"Just that the chimp's got a good head on its shoulders. Now comes the interesting part. You mentioned you weren't satisfied with the solution I gave you."

"I can see that it's right, but it is still self-defeating."

"True, and this enters into the strategy if you play the game more than once. If you play the same opponent repeatedly, you get a very different game called the iterated prisoner's dilemma. This is the interesting game, and it's the primary model for how scientists study the evolution of cooperation."

"How so?" Sameer asked.

"It's like this. If you have a memory of your opponent's last move, you can take advantage of opponents that you trust will cooperate, and can form a mutual cooperation where both partners do better than partners who always rat on each other. The key point is that you have to play the same opponent multiple times to establish trust."

Sameer thought for a moment. "So it's not necessarily the best solution to always defect if you play the same partner more than once. That makes sense. So what is the best strategy?"

"It's a lot more complicated than you might think. Over two decades ago, someone named Axelrod held a huge tournament to test strategies in this very game. The rules were simple. Anyone was invited to submit a computer program that would choose whether to cooperate or defect based only on one piece of information: what your opponent did in the previous round."

"So who won?"

"A remarkably simple little program called Tit for Tat."

"What was the strategy?"

"If your opponent ratted last round, you rat this round. If he cooperated last round, you cooperate this round."

"That's it?!"

"Simple justice. Do unto your coinmate as he did to you. Phrase it however you want. That little strategy won the whole tournament. It wasn't taken advantage of by freeloader programs that always defected in the tournament, but it formed mutually cooperative relationships with programs that were willing to cooperate."

"So that's the best strategy?"

"It was in the tournament."

Jamie pushed another button and the game came back to life. The chimp pressed repeatedly the button on the right again, and before long started getting a single beep with every round. A few moments later, the chimp started pressing the button on the left, and received alternately two or zero beeps. The chimp didn't seem to mind receiving no candy this round. The increased complexity held his interest.

The beeps sounded faster and faster, to where Sameer could no longer follow the gameplay easily. After a period, the chimp slowed down and the scientists could see the chimp was again bored.

"Fascinating," Jamie remarked.

"I don't get it. It doesn't look like he's playing Tit for Tat. He just defected after his opponent cooperated. Yet he's doing reasonably well from the sound of the beeps."

"He's playing Pavlov."

"Pavlov?" Sameer asked.

"Yes. I have the computer set to Tit for Tat, with occasional random errors to keep things interesting. It turns out that the iterated prisoner's dilemma is much more complicated than anyone realized. It has now been mathematically proven that there is no best strategy. In fact, the game is one of the standard models for chaos theory in population dynamics. Every strategy can be beaten, and the strategy that was found over ten years after the tournament to beat Tit for Tat is called Pavlov.

"Pavlov is a strategy that focuses not so much on what your opponent did last round but who won last round. If you won, you play the same choice. If you lost, you switch. It turns out to be, along with a more generous version of Tit for Tat, the only strategy that can dominate Tit for Tat. I've been watching, and the chimp initially was playing that generous Tit for Tat, and then switched to Pavlov when he realized it was more effective. The chimp's strategy has been virtually flawless."

"Is there more to the game?"

"Oh yes! I would love to see how the chimp behaves against complex populations of strategies—whether he can sense the chaotic fluctuations in which strategies are dominant and how to counter them. I'd also like to try another game called the ultimatum game. But this is going to take a lot more programming on my part."

The chimp, bored with the game, began looking around for the package of candy he had been enjoying earlier.

Sameer's cell phone rang, and he began speaking while Jamie walked over to the box of puzzles Sameer and the chimp had been playing with earlier. As she looked over the toys, she stopped abruptly and called out, "Sameer, there's something here you should see."

"Just a minute. It's Roger."

The chimp began sniffing around Sameer, poking around Sameer's pocket that housed the package of candy. Sameer moved the candy behind his back, playing a game of keep away from the chimp while he spoke. "Just a minute!" he said to the chimp with his hand over the mouthpiece. He began backing up toward a bookshelf, holding the candy out of reach behind him. Jamie watched the two from a distance.

The chimp reached one last time for the candy. Unsuccessful, the chimp walked directly in front of Sameer and looked him in the eyes. A second later, the arm of the chimp whizzed across Sameer's cheek, whacking the phone fifteen yards where it smashed against the fence of the compound.

Sameer tumbled backward onto the ground, trying to reorient himself. The chimp pursued him, holding his hand out over Sameer expectantly. Sameer gave him the package of candy, and the chimp scooted away to empty the remaining contents in his mouth, as calm and friendly as he had been a moment before. Sameer's ear was dripping with blood from a laceration the blow had inflicted. He slowly backed away from the chimp toward Jamie.

"Did you see what he did?" Sameer asked.

"I did. Are you okay? We're going to need to stitch that up."

"It hurts like the dickens." Sameer held pressure on the wound with his fist.

"Look at this." Jamie pointed to the cardboard figures Sameer and the chimp had been playing with earlier. The shapes were arranged into a perfect cross.

"I didn't teach him to make that." Sameer said. Looking into the box, he pulled out the Rubik's Cube. "And the last time I saw this, it was scrambled." The cube showed a solid color on each face.

Jamie and Sameer looked over at the chimp, and were horrified to see he was sprawled out on the ground, convulsing from head to foot. Jamie reached his side first, shouting to Sameer, "Help me get this bookshelf away from him!"

Sameer followed her order, then stood passively over the chimp until the seizure activity stopped.

"Has he done this before?" Jamie asked.

Sameer shook his head.

"What's going on, Sameer?"

"We're losing control of him." Sameer's glassy expression was fixed on the chimp. He put a bloodied hand to his ear and walked out of the nursery, motioning Jamie to follow.

"We need to tell Kenji about this," said Sameer.

"If you can find him. I was looking for him all morning—wanted to invite him to the experiment. I don't think he's in today."

"That's odd. He didn't say anything about a vacation. In fact, I can't remember when he's ever taken a vacation."

"Some timing. Let's go find Stiles."

SEVENTEEN

"**NO** way, Susan. Drop it. It's dead. Did you just wake up and say, I think I'll get sued for half a billion dollars today?" Cynthia O'Reilly spread her hands apart with finality.

"Hold on a minute, Cindy. I'm thinking." Jack Merkel was the senior editor for AP's Washington Bureau, and rarely intruded on O'Reilly's editorial privilege. "Look at it this way. The Supreme Court has ruled that in a matter of public concern the plaintiff has to prove falsity to win a libel suit. This is a clear case of public interest."

"Jack, we can't even afford the legal costs to tell that to the judge. A libel suit is a dead certainty, and we can't fund it."

Jack stroked his chin for a second. "Susan, this source smells to heaven. You have to have something to put on the table or this will never float. Did this Carlos guy check out? What do you really think? Is it true? What if you chase it and come up empty?"

Susan looked at her editors, her thoughts racing. After two days of not eating, not sleeping, she had all but convinced herself that this story was the most important chance of her life and she wasn't giving it up without a hair-pulling catfight. "I know it's true, and I can prove it. Carlos checks out. Let me go after it, and if I can't get solid evidence that there's something very wrong going on in four weeks, I'll drop it."

Cynthia shook her head. "This is too sensational. It's probably a poorly veiled attempt to perform corporate sabotage by this Hall guy."

"If Susan could get an ethically valid source to confirm even a few key details, a jury would have a very difficult time awarding damages. What about some convincing footage of this ape, a few admissions by employees, who knows? Scientists are lousy at keeping secrets. If Sue's clever about it, she may be able to verify the key elements of the story. It's a long shot . . ."

Cynthia wavered as she rapped her fingers on the glass wall by which she sat. She thought aloud. "It won't be easy. I could just see a quick DNA test proving he's a regular old chimp, a few expert witnesses testifying there's nothing but chimps in their lab, and AP gets sued for all we're worth. Who knows what kind of goofy deal they might have in Brazil for aftermarket fetuses for research. There's just no proof. Did you ever see the smart horse on Letterman—the one that supposedly tapped its hoof to solve arithmetic but froze up on the air? All it takes is one trick like that with your chimp and the jury will start writing zeroes. There's lots that can go wrong, and with a goliath like Soliton financing the lawyers, I guarantee that it will go wrong."

"How much would you need for an investigation?" Jack asked.

Susan tried to hide her pleasure at this turn in the conversation. "A plane ticket out for myself, a small operating budget—shouldn't be too much."

Cynthia, sensing she was losing the battle, altered her line in the sand. "I have your word that you give this up in four weeks if you can't produce some cold hard evidence to validate the story?"

Susan crossed her fingers behind her back. "I promise."

A concerned look appeared on Jack's face. "I'm worried about this too, Susan. I'm going to grill you on every detail, and I want ethical reporting. No breaking and entering. No bribes. Nothing that will come back to haunt you."

Susan looked at both of them with a smile. "You won't regret this. When can I go?"

Cynthia seemed resigned to the outcome. "You edited the quintuplet and the chemotherapy sketches yet?"

Susan broadened her smile as she pulled two disks out of her pocket.

Cynthia started walking out of the room. As she opened the glass door, she looked back to say, "I hope you can put 'em out of business for good."

Susan mouthed a quick thanks to Jack and bounded out of the office to her desk. Thrilled, excited, scared, and thankful, she punched a few buttons on her computer and had plane tickets set up in moments. Grabbing her coat, she floated out of the office, down the stairs, and to the parking lot. Her silver Lexus clicked open, and she sped out of the lot onto the streets of Washington DC. As she drove, she flipped out her phone and speed-dialed her husband's mobile. "Hi sweetie, if you get this, call me back. Guess who's going to Brazil!"

THIRTY minutes later she had found her destination. After she pulled into a metered parking space, she jumped out, fed the meter, and briskly walked toward the office building looming in front of her. The elevator was fast and ejected her on the twelfth floor to a tasteful office with the words Center for Conservative Values in silver script on the windowed doors. She walked inside.

A lone secretary kept watch at the front desk. "May I help you?"

Susan strode amicably to the receptionist. "Yes, please. I need to see Reverend Jones about an urgent matter."

"I'm sorry, that would be impossible today. May I take your number and a message?"

"Look, I know this is a bit unconventional. Perhaps I should explain myself. You see, I'm a reporter for the Associated Press, and a big supporter of Reverend Jones's work. I happen to know that there is a very unflattering story about the reverend and the center brewing. I think a little notice might serve to dissipate some of the hard feelings involved and put your work in a vastly more positive light. I really do think he'd like to see me." She smiled as she lied to the man behind the desk. With a wink, she added, "I'm taking a big risk being here."

The young man thought for a moment, and said, "Why don't you give me a minute." He abruptly got up, and walked through a door and disappeared. After a few minutes, he returned. "The reverend has graciously agreed to make time for you. Please go on back."

Susan thanked the receptionist and was met just inside the door by a tall, handsome figure in his late forties with a hand the size of Texas and a voice to match. "Howdy, ma'am. It's always a pleasure to speak with the fine men and women of the press. I must say I do believe I recognize your name."

"Hello Reverend. Very pleased to meet you. Thanks for seeing me."

"Come on in and have a seat. Now what can I do for you?" The director's office was elegant. A large oak desk sat on a pleasant beige carpet. Several pictures with classical Christian scenes hung on the walls. A framed picture of the reverend with the president of the United States was featured prominently next to a U.S. flag behind his desk. Two chairs were positioned before his desk, into one of which Susan slid. The crest of the organization and a scripted caption were inscribed on the front of the desk.

"I must confess to a small deception, Reverend," Susan began. "You see, the matter I wish to speak about with you is indeed urgent, but I thought it best not to disclose it to anyone other than yourself."

A hint of irritation was immediately covered up on the man's pleasant face. "Please go on," he gestured.

"It is true that I am a reporter for the Associated Press, and I cover the science and health beat. Recently I have come across a tip for a story of incredible significance, one that might be particularly important for you and your organization. You must understand that what we discuss is to be held in confidence?"

He nodded passively.

"There is a very large company performing biomedical research. I would rather not say which company right now. I have some convincing evidence from an inside source"—she patted a manila folder on her lap—"that this company has been secretly performing research that is morally dubious." Her tone of voice matched her audience, portending a coming sermon.

"As you know," she continued, "there is a growing laxity among our society about where the line should be drawn on medical research. Well, the issue at hand is that this company is working on a breakthrough that may have come at the expense of secret research on human fetuses, grown for the sole purpose of medical research."

"Indeed." The reverend leaned forward, steepling his fingers, a glint in his eyes.

"In fact, the research appears to have a reckless disregard for human life on a number of fronts, and may have as its consequence the creation of intelligent apes that blur the distinction between man and animal, between medical research, and playing God." She paused for effect.

"I sense in you a delicate moral compass, ma'am. Now tell me, is this research that is likely to take the lives of the innocent unborn?"

"In every sense of the word, Reverend. My issue is that although I have become convinced myself through protected sources that this is indeed going on, I'm afraid my research is not sufficient for bringing these crimes to light. It seems that unless someone is able to properly document what has happened, the research may not only continue, but the fruits of the research may be lauded as a reason for continued efforts in a similar vein. The dark background may never come to the light of day."

"I'm listening very closely, ma'am."

"If their discovery is allowed to proceed through normal channels, it will be very difficult to challenge the usefulness of their research. Any effort would be greeted with the suspicion of being nothing more than sour grapes. Now, on the other hand, if we could steal their thunder, so to speak, and present the story in its proper light, there may be a powerful societal backlash against such unethical research that could chill others from trying in the future." She finished with a flourish of her hand.

"How may I help you in your excellent cause?"

"Well, unfortunately, we lack the resources to undertake a proper fact-finding expedition. Now I could pass this story on to the more liberal network media, but the story just might get turned around in the process. Do you understand what I mean?"

"Perfectly."

"A small sum of money would be most helpful in bringing this news to light in the proper way."

"Might I ask for some corroboration of what this evidence might be?" he asked politely.

"Certainly," Susan smiled. She spent several minutes showing him carefully selected documents about the genetically altered chimpanzee.

"Why don't you come with me?" The reverend stood up and beckoned to the front door. When they passed back to the front desk, the reverend addressed the receptionist. "Young man, I do believe this fine reporter has a worthy cause that could benefit from a sum of two hundred thousand dollars, payable immediately."

The shock on the secretary's face was transient. "Yes, sir. I'll see to it right now."

Susan smiled and winked at the secretary, bidding good day to the reverend and thanking him warmly as he disappeared back through the door.

"Please keep me posted," the reverend waved.

ONCE again outside, Susan opened her cell phone and dialed a number. There was a short pause. "Carlos."

"Hello, Carlos, this is Susan again. I have your fee, and I'm on my way."

"That is good news, Ms. Archer-Bentham. I shall greatly look forward to working with you. I will make the arrangements we discussed."

"That would be wonderful, Carlos."

"Ms. Archer-Bentham, there is one other thing. I have a most interesting new development to speak with you about. When you arrive with payment, I think you will find it particularly useful."

EIGHTEEN

JEREMY Evans stripped off his bloody latex gloves and tossed them in the garbage. "We've got a pretty good signal in the art line, Rog. Why don't you drop the propofol down a bit and see if we can't get him a bit less sedated."

Roger Stiles pushed a few buttons on an IV pump, and stared at a monitor over the chimpanzee's head. Jeremy had just placed a catheter in the femoral artery, and the sawtooth waves of the chimpanzee's blood pressure tracked in synchrony with the ECG directly above on the monitor. There were two monitors mounted above the exam table. One monitor showed horizontal tracings of heart rate, blood pressure, oxygen saturation, and respirations, one above the other, each in different bright colors. To the right of each tracing were large digital numbers showing average values for each parameter. On the other monitor were sixteen different horizontal tracings showing apparently random brain wave fluctuations.

"You recording yet?" Stiles asked back.

Jeremy sat down at a computer terminal a few feet away and started typing. "EEG's on continuous record," he answered back. "Wish we'd seen the seizure; Sameer couldn't even remember how it started."

The chimpanzee with the blue collar lay motionless on the exam table. Each wrist and ankle was attached to a soft cloth restraint that was tied down to the table. A face mask was connected to an oxygen outlet in the wall. Two IV lines snaked from the chimp's groin and forearm, one to a small transducer box attached to the monitor, and the other to a blue IV pump containing a milky white syringe. Another wire traced from a belt around the chimpanzee's chest to the monitor above. A dozen or more wires led from a computer to small electrodes stuck to the chimp's head.

The door opened, and Jamie and Sameer walked in. He asked, "How's the chimp?"

Jeremy answered first. "Aw, he's fine. It was just a seizure or two. We found out that in addition to the one Sameer saw yesterday, there was one last week that a security guard witnessed. He's just sleeping right now. Say, you guys talked to Nakamura lately?"

Sameer shook his head. "Nobody's seen him, or Simons, or Michaels for a couple days. It's weird, like they all took off on a retreat somewhere. I've wanted to let them know that there's something funny going on with the chimp colony lately too. The political dynamics is all off. The dominant male is dead this morning, and the whole pecking order has changed. I don't get it."

Jamie kept looking at the motionless chimp. "He's tied down?"

Jeremy answered, "Yeah, we slapped a four-point re-straint on 'im. Don't want him pulling out his arterial line or he could bleed to death in minutes. And when I take the line out, I don't want that beefy arm pounding me while I'm holding pressure should he happen to wake up too fast. Chimps may look small, but their upper body strength could easily match a heavyweight wrestling champion."

Stiles looked at Jeremy with a sly grin. "You're just jealous. You have to admit he cuts a pretty imposing fig-ure, as long as you like short, furry types who drag their hands when they walk, that is."

"So what exactly are you doing?" asked Sameer.

"EEG. It's more complicated when your subject can't follow commands very well, doesn't exactly trust you, and could deck you with one swat of his arm," Stiles re-sponded. "An EEG's really the first thing you want to check in someone having new seizures. We already had him in the scanner just a week ago, and there's no vas-culitis, infection, or anything screwy on the films. We're probably looking at a seizure focus."

Jamie pointed to the EEG monitor. "What are these tracings telling you?"

Jeremy pulled out a piece of paper and drew a round cir-cle with two ears. He started sketching lines with Xs at var-ious locations on the circle. "The Xs mark where we have placed electrodes on the chimp's scalp. Is that clear?"

"I think so," Jamie said.

"What's most important," Jeremy continued, "is the frequency of the waves we see. A normal awake subject has activity mostly in what's called the alpha spectrum, from about eight to twelve cycles per second. These waves tend to be most prominent in the back of the brain and on the sides here and here. That represents these four tracings on the monitor."

He pointed to four of the green tracings on the screen, then continued, "In the front part of the brain, you tend to see more beta waves, which are faster than 12 Hertz. Those are the bottom tracings on the monitor. Right now we don't see much alpha or beta activity. That's because he's sleeping, so the brain waves are much slower, mostly in the theta and delta spectrums, or about 1 to 7 Hertz."

"I see lots of blips in the signal that look like something big is happening," Jamie commented.

"You mean that blip right there?" Jeremy pointed. "That's from an eye blink. You'll see lots of those. That big signal right here is called a sleep spindle. When a subject is sleeping they periodically have these waves of activity that sweep across the whole brain. In general, it is synchrony and order that we're looking for. Usually in the brain, chaos is good, and rhythm is bad. When things are very orderly, it usually means that seizure activity is more likely. There are some characteristic patterns we might see as well that clue us in that we're looking at a brain that is prone to seizures."

The screen suddenly erupted with activity, and the chimp let out a bellow.

Jeremy reflexively took a step back. "Looks like he's waking up. That was all motion artifact from moving muscles. Take a look at those top few tracings; see the faster alpha rhythm coming back?"

As the chimp returned to alertness, it began to make furtive glances toward the scientists. His eyes lingered on Sameer. A pleading, longing expression directed at Sameer was accompanied by a soft, pathetic moan. Sameer returned the chimp's stare with detachment, holding the same scientific aloofness as his colleagues. The chimp, more desperate, began slamming his body against the restraints on his legs, his eyes open wide as he struggled against his harness. Eventually, the chimp ceased pulling against the restraints and lay motionless, his eyes moving from one person to the next.

Stiles took a few steps and plugged in a small handheld instrument with a long cord. He stood in front of the chimpanzee. "I think it's time to pull out our toys," he said. "We have a few tools to induce seizures and hopefully catch what part of the brain they're coming from. One of the best is a strobe light. Watch the third and fourth trace from the top when I turn this on. That part of the brain we already know processes vision in this chimp from our fMRI results. We should see waves of activity at 20 Hertz, the same frequency as the strobe light." He flipped the switch.

The two tracings he mentioned almost immediately began showing a fast sawtooth wave. After a few seconds this disappeared and was replaced by a slower, high-amplitude wave.

"Who's your daddy?" Jeremy said, turning to high-five Stiles.

"What do you see?" asked Sameer.

"The strobe light drove the visual part of the brain for a while like we would expect, but then this big old signal showed up. It's called a spike and wave, and is characteristic for epilepsy. If we let it go long enough, it might spread through the whole cortex and produce a seizure."

The chimp began moving its arms and legs more frequently, occasionally tugging hard against the restraints.

Seeing the futility in the efforts, he subsided and remained mostly still.

"Switch to 100 percent nitrogen," Stiles said.

Jeremy moved to the gauge on the wall and rotated a dial, leaving his hand on it.

A few seconds later the monkey started breathing more heavily and rapidly. A beep sounded a few seconds later from the monitor and the blue oxygen saturation curve became erratic. The number to the side dropped from 99 to 95 and then continued down to 87, when it started flashing red. The EEG tracing started pulsating with rhythmic activity and the monkey's left arm began to tremble.

"That's enough," Stiles ordered.

Jeremy quickly flipped the dial back. Within seconds, the flashing red number started to climb, and the chimp started breathing more easily. Soon the EEG returned to its chaotic state.

"Very interesting. When you hyperventilate or lose oxygen to the brain, you can often provoke a seizure. What we saw with that little episode was two things. First, it is very easy in this chimp to provoke seizures. Second, the episode had a totally different signal from the strobe light episode. It started in a different spot in the brain."

"What does that mean?" Sameer asked.

"It means that there are probably multiple anomalies in the brain that can trigger seizure activity. It's probably the way the cortex is wired up generally rather than one small problem spot," Jeremy responded quickly.

"It means it's time to get a biopsy," Stiles said.

"A biopsy of the brain? Are you serious?" Jamie asked.

"Absolutely," Stiles said. "What this means is there is

probably something very interesting about the circuitry in the brain that is causing this chimp to be vulnerable to multiple types of seizures. If we drill a small hole in the skull, take a few square millimeters of the cortex, and look at it under the microscope it will probably be fascinating. I already have preapproval from Nakamura, since I sort of expected this to be the case. It's a small piece of brain. The chimp will never miss it."

ONCE the scientists were engrossed in their discussion, the chimpanzee looked across at the stand filled with instruments and syringes, then carefully down at his wrist straps. He curled his fingers up slowly to the leather straps and buckle on his wrist. One finger at a time, he slid the free leather end through the metal clasp. Without looking down, the chimp moved his wrist until the metal prong of the buckle worked its way out of the strap.

Flexing his wrist, the chimp was able to pull some slack into the buckle until he could quietly slip his wrist out of the strap. The chimp then slid his arm over to loosen the corresponding strap on his right hand. A hand crept up carefully to the buckle on his collar, but then slid down as Sameer turned his head back toward the chimp.

SAMEER furrowed his brow. "Brain biopsy. I still think it's too dangerous. You know how important this chimp is . . . to all of us."

Stiles shrugged. "Well, I wouldn't want to do it to my mother, but I've done it a dozen times in animals. With good sterile technique and the proper instruments, it's a very simple brain surgery. The chance of mishap is probably not more than a couple percent. It would also give us the chance to do some extracellular recording while we're in there. That would be most useful. Unfortunately, it may take a few days to get the necessary instruments here. That should be it, Jeremy. We have what we came for. Let's put him back under."

As Jeremy reached for the propofol drip, the chimp sprang into action, wresting the milky white syringe off the tubing on the table. In one movement, the chimp stabbed the needle onto Jeremy's exposed shoulder and depressed the plunger. Jeremy shouted in pain as he staggered back.

Jamie screamed. Stiles's horrified expression faded instantly as he sprinted to the back of the room and emerged carrying a feathered dart. The chimp watched Stiles as he crept down to fuss with the straps binding his legs. Stiles circled the chimp carefully and lunged toward him, implanting the dart in his left thigh, then diving to the ground and rolling to the side and behind the chimp as the animal's arm swung outward on an arc, just missing Stiles's head.

The chimp was livid with rage, thumping against his remaining straps until he became less and less vigorous and finally collapsed down motionless onto the chair.

Jeremy crawled slowly to the chimp's side, obviously drugged to the point he could barely function. He leaned back against the computer and took slow deep breaths, his eyes staring at the floor. Stiles joined him in a moment and bandaged his shoulder, which was still bleeding from the wound.

Jamie studied the calm chimp until her heart descended

from her throat. She was the first to speak. "Now what do we do?"

Sameer answered, "We've got to get him outside while he's sedated and we can order some more reliable containment equipment. Something tells me experiments are going to be a lot more difficult now. I'll let my staff know to be careful with him. I don't understand what's going on."

A bright moon streamed down yellow light through gaps in the trees. Silently, a lone chimpanzee scurried into a clump of trees and began yanking on a low-lying branch. With great force, it snapped off, sending the chimpanzee tumbling to the ground. Slowly, the chimpanzee got up and retrieved the broken branch.

The chimp then crawled through the underbrush, dragging the branch behind until he came to a metal shed. The chimp looked around carefully. He slowly made his way to a tree about twenty meters from the shed across a small clearing in the trees. He skirted around the outside of the clearing for several meters and looked up. A metal canopy was nestled in some leaves about two meters off the ground. Inside the canopy around a large trunk was a small camera.

The chimp hoisted the branch above his head and with enormous strength swung around the branch to crash down on the camera. His aim was perfect, and the camera smashed under the impact. The chimpanzee bellowed with pleasure and retrieved the large, heavy stick. He slid through the clearing to the metal shed. A corrugated metal wall had inset an unmarked door frame with a metal door. A small keyhole was visible below a doorknob.

The chimp hoisted the branch high above his head. As he stood, moonlight streamed down onto the chimp's muscular body. With a sudden grunt, he sent the branch crashing down against the metal door, making a small dent in the door. Once again, the chimp lifted the branch up and smashed it down again. Time after time, the chimp beat on the door with growing intensity, a fury mounting with each violent stroke. With a loud crash a screech of metal resonated through the forest as the mutilated metal door of the supply shed creaked in then popped outward. The chimp dropped the branch and fell to the earth, breathing heavily. His left arm began to tremble and he sat on the ground, watching his arm. The twitch gradually subsided as the chimp breathed deeply and slowly.

The chimp again stood and pulled open the door far enough to slide inside. From outside the door, a bunch of bananas was ejected from the small opening. Another bunch of bananas flew out, then another. Soon a huge stack of bananas had formed outside the opening. Within a minute another chimp arrived, grabbing an armful of bananas. Two more came immediately after, then five more. The bananas disappeared as fast as the chimp could throw them out. Grabbing the last armful of bananas himself, the chimp emerged from the shed and made his way into the darkness of the trees.

DIEGO Garcia was making notes in a logbook in the security control room. He glanced up on a large wall of monitors and cursed under his breath. On the right side of the wall, two of the monitors showed only static. Diego picked up the phone and dialed a number. After about eight rings, a sleepy voice answered on the other end "This is Skip."

"Mr. Jordan, I wanted to let you know that cameras forty-three and forty-four have no signal. I can get only static."

"You have a soccer ball for a head or what?! You woke me up to tell me that two little cameras are malfunctioning? We'll check it out in the morning. Now don't bug me again!" The phone slammed and went dead.

Diego shrugged and began examining the other monitors on the wall. He scanned with his fingers across row after row of cameras, and came to the bottom row where he started and looked back. *Deus meu.*

Next to the dock, half a dozen boats were floating loose in the harbor.

He picked up the phone and hurriedly dialed a number.

"Diego, if that's you again I'm going kick that soccer ball of a head so far . . ."

"Sorry Mr. Jordan, but it appears that all of the boats are loose from their moors in the dock."

A silence came at the other end. "All right, Diego. It's those damn kids again. Let's go take care of it. I'll meet you at the dock. Bring some tear gas."

A few minutes later Skip Jordan emerged from the trees and joined Diego standing at the riverside. Next to the dock, boats were floating aimlessly in the bend of the Amazon. "Well don't just stand there," Jordan said. "It looks like they loosed the boats for a stunt and left. Help me get the boats back in place."

"I think there is another problem, sir." Diego pointed to the river.

Skip Jordan looked a hundred yards downriver to a ferry drifting in the water. The boat swayed under the weight of at least forty chimpanzees jumping up and down and scooting back and forth along the large craft. One chimpanzee stood with an oar at the back of the boat.

As Jordan looked on, one of the chimpanzees began walking around the edge of the boat eating a banana. He looked right at Jordan, and bellowed out a gleeful shout just audible to Jordan and Diego. Suddenly, he lost his balance and fell, arms flailing, into the water. The chimp at the back scrambled to reach over the side and pull the soggy chimp back into the boat.

Jordan began charging down the river, his chest bouncing with each awkward step. Diego followed closely behind, already removing his pistol from its holster. Just as he was taking aim on the bulwark of the raft, the chimp at the back put down his oar and reached into the boat. A moment later a large stone came hurtling by Diego. Startled, Diego and Jordan dove to their hands and knees. The chimp whirled another stone that struck Jordan on his right flank. He doubled over in pain, holding his rib cage.

Wincing to Diego, Jordan ordered breathlessly, "Hold your fire. If we bring these chimps down here, they could kill us. We need support. You got your cell phone? Get me Nakamura now."

Diego dialed the number. "There's no answer, sir."

"Give me that phone." Jordan switched it off and dialed again.

"Hey, Johnson. We got a real problem here. I need Nakamura, Mercer, someone on the horn yesterday."

The voice on the other end sounded relieved. "So you

know already. Mercer's right here. He just asked me to call you."

"Know what? How could you know about the chimps already?"

"Who said anything about chimps? We have three dead bodies here in Nakamura's lab, boss. Tech just found them three minutes ago."

"Johnson, I don't need games right now. Did you say three dead bodies?"

"You'd better get over here now. Oh man, someone open a window!"

"Who are they? How did they die?"

"It's gonna take some time to put the pieces together, boss. Like I said, you'd better get over here now."

CARLOS Escalante was lying in his tent with a set of headphones over his ears reading a book. He suddenly put down the book, listening very carefully. He kneeled up, scrambling through his pack and producing a pad of paper and a pen. He began to take notes furiously, then stopped suddenly. *Holy shit.*

NINETEEN

CARLOS examined the cash and tucked it into his pocket. He turned around and walked toward the door of the airport without a word.

Susan felt the color drain from her face. *A scam? After coming so far?*

She looked around helplessly. Finally, Carlos turned his head and asked simply, "Are you coming, Ms. Archer-Bentham?"

"Susan," she said nervously, catching up to Carlos. Susan walked with him along the sidewalk a few paces, then asked, "Are you going to tell me now about this new development?"

Carlos lowered his voice. "Developments, now, at no extra charge. Here is the first." He pulled out a small tape recorder, and turned it on. It replayed the voice of a woman speaking on Nakamura's answering machine: "Kenji, where are you? Never mind, I sent the embryos—about three hundred, good condition, diverse population from my IVF clinic, just like you wanted. That should be plenty to get enough viable pregnancies to sacrifice one a day during the third trimester. We should be able to pin that last transcription factor down exactly. Call me."

Susan gasped out loud. "Carlos, that's perfect!" Her eyes lit up, all of the indecision gone. "Do you know who that was?"

Carlos shook his head. "Real tough to trace. I might get phone logs if I can figure out who to bribe."

"Carlos, you're a genius! That's exactly what we need!"

Susan's expression sobered as she thought out loud. "Unfortunately, that's probably not enough evidence to go on. There's too much at stake to rely on a phone message without any proof of the cargo to back it up."

"Right," Carlos agreed.

"What about the chimp? Any word about the chimp? There has to be a way we can sneak in and get some footage of the chimp, get something convincing to back us up . . ."

Carlos punched the tape recorder on again, and another voice sounded, this time more emotional, even desperate.

"Absolutely bludgeoned, Mr. Jordan. Almost unrecognizable, but we're sure this one's Nakamura. His ID card is in his pocket."

"Yeah, that's him all right. And these two look like Michaels and Simons. Senior scientists. Who the hell did this?"

A third voice on the tape spoke with a heavy Brazilian accent. "The tech says it's the chimps. All those empty cages. He says they're vicious, almost got him a few times while he was feeding them."

"We'll see about that. All the same, glad I didn't chase down that boat."

"Boat, sir?"

"Bunch of chimps went joyriding on one of our ferries. Must be three dozen of those buggers on it, including that one with the collar. Man, I tell you nobody deserves this, but I'd almost rather face Nakamura this way than tell him I lost the one with the collar."

"Well you're just going to have to get it back, aren't you? You can track him. He's got that radiocollar."

"Screw you, Mercer."

"Someone get me Gupta."

"Mercer, you don't get it, do you? Kenji's dead! Forget about the chimp."

"I said, get me Gupta. And everyone else who's been working with that chimp. Right now."

Carlos switched off the recorder.

Susan's eyes doubled in size, silent for a long moment as she digested what she heard. "Carlos, that's it! We'll find that chimp first! If we could capture it we would have the story of the century. With the evidence we have and that chimp for visuals, this will be on every front page and evening news in the world. We have to get that chimp first! It's perfect!" She pulled on Carlos's arm in excitement.

Carlos raised one eyebrow.

Susan's mood again soured. "But how are we going to do that? How do we capture a wild chimpanzee that could be anywhere within two hundred miles in the Amazon jungle?"

Carlos hailed a taxi. "Are you out of cash, Ms. Archer-Bentham?"

Susan shook her head.

"Good, because we're going to need it when we meet our guide in a few minutes. Let's just hope that we can find that chimp's frequency soon."

Carlos stepped into the taxi, with Susan close behind.

"JAMIE! Wake up!"

She rolled over.

The knock came again. "Jamie!"

What time is it? She rubbed her eyes, then glanced at the clock. She put the pillow over her head.

"Jamie!"

She threw the pillow at the door. "Sameer? Go away."

"He's gone, Jamie! Wake up!"

This had better be good. She sat up, then shivered. After two years in the humid jungle without air conditioning, she had adapted by adding blankets, not clothes, when she slept. She stood up and put on a shirt and pair of shorts.

"Jamie!"

She opened the door. "What, already?"

"He's gone. The chimp. He escaped on a boat."

"Why didn't you tell me?" She sprang to action.

"Come on. Mercer's waiting."

"Does Kenji know?"

"Kenji's dead."

"What?"

"He's dead, Jamie. So are Simons and Michaels. Some kind of accident. I just heard about it."

"All three of them?" She fell into step behind Sameer, all trace of sleep gone.

"Look, I don't have the details, but I heard it straight from Mercer."

"You don't think someone . . ."

"I don't know, Jamie. Mercer said he thought they were killed by one of the animals. Just keep your eyes open. I don't know what to think." They turned the corner from the living quarters and passed the cafeteria and mail room.

Jamie walked in silence. *Why would all three of them have been killed at the same time? That meant every scientist who had worked on the chimp project was . . .*

She didn't trust Mercer. She was going to do a lot more than keep her eyes open.

"Hey! What's going on?" Stiles's voice came from behind her. She stopped.

"Roger?" She could now see Stiles and Jeremy jogging to catch up. Stiles looked as dazed as she felt, Jeremy even more so.

"Mercer just called and said there was some sort of emergency meeting. Will someone please tell me what in blazes is going on here?"

Jamie and Sameer waited for the two to reach them, then started walking again.

"It's Nakamura."

"He called the meeting?"

"He's dead."

Stiles stopped abruptly. This time the others kept walking.

"Did you say dead?" He jumped back into step.

Sameer, now out of breath, recounted the story he had heard thus far.

They moved single file onto the staircase and ascended to the main floor toward Nakamura's office. There was a crowd of security guards standing by the door.

"Where's Mercer?" Stiles blurted out.

"Please step back. This is a crime scene. No one goes in without . . ."

The door opened, and David Mercer stepped out.

"Why don't you take it from here, Skip. I'll check back in a little while." He motioned everyone inside as Skip retreated out the back way. "Perfect. Everyone's here."

"David? What happened?"

Mercer looked at the closed door to the lab. Muffled voices could be heard from behind the door. Jamie leaned against the wall, watching the reactions of each of the men in the room.

Stiles sat down in a chair by the desk, taking fistfuls of his hair between his fingers with his head down on the desk. Jeremy sat close by. He looked awful, like he hadn't slept for a month. *Not a good one to wake up early.* Sameer sat down on the office floor and stared off into space.

Mercer took a few purposeful steps to sit on the corner of the desk. "I know you're all feeling the shock of the whole situation as much as I am. Especially you, Sameer. You've worked with them nearly as long as I have. But there's some urgent business we need to discuss before the grieving takes over."

Jamie clenched her fists. "Business! I'll say we have business. Three people are dead!" She took a step toward the door.

Mercer looked directly at Jamie. "I'm sorry, Jamie. I know this sounds abrupt. I'm sure you're thinking this isn't the right time to talk . . ."

"Damn right it does."

"Let me start over. I assure you I'm absolutely sick over this terrible accident. It's my job to tell Kenji's family what happened. I was one of the first ones on the scene. But there were two accidents tonight. I wasn't sure if you heard about the other one."

"You mean about the chimp? We'll just have to get him back."

Stiles broke in, "Well I bloody didn't. Would someone care to please tell me?"

Jamie leaned back against the wall. Feeling self-conscious about her nightshirt and shorts, she tightened the shirt in a knot at the bottom while Mercer explained.

"The chimp—the one you all have been studying—escaped tonight. On a ferry. With at least a few dozen other chimpanzees."

"No. You don't think *he* killed them?" Stiles anticipated. "Killed them and sped off in a bleeding ferry like some kind of gangster?"

"We're not ruling anything out at this point," Mercer continued. "But the facts are, every scientist that worked to create the chimp is dead, and the chimp is gone. We have to decide what to do about it."

Jamie cocked her head. "Like I said, we have to get him back."

"Well, that's why I called you here. As far as I know, you are the only ones who know the whole story about that chimp. Every one of you has told me that it was the opportunity of a lifetime. Clearly Kenji thought so as well. If we have any chance of bringing him back, we have to move quickly."

"Bring him back? So he can kill us too?" Jeremy raised his eyebrows.

"Hear me out. We don't know who killed them. There were a number of chimps housed beneath Kenji's lab, some of which are still there and some aren't. I don't know what happened. But I do know if we don't get that chimp the game is over for all of us."

"How does this affect you?" Jamie asked.

"There's something that you probably don't realize. BrainStem Therapeutics is out of capital."

"What?" Sameer's eyes narrowed.

"Finished. We're being totally floated now by credit. Soliton's done bankrolling us unless we come up with a cash cow soon. Drake told me as much last week on his visit. The only way I could keep him from dissolving the whole company on the spot was this chimp. I didn't tell him much, but enough to catch his interest. And it worked. He's given us enough wiggle room for another six or eight months, enough time to launch the initial public offering. If I can't show him something concrete soon, it's over. If he finds out we lost that chimp, BrainStem is as dead as Kenji and the others. That's what this is about."

"You're serious?" Jamie asked.

He nodded.

"Wait a minute. You mean you're seriously thinking about wandering out in the jungle like some kind of action figure and tracking the chimp? Bringing it back?" Jeremy asked.

He nodded again. "I have my whole career tied up in this company. If you can't take a risk, you can't run a major corporation. If BrainStem folds, I'm on the fast track to managing the local UPS office." His eyes looked apologetic, pleading. "That's not everything. I want this to work, too. The chimp's important. Every one of you said so."

Jeremy lowered his voice. "Look. I know I'm just a postdoc here. And I agree. That chimp isn't a project. It's the most important scientific discovery in history. I grew up on a diet of science fiction. Aliens taking over the world and all that." He wiggled his fingers and flashed his eyes as he spoke. "Well, that isn't how it's going to happen. Aliens aren't going to fly in on saucers; we make them right here. We already made them. A new sentient race. That's what we're talking about here. But why go get him? Isn't there something you're all forgetting?"

Jamie stared at Jeremy in anticipation. "Forgetting?" asked Mercer.

"Yeah. We have the blueprints. Even if the company folds like toilet paper, what's to stop us from going through Nakamura's notebooks now, getting the raw materials, and starting over? We just make another one. The five of us. Hell, I'll work for free. The hard part's all done."

"I'm afraid it's not that simple," Mercer said softly.

"The boy's got a point," Stiles countered. "It's just not that expensive to make a transgenic chimp once you've isolated the DNA."

"Like I said, it's not that simple."

"Then enlighten us. What's so hard about it?"

"Because I've looked."

Jamie asked, "What do you mean?"

Mercer stood up and paced away from the desk. "I mean I've looked through everything. I searched his files, his notebooks, at night, real secret-like. I tried during the day to get him to archive the information. The more I seemed interested in the chimp, the more suspicious he seemed of me. I've been trying to learn more about this chimp for weeks, and the lab records don't say anything about this whole chimp business. Same thing with Michaels's and Simons's records. Samples in the freezers are labeled with some cryptic numbering system that tells me nothing. And there are thousands of them."

Jeremy whistled. "That is not cool."

"It's totally unethical. I know, so is rifling through Kenji's office at night. But I had no choice. The fact is, everyone who knows how this chimp was created is dead. Either we find that chimp, or we just pack up and go home. Is that what you want to do?"

Jamie stared at Mercer, her eyes softening. Maybe she had misjudged him, not about being a self-centered stuffed suit, but he was clever. Maybe he went deeper than his tailored appearance. What he was suggesting took guts.

Stiles answered, "I say we haul his hairy little frame back and double the locks. But I don't have the experience to lead the expedition."

Jamie looked at the faces of the other scientists. Without exception, each one was looking at her. She knew why. Of the five of them, she was the only one remotely capable of leading a search party into the rain forest.

She took a deep breath. "All right. I want that chimp back too. But not right now. We do this sensibly. I don't want to underestimate the chimp again. We take a day or two to get supplies, make a game plan. You don't wander out into the Amazon unprepared."

Stiles and Mercer nodded enthusiastically.

Jamie looked at Sameer. "What's the range on his radio collar?"

"About ten miles ground to ground in the jungle. Should have several months of battery life left."

Jamie thought for a moment. "We'll send out a speedboat, tonight, have them follow the ferry. Then we'll know where the ferry is beached. We'll need provisions for at least two weeks and topographical maps of the forest within seventy-five miles of the chimps' landing site. We'll take low-velocity sedative guns, medical supplies, light-weight tents, and light firearms. Everyone who comes carries a pack. The chimps are likely to meander around from wherever they land, and we could probably overtake them in a few days overland with a more direct route. I will choose the expedition leader and any personnel I feel are necessary. Is that agreed?"

Mercer shook Jamie's hand vigorously. "We'll get him."

Jamie nodded. "If the jungle doesn't get him first." She looked over the group and added, "I think I've finally come up with a suitable Turing test for the chimp. I propose a head to head duel in the most ancient of all human games—the hunt. May the best species win."

"**AH,** so this is not only a safari, but a race. And who are our worthy opponents?"

"It's a group of scientists. We know five of them. The most experienced are probably their primatologist, Sameer Gupta, and a field biologist, Jamie Kendrick. None of them have deep jungle experience, as far as I can tell," Carlos summarized for their new guide. Susan nodded in agreement.

They were seated in a cabin on the outskirts of the city. The room smelled gamey, the wall lined with the heads of exotic predators. Most striking was a full-size stuffed jaguar mounted as though at full run. A finely polished rifle dangled from hooks on the wall above the jaguar. Exotic birds in cages warbled around the room, giving the den a hum of life. Seated in a leather chair that looked uncomfortably like snakeskin was a small, thin woman with short brown hair, a sharp nose, and quick eyes. Ayala Goren cocked her head as she looked at her two visitors.

"Well, that will cost you extra. For an expedition such as you propose, I wouldn't take less than thirty thousand U.S. dollars. Now, do we have anything else to talk about?"

Susan pretended to look astonished. "Thirty thousand dollars for a few days?"

Carlos's face was silent.

Susan softened her expression. "If I agree to the fee, does that see us through until we find the chimp? No other costs?"

"Oh you'll find your chimp alright, but the jungle's a dangerous place, and nobody is going to guarantee you that your chimp, or your scientists for that matter, will still be alive when we get there," Ayala said acidly.

"JAMIE, you're back." Paolo did a double take as he opened the door.

"It's good to see you again, Paolo." Jamie's smile was genuine.

"Come on in. I've been waiting to hear from you." Paolo led her into the cabin, pausing to close a window to the ambient sounds of the jungle.

Best to come right out with it. "Paolo, I need your help leading an expedition into the forest."

"I see. So much for small talk." Paolo cocked his head to one side.

"It's tough to know where to begin," Jamie continued. "The last few weeks have been intense. I've stumbled onto something big, bigger than anything I've ever worked on, or heard about."

She described how she had stumbled onto the chimp, how they had tested it, how it had surpassed even her wildest expectations. Paolo stared back at her in stunned silence as she spoke.

She finished her account. "It's the most incredible thing I've ever seen, but he's gone. Escaped into the jungle. Just last night." She paused to breathe.

"Why should he want to escape?" Paolo inquired tentatively.

Jamie looked down. "I suppose I can't blame him, but the implications are too big to just let him go. Besides, he's hardly prepared to survive alone in the jungle, having grown up dependent on human assistance. It's in everyone's interest to get him back."

Paolo breathed deeply and looked directly at Jamie. In a soft voice he asked, "Tell me more about the chimp."

"He's incredible. I'm convinced he's as smart as a human being. And yet different. He does things that are so surprising . . . and yet at times he seems so human."

Paolo was thoughtful for a moment, and asked, "Don't you wonder, Jamie, if it's right to study the chimp like that if he really is as conscious as you or me?"

"Sometimes. I guess I feel like most of what we're doing is teaching the chimp, showing him his capabilities. I don't think he'd be happy either, swinging around with other monkeys. He knows he doesn't fit in." *Did she really believe all that?*

Paolo pressed her further. "You know, human society has never faced anything like this before. Should the chimp have basic human rights? I don't see why not."

Jamie turned around and paced across the room. "Paolo, I've spent my life trying to answer big questions, the kind that change the world in a good way. It seems like everyone else is content asking easier questions that don't matter. For once in my life, I feel like I'm close to a really important question, and actually finding the answer." Jamie wiped her eyes. "I need this. I need you, Paolo."

Paolo covered his face in his hands, thinking. He looked up. "What if I refuse?"

"I'll have to lead the expedition myself. I'd feel better if you were there," she replied. Jamie felt tense, wondering if Paolo's hesitation was about the chase or about her.

"Jamie, I have thought a great deal about our conversation before you left."

"As have I."

"I haven't often spoken so freely. I hope I didn't scare you away."

Jamie's eyes opened wider. "Not at all."

"You seemed in a bit of a hurry to get away."

Jamie felt defensive. "I suppose I was a bit overwhelmed. So much to think about . . ." She added honestly, "So many emotions."

Paolo nodded. "I have to know why you're doing this."

Jamie spoke deliberately, her eyes pleading to Paolo, "I have to find out who he is. I can't ignore what I've seen, and I need some answers. You're the only one I trust to help."

They both stood silent for a long moment. "I'll help you, Jamie," Paolo finally said.

"Thank you," she whispered.

TWENTY

WITH her mask and snorkel just above the surface, Ayala Goren's muscular frame slid along the surface of the water, now around a jog in the river and out of sight from the fishing boat. She swam effortlessly, her mind focused on the terrain ahead and the waters around. She had spent enough time in the Amazon River to know better than to let down her guard while alone in the water. Nevertheless, it was exhilarating to swim in a place so teeming with life, and with danger.

Her life in the Amazon had initially been a retreat. Shaken to the core by her service as one of Israel's elite special operations officers, she had escaped to Brazil from demons that were omnipresent in Israel. After three years on active duty on the West Bank, she had seen horrors that most soldiers didn't believe existed in modern warfare.

The nightmares were never of the exposed border

patrol beats or the occasional gunfight. They started only after her stay in the Hamas Hotel, as she called it. Captured by Palestinian extremists, she had spent two weeks of inexplicable terror in the hands of her enemy. Such events as she experienced were never discussed in the international press or even known about but by a very few. There were plenty of open hostilities to discuss in public; the more secret intelligence war behind the scenes was infinitely more important, and more brutal.

Her release had been pure serendipity, as her captors had been discovered by a roaming Israeli patrol that was far off its route. Her assailants had simply fled, leaving her tied, unclothed and bleeding, to a chair in the sparsely furnished room. After an intense debriefing almost more traumatic than the events of the preceding two weeks, she had been released from further service in the military, and given an apartment and a living allowance with little else but an order of secrecy.

There are few afflictions more poorly understood or more psychologically devastating than post-traumatic stress disorder. Some who do not wrestle with the condition know of the flashbacks and nightmares that the victims experience, but expect that eventually people "get over it." Very few know of the entire lives lived in terror that mark severe PTSD, with victims afraid to leave the house or speak to other people. Ayala Goren lived such a life, where sixteen hours a day asleep was only a compromise between the terrors at night and the chronic pain during the day.

She fled to a place as far away as she could imagine, someplace that couldn't remind her of home—and she kept busy. Initially she trained as a tour guide in the forest, and in the off-season spent her time as a nomad wandering through the jungle and becoming bewitched with its mysteries and peoples.

The rain forest breathed new life into her, and she recovered a semblance of the courage and mettle that had marked her short career as a soldier. She became less and less interested in routine expeditions, and began leading extreme vacationers deeper into the jungle seeking more exotic experiences. Now, ten years later, she had been reborn. But she never, ever forgot.

This was unexpected fun. It wasn't too often that an assignment was unusual enough or with people charismatic enough to make her feel adventurous. She held a gloved hand to her forehead and blew through her nose to clear the puddle of foul water out the bottom of the mask. She blinked twice and surveyed the scene ahead with the trained eye of a soldier as she approached the dock. There were a dozen craft of varying sizes, but the pier was otherwise empty of life. She scanned the perimeter, and could not make out any surveillance or security stations.

She kicked one leg over the pier, swaying with the rolling motion as she stood and crept up and down the dock examining the boats moored to its side. She slid the mask down around her neck and rubbed the muddy brown water from her face. In this part of the Amazon, the visibility was zero, and the mask was more for protection than navigation.

She passed several small speedboats with the characteristic BrainStem logo on their flanks. Then she paused next to a larger ferry near the shore. Inside she could make out the shapes of a series of backpacks lined up along the starboard wall. She glanced quickly over her shoulder and leapt across the bow in a single jump.

A blaring siren pierced the night with a wailing cry from the ship's loudspeaker and flashing lights from the bow and stern.

Ayala scarcely had taken a breath before she purposefully ducked down by the first of six backpacks and unzipped the major compartment. She rifled through the contents. Then she rezipped the pack and examined two major side pockets.

Replacing the pack, she stood and scanned the horizon. *Still clear.* She examined the second pack. It had a long canvas container along its side wall, which Ayala slid out to examine. Her fingers stopped unwrapping at the sound of voices, distant but rapidly approaching. She inspected the small dart gun inside the canvas bag and quickly slid the gun back into the canvas sheath and set it on the floor. Then she zipped the pack shut and moved to the third.

The voices were now loud enough that she could make out two distinct voices. "Hold right there! Security!" said one breathless voice. The other, more calmly, said, "Looks okay, boss." Ayala's fingers dug into the contents, feeling, probing, as her eyes scanned each item. She grabbed an oblong metal box from the pack and rezipped the main pocket, letting the pack fall back against the bulwark. A flashlight beam drifted over the port side and she dropped prone on the floor of the boat.

"Diego, I have my orders. No monkey see, monkey do." The voice spat out short phrases between breaths. "Mercer's gone tomorrow—then we sleep." The voice was only a few meters from the dock.

Ayala grabbed the canvas bag and metal box and crept on all fours to the bow. In one fluid movement, her black shape slid over the railing and she hung from one arm along the exterior of the boat, her other arm clutching her spoils tightly to her chest. The instant the first of the two figures stepped into the boat, she released her grip and dropped into the water with little more noise than the tide breaking against the bow.

With a single scissor kick, she halted her fall without submerging and managed to hold the objects above the water. She pulled herself underneath the hull and by the time the two figures were on board, the only part of her above water was the tip of her black snorkel and one gloved hand carrying the box and canvas bag, pressed tightly against the side of the boat.

The siren stopped abruptly. "All right—looks like it was just a big wave or something. All the same, Diego, tomorrow morning can't come too soon for me. I've taken a lot of heat for this. Just a bunch of monkeys, I say. Not like we don't have enough already. Let's go."

Diego peered over the side of the boat directly above Ayala's snorkel tube, then retracted his head and stepped onto the dock. The sound of footsteps faded down the planks and disappeared. Ayala's wetsuit drifted away from the boat, her pillaged goods held with one hand above the water as she sidestroked into the distance.

SUSAN Archer-Bentham was sleeping along one side of the fishing boat when she woke with a start as Ayala's dripping figure jumped into the boat. As she regained her presence of mind, Carlos tipped up his hat and studied Ayala.

Ayala silently examined the metal box, then with a click, a spring-loaded frame snapped into place and Ayala was holding a pistol-shaped handle with three metal crossbars extending four feet to either side.

"What is that?" Susan asked, bewildered.

"That," Ayala said, pointing to the digital readout on the handle, "is your chimpanzee's frequency." She slung the canvas bag over her shoulder. "Now, I believe we have a flight to catch."

TWENTY-ONE

JAMIE stretched back in a deck chair as the early sunlight baked her neck and arms. The forest never slept, and the hum of insects Jamie had never quite learned to ignore had greeted her shortly after sunrise as the expedition had met at the boat. Now, she lazily looked over the mangroves puncturing the water on either side of the dock. After three intense days of planning every detail of the expedition, she felt strangely like a tourist settling in for a jungle cruise.

Diego Garcia loosed the mooring and idled the motor as the ferry slowly drifted away from the dock. Inside the ferry, Jamie turned her attention to the resolute faces of her seven colleagues, each contemplating the journey ahead. On her side of the boat sat Paolo Domingo, Roger Stiles, and Jeremy Evans. A few feet away on a bench sat David Mercer and Sameer Gupta. In the bow next to Diego sat Juan Miguel Santos, another member of the security detail at BrainStem Therapeutics.

Along one side of the boat, six packs were lined up, and a tarp covered a loose collection of supplies in the bow of the ship. The waters were unusually calm, the languid current all but imperceptible in the reflected morning sun. Jamie breathed deeply the humid aroma of rain and dead fish. The far shore was completely invisible, shrouded by the mist that hung in the air.

The expedition underway, she sensed the eyes of the crew turned toward her, toward Paolo, seeking information. She sat up and spoke. "For those of you who haven't been introduced, this is Paolo Domingo, who will be the field leader on the expedition. He has ten years more experience than anyone else here in the rain forest, and has the final word on all aspects of the mission. This might be a good time to review some basic precautions about going into the forest."

On cue, Paolo surveyed the crew with a confident smile. In a voice that betrayed both wisdom and genuine concern, he introduced himself and memorized the names of the crew members. After a brief discussion of the background of each member, he laid out the ground rules for the expedition.

"First, it is absolutely essential that no one at any time or under any circumstances, be alone in the rain forest. Groups of two or three are required, and each group should always have both a sat phone and a GPS locator. The biggest danger in the forest is not finding your way out. Second, no matter how important the mission, the safety of the crew is more important.

"A bit about myself. I have lived in the forest for fifteen years. I've thought many times in those fifteen years that I've seen every wicked demon the jungle has to offer, and each time it hasn't taken long to find a new one. If you want to have any chance of getting yourselves, and your chimp, home safely, we need to work efficiently and quickly.

"While I have not been tracking before with the benefit of a VHF antenna, it should be a welcome tool. I understand we have a ground-to-ground radius of about ten miles in the forest?"

Sameer answered, "We're not exactly sure. The radio tracking collar was designed for use in the compound, and we haven't field tested it for range. We've never had a problem on the compound, but that's only about ten miles in diameter and pretty level terrain. The antennas are tricky to use, and the range can be cut very short if the subject goes behind a hill, underwater, or underground. Our best guess is that we should have ten miles with our three-element Yagi antennas, maybe a bit more range if he's high in a tree."

Paolo nodded and asked, "How many antennas do we have?"

Jamie, who packed most of the supplies herself, answered, "We brought three antennas, for a worst-case, allowing three teams of two, and two staffing a base camp at the takeoff point." She nodded to Diego and Juan Miguel.

Paolo continued, "I have been so focused on the logistics of getting in and out that I'm a bit unclear about the plan once we find the chimp. What equipment do we have for neutralizing and sedating the target? How do we transport him once we find him?"

Sameer said, "We have some ketamine darts for induction. They should take effect within one minute and last for maybe twenty minutes. After that, we'll be using

mostly shots of benzodiazepines and restraints for sedation until we can get back to the base camp. It's safer, easier to monitor, and relatively longer-acting. We have
compact fold-out stretchers that should be managed easily by any two of us for transport."

"We should be within a day or two of the base camp
when we locate him—the sedation will not harm him
over such a time period?" Paolo asked.

Sameer responded, "A couple days is not ideal, but we
can definitely keep him sedated that long. We just need to
watch his breathing and protect his airway. We have a few
oral airways that we can tape in place. For an emergency,
whoever is carrying him should have a bag-valve mask
handy. We have some compact ones packed. Shouldn't
really be too much of a problem once we find him. The
trick is getting there."

Sameer took a few minutes to show the crew members
the technique for airway insertion, mask-breathing, and
administration of the ketamine darts and ativan shots. Jeremy and Stiles began to look bored, and Sameer ended
his demonstration.

Paolo asked one more question. "What is the range on
the darts?"

"Probably fifteen to twenty meters. That will be the
hard part. We might need to either catch him sleeping or
surround him. Chimps sleep in nests in the lower canopy,
and usually make a new nest every night. We have to be
careful not to sedate him where he's going to have a dangerous fall, so that may mean trying to get him on the
ground while he's awake."

Paolo addressed the entire group again. "We can survey the terrain once we've located him, and make a more

specific plan. Visual confirmation before sedation is essential, since there are at least two dozen chimps on the loose, and we don't have an endless supply of anesthetic. Have the sat phones been field tested?"

Mercer answered, "We have four satellite phones in excellent condition. Communication will not be a problem anywhere in the rain forest."

Jamie said, "We have rations for two weeks packed, and another three at the base camp. If we have to split up, each group should have a medical kit in addition to the phone, GPS, and field equipment. The biggest danger is malaria, and there's no way of knowing whether we're likely to find chloroquine-resistant malaria, so don't be too smug that you're taking antibiotics. There are probably as many diseases in the rain forest that haven't been described as those that have, so don't treat any unusual symptoms lightly."

Stiles asked, "How exactly do these tracking antennas work?"

Sameer grinned proudly. "We are using a Stealth Yagi springloaded antenna—the latest in compact, reliable hand tracking. Would you show me an example, Jamie?"

Jamie began fishing through the pocket on her pack. *Where was it?* "I know I had one in my pack. I checked everything twice." She quickly checked the other packs. Embarrassed, she handed a handheld device to Sameer. "I can only find two. I don't know how this could happen. I was sure I had everything packed."

Paolo raised one hand in reassurance. "Two antennas will be more than adequate. It is not worth the time to retrieve another, since I do not intend to separate into more than two groups."

Sameer grabbed the antenna and held it out away from the group. "This button releases the antenna." With a push of a button, the small pistol-shaped device unfolded into a long, handheld rod with three parallel, horizontal, metal crossbars. A faint static came from the speaker on the device. On the stock, a digital readout showed 150.726 MHZ.

"The frequency is autoset into the antennas. No need to change it. When you detect a signal, it will be a short, audible pulse every second. You'll need to slowly sweep around 360 degrees to find the maximal signal, and head toward it." He demonstrated a very slow sweep-around. "The antenna should be held parallel to the ground. The forward–reverse axis is highly polarized, and you don't need to rotate it." He folded the antenna back and handed it to Jamie.

Paolo looked around at the group members. "Any other questions?" No one spoke.

Diego looked over his shoulder, one hand on the steering wheel. "Probably take us another hour at least to reach the chimp's landing site. The ferry's homing beacon is still a good ways downriver." Diego had traveled with Mercer in a speedboat the night of the chimps' escape and found where the ferry had been beached. The homing beacon was intact per his report.

The other passengers settled down to wait. Jeremy walked to look over the side of the ferry. Paolo spread out a topographical map of the area and began studying it intensely. Mercer closed his eyes and sat motionless on the ferry. He was sweating and had looked particularly queasy ever since the boat had left the dock. Stiles stretched his arms and crossed his ankles, looking out at the brown river.

After a few moments, Stiles straightened his posture. He turned to Sameer, and loud enough for Jamie to hear said, "Look over there. What do you see?"

Jamie followed Sameer's gaze over the calm waters. After a moment, a splash coincided with a dolphin leaping out of the water in a large arc. "That a porpoise? In the river?" Sameer asked.

"Pink dolphin," said Stiles. "They're indigenous here. One of the few places in the world you can find them. Remarkable creatures really. May be smarter than little Ken Jr. even. No one knows."

"Smart, maybe, but I don't think he's anything like our chimp."

Stiles's voice was dreamlike. "Imagine a creature whose entire world consists of play, relationships with other similar creatures, and introspection. Food is abundant, almost without effort to obtain. Imagine a creature with no predators, no real danger in its natural environment other than man. This creature has language so developed it has the capacity to project exact replicas of three-dimensional objects instantly to the mind of a colleague through ultrasound. It has no need for sleep, spends its entire day frolicking in a watery paradise, and having sex. Tell me, who's the smart one?"

Jamie looked toward Stiles and cut in, "Very romanticized, I'm sure. But I hardly think the dolphins are busy with differential equations in their spare time. Sometimes you sit and think, and sometimes you just sit."

Stiles shrugged. "When you compare brain size to body weight or surface area, there are two animals that are equivalent: humans and dolphins. Other primates are a distant third. Dolphins even have brain folding more complex than humans, and probably have as much of their brains devoted to abstract thinking as humans. It may not be as far-fetched as you think. Just because you can't communicate with them doesn't mean you know what they're not thinking."

Sameer said, "Well, we know our chimp is smart, and I'm quite sure he's not as harmless as those dolphins. I just hope our fearless leaders understand that the chimp may well have the upper hand in this hunt. It's his backyard we're invading, and I don't really think he'll be excited to see us again."

Jamie nodded, then glanced over Paolo's shoulder at the map he was studying. "Should be good for tracking," Paolo turned and said. "Mostly level terrain for the first ten miles inland. Probably pretty dense forest, but doable. I'll bet they're not more than a few miles from the river. They're used to living in a small range."

Jeremy looked transfixed on the horizon, standing against the railing. He turned back to the group. "Looks like a helicopter ahead. Wonder what they're up to."

Jamie searched the sky. "Mostly photography and filmmaking. It's a big business here. I used to hear them all the time in my field research. Supposedly, there's quite a helicopter tourism business, too. Next best thing to the Grand Canyon in adventure travel."

JUAN Miguel pointed in the distance and asked Diego, "Should be right over there, no?" Diego turned the wheel and headed toward the far shore, where the distant image of the beached ferry was just visible.

"Looks like we're here," reported Diego to the group.

Slowly, the passengers began stretching, awakening from the hypnotic trance of the river. Jeremy and Sameer inspected their packs one last time, adjusting a few items. Jeremy gave a quizzical look, to nobody in particular. "I thought I had some ketamine darts in my pack. I don't see them here anywhere."

Jamie furrowed her forehead. "You're kidding me. I don't know how that's possible. I swear I checked everything twice yesterday. Sameer, you missing anything?"

"Don't seem to be. Darts and antenna are both intact. Everything else looks right. It's probably not a big deal. It must be in another pack. We'll sort it out—we have plenty of ammunition anyway between me and Stiles," Sameer said.

"I just hope you remembered my shower massage," said Stiles.

The boat pulled into a small beachhead twenty meters from the deserted ferry, and Juan Miguel hopped out with a tow rope. He lashed the ferry to a tree branch, and the crew began to disembark while he moved to anchor the chimps' boat. Paolo began to organize the group. "Diego, you and Juan Miguel can set up camp here. Remember we're coming on to flood season and the shoreline is pretty variable. It could change by half a mile in two weeks, and this could all be submerged, so be sure and set up quite a ways inland. Sameer, why don't you see if we can get a read on the chimp."

While Sameer fussed with his pack, Stiles scanned the forest and said, "I suppose this would be a good time to compliment old Kenji on his decision not to engineer a very smart jaguar for us to chase."

Sameer pulled out his antenna and popped open the

crossbars as the rest of the group shouldered their packs. He slowly made a half arc around the river. After about thirty seconds, he stopped for a moment and backtracked, only to resume his slow arc. Finally, he shrugged. "Not a blip. He must be out of range."

At that moment Jeremy called out from the beach he had been exploring, "Guys, I think you'd better come see this." He pointed downriver, where a small fishing boat was moored. More precisely, he pointed to the shape of a body stretched out next to the boat.

The scientists jogged down to the site, with Jamie's long stride reaching the boat first. The boat was in fair condition, without any structural damage; however, the contents were a picture of entropy, scattered around the cabin with abandon. A few remaining fish heads and tails were strewn about the torn fishing nets on the floor.

Next to the boat a single lifeless figure lay rotting on the beach. His frozen expression, twisted permanently to one side, showed little of the terror he must have felt in his final moments. One arm was disarticulated, and lay a few yards inland. Jeremy went over and kicked it with his foot. Scratches and bruises covered the arm, and the upper third near the shoulder showed obvious evidence of teeth marks from something gnawing on the flesh.

Jamie clutched her stomach at the grizzly scene. *Keep it together.* "Jaguar?" she managed.

Paolo shook his head grimly. "Not a chance. This isn't their style, and they rarely attack this close to shore. Besides," he paused to show some coarse black hairs he had picked off the ground, "jaguars don't leave chimpanzee hairs at the site of their attack."

Sameer said, "No way. Chimpanzees don't behave like

this. It's too aggressive, even if they were threatened or needed food."

"It seems, Sameer, your chimps are under new management. They have a new alpha male, one that doesn't give a damn about how chimpanzees are supposed to behave."

The group looked at the carnage for one final moment, and walked back to their landing site as Paolo phoned the Manaus police to report the "accident."

Paolo divided up the team. "We can cover the most ground in two teams, each at a forty-five-degree angle to the riverbank. Check your compass frequently to keep your bearing. If we don't detect a signal by tonight we'll talk again. Jamie, David, and Jeremy: you head southwest. Roger, Sameer, and I will track southeast. Keep your phones handy and make contact as soon as a signal is detected. We should be able to cover ten miles today. Good luck."

He took a quick compass read, and started walking into the undergrowth. Stiles and Sameer followed him. Jamie and Jeremy started off in the other direction, leaving Mercer to sigh and follow their footsteps, swatting the mosquitoes that hovered over him.

TWENTY-TWO

AYALA Goren ducked her head into the wind as the deafening chop of the rotor clamored overhead. Susan followed Ayala and Carlos into the belly of the chopper waiting on the private airstrip. Inside the crowded interior, Susan looked over at the pilot, trying to decide if he was dead or simply motionless.

The short Brazilian pilot was well into his sixties, by appearance, and betrayed he was alive only by an occasional movement of the toothpick in his sparse teeth. He was dressed in a worn, beige, collared shirt with snaps up the front and jeans. He wore goggles that hid what Susan imagined were squinting eyes.

"Vamos embora!" Ayala shouted to the pilot, and the helicopter lifted off the ground. As the grassy airstrip faded into obscurity, the tall skyscrapers of Manaus rose and then receded from the heart of the adjacent city. The meandering course of the Amazon and the Negro could both be seen from the air. On the far side of the Amazon, a dense green carpet stretched out of sight in the distance.

Although no stranger to traveling by helicopter, Susan had severe misgivings about the aged pilot, and asked Ayala what she knew of the man.

"Don't let the old fossil fool you. He's spry as they come. Closest thing to a fighter pilot in the Amazon." Ayala had to shout to be heard.

"That's what I was afraid of!" Susan shouted back.

Carlos scanned the landscape below. "How do we find the landing site?" he asked.

Ayala pulled out a pair of binoculars from her pack, and rested them on her lap. "The scientists should lead us right to it. All we have to do is find their boat."

"They're moving today? How do you know?" asked Susan.

"Surprising what you can hear when you hang out under the right boats."

The pilot, having reached the Amazon, turned and began to follow the course of the river upstream, keeping altitude within fifty feet of the tallest emergents. The passengers carefully scanned the river, which was dotted by a handful of boats of various sizes. The largest ones were easily visible, and likely represented smaller cargo ships, since the tankers and container ships rarely navigated upriver past Manaus. The smaller vessels were just visible without magnification.

Susan examined the river as the outline of the city faded farther into the distance. Clearings in the forest near the riverbank that signified villages, native settlements, or small ports began to appear less frequently as the chopper moved farther from the city.

Some time later, Carlos shook Ayala's shoulder and pointed to the northern bank. "That should be the complex up ahead. You can just see the main building."

Ayala aimed her binoculars where Carlos had pointed and began speaking again to the pilot in fluent Portuguese, "Ali. Voa perto do edifício mais grande."

The chopper hovered over the river adjacent to the complex and began to slowly descend. Ayala's gaze was fastened on the dock at the mouth of the complex. Soon she lifted her binoculars, satisfied, and announced, "Perfect. They've already left. Now we will see who are the better trackers." She addressed the pilot rapidly, "Temos que achalos! Segue o rio e fique em baixo dos árvores." He nodded back, the toothpick in his teeth lazily flipping up and down.

The helicopter circled 180 degrees and began moving downriver, keeping an altitude below the treetops lining the river on either side. After several passes down the river, Ayala had identified several possible boats of interest. She guided the pilot to circle over each as she peered down through her binoculars.

Each time a candidate boat was rejected, she wrinkled her face in disgust. Susan sensed she was annoyed after three unsuccessful passes down a thirty-mile stretch of river. Ayala gave the pilot a command to circle back again when she started and yanked the binoculars back to her eyes. Susan looked across at the southern bank of the river and stared only an instant. She turned her gaze toward Ayala. She admired the woman's self-assuredness. What she wouldn't give to have that confidence.

"We have them," Ayala said. In one movement, she unloaded the pistol-shaped object she had retrieved the night before, and snapped it into operation. Turning a knob on the stalk, she switched on a coarse static from the speaker. She climbed up next to the pilot and pointed eastward. The helicopter ascended and angled to the right over the forest. The static continued unabated. When Susan realized her fingers were going numb as she gripped her seat she relaxed her hold.

Ayala made some unintelligible suggestions to the pilot, and the copter began a long wide circular arc into the forest. It continued in its arc until a couple minutes later it returned over the spot where it had left the river. Again the helicopter swung out into an arc, this time wider, following an oval path along the shoreline. After sweeping eastward from the crash site, the pilot began flying straight west parallel to the river.

Quite suddenly, a faint beeping coarsed through the static on the antenna. Within a few seconds the beeping became clearer and unmistakable: one pulse every second like the sound of a soft alarm clock. Carlos looked at Susan with a broad grin. "'Alo, chimpanzee," he called.

Ayala continued to focus on the sound. Within thirty seconds, the beeping began to fade, and then disappeared as suddenly as it had come. She directed the pilot to fly a crossing path perpendicular to the river where the beeping had peaked. As the helicopter swung out across the river and reentered the forested carpet, the beeping began again as abruptly as it had before. This time the signal intensified even louder. But a moment later it rapidly decreased.

Ayala prattled with the pilot again, and the aircraft deftly turned about face. The signal instantly became louder. The pilot continued straight ahead. Suddenly the signal went dead. Ayala raised a hand to the pilot and the helicopter pulled up, hovering over the spot. Above the hum of the blades, the crew could barely hear a faint pulsing signal.

Ayala lowered the antenna's tip until it was pointing straight at the cockpit floor. The pulsing signal bounded loudly through the cabin, and Susan beamed at her partners. Ayala pulled out a handheld navigation module and quickly recorded their position. She then shut off the antenna's beeping. She stooped up and moved to the back of the cabin.

"How do we get there?" Susan shouted.

"Easy. We jump!"

She had to be kidding. "What the hell are you talking about? We can't jump. Have you looked down?"

"Do you want your chimp or not?"

"When I said 'dead or alive,' I was talking about the chimp, not me!"

Carlos interrupted their conversation by pointing about a mile to the southeast. "There is a small tributary over there. It would make a good landing site."

Ayala nodded, and the pilot flew above the trees to a small clearing over the riverlet. The helicopter descended slowly to about one hundred feet off the ground, but could not penetrate the lower canopy with its many outcropping branches. Ayala shouldered a pack, and then tossed one to Susan as Carlos picked up a third. She grabbed a sturdy crate in the back of the cabin, lashed it to a chute, and opened the door of the helicopter. The wind rushed in and left Susan gasping for air. Ayala hoisted up the crate and tossed it out the window. Susan watched it tumble down with terror, expecting to see it smash into the river. The parachute slowed the fall of the crate, and Susan watched it thud into the shallow bank of the river more or less intact.

"It's a little tougher for us!" shouted Ayala to Susan and Carlos. She grabbed a rope from the back of the chopper and hooked the metal bolt at the end of the rope onto a metal clip on the helicopter floor. She then tossed the rope out of the helicopter where it unfolded down until it reached the ground several seconds later. Ayala reached under the seat and surfaced with three pairs of gloves. "Just grab the rope with your gloves and use them to slide down it. Hold on tight and the friction will slow you down."

"What are you talking about?!"

"Try not to land with your knees locked; and try not to land in the river!" Ayala waved and then dived out of the copter. Her body threaded gracefully along the rope until she landed on her feet on the riverbank a few seconds later. She waved from the ground.

"You go next," shouted Carlos to Susan.

"You go to hell!"

Carlos gave her a gentle prod and Susan gingerly put one foot on the door frame. The wind ripped at her eyes. She looked over her shoulder, feeling starved for air. Carlos nodded, and she grasped the rope tightly with her gloves. She climbed to the edge and stepped off into the air.

The wind tore at her face as her shirt filled with air, lifting off her chest and over her face. She couldn't breathe, drowning in the sea of air jetting across her body. Her freefall continued unchecked, her terror fading into numbness as she clenched tightly onto the rope. Her field of vision was consumed with the ground racing up at her, and she realized she was headed directly into the river.

She frantically tried to assemble a plan for how to land, but had scarcely begun doing so when she smacked into the water and plummeted underneath the surface, still clutching the rope in her hands. She thrashed under the surface, her hands refusing to let go of the rope until she felt like a fly suffocating in an underwater web. Without any conscious effort, her head bobbed to the surface, then under again, then back to the surface as the river carried her rapidly downstream.

Glancing up, she saw a huge boulder racing toward her. She dropped the rope and began paddling with her arms, but continued moving straight toward the hulking triangular rock. Water coursed along either side of the sharp facing edge. The weight of the pack pulled her underwater, taking all her strength to resist.

As the rock loomed over her, she grunted and turned her body feet first, pushing off on one side of the wedge, sending her headfirst over the rapidly coursing water. The water poured into her lungs as she coughed and sputtered in the cold rapids. She felt the scrape of something hard against her left hand and reflexively grabbed out.

Her gloved fingers closed on a protruding root, and she swung her other hand to pull her up against the torrent of water trying to pull her downriver. Swinging her feet over she found bottom and managed to stand up in the chest-deep water, pulling herself arm over arm until she collapsed on the riverbank, panting heavily.

She looked up to see the figures of Carlos and Ayala racing along the riverbank toward her. Carlos reached her first. Susan stared him down venomously. "You're both fired," she said feebly. Carlos grinned in relief.

Ayala reached her side a moment later. "Nice work—

we're probably within a couple miles of the chimp. Not bad for a first jump."

Susan was exasperated. Fumbling for words, all she could manage was, "I'm completely soaked!"

"Get used to it," Ayala replied. "You're right in the middle of the Amazon Basin; it rains here two hundred days a year."

Susan took inventory of her body, wiping the oozing blood off a scrape on her left forearm. Her fingers were caked with mud, and stung from the tight grip on the root. Her ego crushed, her body aching, and her heart still pounding, she brushed herself off and said, "So let's go get him."

Carlos and Ayala had already turned upriver.

TWENTY-THREE

THE forest floor thudded with the methodical fall of Jamie's hiking boots. She felt confident, purposeful, as she led her party deeper into the jungle. Her leg muscles responded promptly to each command, and the rhythmic sensation of her thighs against the cloth of her cotton shorts made her feel energetic, youthful. She was at home in a jungle where only the fit survive and belong.

Periodically, she looked back at Jeremy and Mercer, who struggled to keep up with her elfish movements. More than once, a glance back caught one of her fellow travelers watching her hips as she walked. *Let them look.*

The forest had become stately and elegant, nothing like the thick undergrowth by the river they had tediously thrashed their way through earlier. For at least a quarter mile along the riverbank, the forest was very different from the interior, where tall trees ascend out of sight into a twilight sky of green and the forest floor is surprisingly clear. The dim light filtering through the canopy allowed little to grow in the soil, and apart from the humus of fallen sticks and leaves, and the ubiquitous insects that lived in it, the ground was barren of all but sparse grasses, flowers, and ferns.

Trees of striking diversity, but monotonous similarity, rose on every side like the columns of an interminably large, forgotten Greek temple. Occasionally, a stream of light would break through as a fallen tree opened a peek-hole to heaven, or a cluster of smaller trees or ferns would be seen. Most of the trees were of respectable size, a few feet in diameter, others surprisingly thin, and some had trunks so massive that the three hikers fingertip to fingertip could not encircle them if they tried. Many were buttressed with large roots, a foot in diameter themselves, that spiraled out from the trunks.

Jamie felt ecstatic to be out of the lab, back in the jungle. With the excitement of discovering the chimp, experiments bolder than any she had dreamed of, and the frantic preparations for the expedition, she hadn't realized how much she missed the forest. She missed waking up to the thrum of life, smelling the damp air, feeling free. Her thoughts roamed to the chimp. *What would he be doing?* She wondered how much longer they would need to study him before she really understood him. One thing was for sure; nobody would believe her experiments, and the shocking implications about the soul, unless she had the chimp in her possession to prove her claims.

Beads of sweat collected on Jamie's forehead, and she noticed that Jeremy and Mercer were breathing more rapidly as they fought to hold their pace with dignity. The air had a dank scent, strangely familiar, like a primitive recognition of a primordial birthplace bred into the species. The weather was humid, less so than on the river.

The forest was well enough lit for Jamie to see where she was walking, but no more. The perpetual dusk in the deep forest only darkened at night, something that Jamie was used to, but she suspected unnerved her companions greatly.

The canopy above was a totally different world, where collections of exotic, colorful plants unfolded amidst tangled vines and the traffic of butterflies, birds, and bats, all invisible to the forest floor. Most species in the canopy, where most of the animals lived, never left it in their lifetimes. Only a fraction of the more adaptable species ever ventured to the ground level.

From experience, Jamie knew that animals are frequently heard, but infrequently seen in the forest interior, where plants reign, encastled in intricate and exotic defenses. Hundreds of thousands of toxins, thorns, and evolutionary gambits had protected the rain forest plants from being ravaged by animals, and a hardy symbiosis existed among the animal and plant survivors that made the forest their home.

Jamie's pocket compass bounced on its necklace against her canvas shirt. She occasionally picked it up, reoriented herself, and strode off again toward a distant landmark. More infrequently, she checked her palmtop GPS and gauged the distance they had traveled. Jeremy had been talkative at first, but after a few attempts at conversation, he acquiesced to maintaining their march in solitude as he became more winded. Mercer marched without a word of complaint, bearing his exercise with dignity and patience, not even stopping when he periodically sipped from his canteen.

After several hours of marching, Jamie saw Jeremy stop to stretch his shins against a tree. She noted tightness in her own calves, and realized the others were probably much worse off. She stopped as well and hoisted her pack off her damp shirt. She pulled out their antenna and snapped it open as Sameer had done before. Not sure what to expect, she held the antenna at arm's length, and flipped on the audio channel. She slowly rotated the device around her, pausing only occasionally, and then repeated the entire motion. Was she doing something wrong? She shook her head and replaced the antenna in her pack.

Mercer gave a self-deprecating look to the others, indicating that he was ready to proceed, but could not fully hide a trace of appreciation when Jamie said it would be a good time to break for lunch. He removed his pack and sat on it next to the others.

Jeremy unwrapped a granola bar and sat on a fallen tree, massaging his ankles with his other hand. He looked at Jamie. "You ever get lonely working out in the forest?"

Jamie smiled warmly and looked away. "Not as lonely as I used to get at Princeton. Isolation here can be spiritual, unlike a cramped dorm room."

Jeremy nodded and remarked, "There's something spooky about this place, don't you think? I mean, it's like some kind of fairy tale missing the story."

"Maybe that's what we're doing here."

Jeremy turned to Mercer. "One question I've never really had answered. What's the point of all this anyway? I know what that chimp means to us, but I don't understand

Kenji. What was he hoping to do? I mean, why did he make the chimp in the first place?"

Mercer shrugged. "Never got a straight answer out of him. And now . . ."

Jamie finished his sentence in her mind.

Mercer continued, "No, I was never in the loop until just recently, when Kenji needed to hire you folks to work on the chimp. For me, it's about money at this point. I see potential for a product. I don't know what he had in mind."

"Guess it doesn't matter anymore. I just like to know what motivates people. For me, science is a game: the best game in the world with the toughest opponent. I love games."

Mercer opened his pack and retrieved some dried fruit and meat. He ate ravenously, withdrawing from the conversation. The others followed suit and turned their attention to lunch.

After a moment, Jeremy turned again to Jamie. "So what's the coolest thing you ever saw in the rain forest?"

"So many things . . . I once saw from a tree a colony of army ants. It was a swarm you could see from a hundred feet up: I watched it most of the day sweeping across the forest, laying waste to everything in its path. The ants even crossed a small river by forming a chain and climbing across each other. It blows your mind to think of so much power in the clutches of so many tiny ants. Each one seems so insignificant."

The three ate in silence their brief meal, each grateful for the rest. Jamie insisted then that everyone remove their shoes and inspect their feet. She removed hers first and checked over her slender feet. "One of the biggest threats to this trip is going to be foot ulcers."

She instructed everyone to change into fresh socks, and hang the old ones to dry on their packs. She also gave them some nystatin powder to put in their shoes to stop molds from growing. "Get used to the ritual. It may be overkill, but I want everyone in dry socks three times a day."

Jeremy grinned. "My mother only makes me change twice."

Satisfied when they had all finished the inspection, Jamie stood and shouldered her pack. She pulled the compass from off her chest, looked into the distance, and began walking. Jeremy replaced his pack with a groan and followed after Mercer, who was already close behind Jamie.

PAOLO, Stiles, and Sameer walked briskly through the maze of trees that surrounded them. Where possible, they walked three astride; when the trees were too dense, Paolo would lead and Stiles and Sameer followed. On one such occasion during the late morning, Stiles commented, "You know, we look like a bloody Star Trek landing party in here. Does anyone else feel out of place?"

Sameer answered, "I think it's magnificent. Like the forest back at the compound, but so much less confining knowing there is no wall around us."

Paolo disregarded Stiles's intermittent complaints. The forest seemed to infuse him with a tranquil energy as he led the party deeper into the jungle. Once they had cleared the secondary forest by the river, they had been making excellent time. *We should be able to cover ten miles today,* he thought with satisfaction.

Stiles prattled on. "So let me get this straight. Suppose we find this chimp's signal and track him down. Exactly how are we going to go about getting those little darts into him? I don't suppose he's going to want to come down for a biscuit and a chat when he spots us."

Sameer answered, "It all depends. Our best bet will probably be to climb a tree and sedate him in his nest. I think we could manage it if we're quiet about it."

"Oh right. Wait a minute. Now what was that about climbing trees again? The branches are fifty feet up if you haven't noticed."

"What about the stories of your summers as a lumberjack?" Sameer said.

"You're on thin ice, pal."

"All it takes is a good safety harness, shoes, and gloves. I've done it many times to plant food up in a tree when trying to get the little blokes to climb the right trees. It shouldn't be too difficult."

"You know this would be a lot easier if Frankenstein had engineered the little monster with a fear of heights built in," Stiles said.

Paolo looked to his companions and asked, "I've been thinking a bit, and I'm curious about how it will be received when you publish your findings."

"What do you mean, exactly?" Stiles asked.

"Think about it this way," Paolo said. "Human beings don't have a very good track record of tolerance when it comes to sharing the spotlight. If it turns out that the chimpanzee is accepted as intelligent, what then? Is he going to be allowed to reproduce? Does he have any rights?"

"What happens in the privacy of a chimpanzee's bedroom is his business. I won't get involved," Stiles said.

"Seriously, could human society tolerate another race of intelligent beings, possibly superior to ourselves in many respects? What kind of impact would that have?"

"I don't know. It's an amazing story, but people have a way of ignoring important news after a while. You ever hear of Oliver?"

"No," Paolo said.

"Some enterprising chap nearly forty years ago found a particularly human-looking chimp and taught it to walk upright and mix drinks. He called the chimp Oliver. Well, Oliver went from owner to owner in California as a sideshow attraction. He hit the big time when a Japanese TV broadcast speculated that Oliver was really a chimp-human hybrid, and claimed he had forty-seven chromosomes, intermediate between chimps and humans. Utter nonsense, of course, but Oliver became a literal media circus. It finally got enough attention that in the nineties Oliver aired on a telly show called *Unsolved Mysteries* devoted to such things. I guess someone got fed up with it all after that and demonstrated that he in fact had forty-eight chromosomes and was a regular old chimp."

Stiles slipped back behind Paolo as they stepped over a large, buttressed tree trunk. He continued, "Anyway, such curiosities are great over a beer or two, but the public at large really doesn't give a banana in the long run. It might be the same way with our chimp here. There will be some hype, some protests, and then everyone will just forget about it, except for a few scientists. Those scientists are going to make some pretty amazing discoveries about the brain, which also will be known by almost nobody until something useful comes out of it all. The chimps will be like every other genetically modified animal: bred in small numbers for research but not released to the wild or mixed with native populations."

"You seem very sure of that," Paolo commented warily.

"Listen, I know how these things work. If it isn't an aphrodisiac or makes someone money, the public just won't care about it. Not for long, anyway. Jamie thinks differently."

"What does she think?" Paolo asked quickly.

"To her it's all about God. She thinks if we can prove this chimp has all the elements that make up a human soul, she's proved that the soul isn't some immortal ghost that lives inside us."

Paolo froze at the comment. *Why didn't she tell me?*

Stiles looked back, and Paolo started walking again.

Stiles continued, "She's got a point, you know. Not that I really care. I haven't believed in God since I was in diapers. And no matter what we find, I bet most people will completely ignore the whole affair."

"Yet you're willing to risk coming in here to track that chimp down?" Paolo asked.

"Don't get me wrong. That chimp is the most amazing thing ever created by mankind, and I'm bloody well going to get him back. When Kenji first showed him to me, I thought, 'Well Sir Ken, you've outdone yourself: it's a monkey.' But I've changed my tune. I tell you that chimp is one smart banana. It's every bit as smart as you or I."

Paolo thought for a moment and said, "You underestimate the problem. I think this chimp is different from genetically altered animals created in the past. If it truly is sentient, the public will not forget it, nor will it be easy to contain in a laboratory. Your present situation should testify to that."

Stiles shrugged. "They should pay attention. The greatest danger humanity ever faces may not be nuclear weapons or disease. It may be obsolescence."

"Obsolescence?" asked Sameer.

"Exactly. Forty thousand years ago, as the story goes, Neanderthal man was king. A short time later, he was extinct. It wasn't because of bombs or wars or meteorites. It was because of Cro-Magnon man. Neanderthals became obsolete. Now I'm not saying something silly like these chimps are going to take over the world. But this is only the first experiment. Others may be smarter, more adaptable, or just more vicious."

Sameer said, "Maybe if we created something better than ourselves it would deserve to replace us. Maybe God hasn't finished his creation and man is just winding down as the next stepping stone in His plan."

Paolo's response was immediate. "I can't believe that, nor do I want to see mankind traded in for a newer model."

Paolo continued on in silence, then abruptly paused, signaling for the others to stop as well. Above the ambient noise of the forest a high-pitched cry sounded from a distance.

"Just what is that?" asked Sameer.

"It's a jaguar cry. Nothing to worry about. She would never attack us without provocation."

"Somehow that's not too reassuring," Stiles muttered.

As they walked, Sameer reached a hand into his pack, unzipped a pocket, and pulled out the antenna. He flipped it open and began sweeping it from side to side. After a minute or two with no success, he put it back into his pack and continued walking.

A large, brilliant yellow butterfly sailed past the hikers. "Amazing," said Sameer, "how all the butterflies really do look alike in one region. Then every little while it changes and all the butterflies look completely different."

A large animal scurried across their path.

"Was that a rat?" asked Stiles.

"They get pretty big here," said Paolo without emotion.

"Seems like he's a long way from the subway. I guess there's plenty to eat here, too."

"Speaking of food, I have always wondered how many of these plants are edible," said Sameer.

"You mean how many of them taste good, or how many won't kill you?" asked Paolo.

"It seems there are a lot of fruits and flowers here that I do not recognize," Sameer clarified. "I wonder if our little chimps will try some of them."

"Can't tell you exactly, but that one you're looking at over there is a mixed blessing. It's called a passion flower. Beautiful, sure, but the foliage contains hefty concentrations of cyanides. Supposedly it's something of a hallucinogen when smoked as well."

"About the last thing someone would need in here is a

nightmare. My imagination is plenty active on its own," Stiles said.

"I wouldn't go arbitrarily tasting plants, and I hope your chimps are smart enough to do the same. If not, they'll learn soon enough," said Paolo.

"Let's hope not too soon," Sameer said.

TWENTY-FOUR

AFTER three hours of hiking from the riverlet where they had jumped, Ayala, Susan, and Carlos struck gold. They had spent their first hour tracking in entirely the wrong direction. Ayala had found a weak signal at the jump site coming from downriver and begun tracking it.

After the signal had grown slightly weaker an hour later despite a vigorous pace, Ayala stopped and moved the antenna full circle again. She cursed under her breath when after a careful pass she discovered that the signal was actually more intense when they turned 180 degrees. They reversed course and heard a steady enhancement of the signal as they traveled upriver.

Each of them carried a small pack, suitable for camping, rations, and equipment for sedating and capturing the chimpanzee. It was Ayala's express hope that they could capture the chimp the same day and make a quick exit, but the extra supplies were available should they need more time. An inflatable raft was at the jump site, along with other, less portable supplies. Carlos had recorded GPS coordinates of the site with his handheld. In the rain forest, he had explained, measurements could be expected to have an accuracy within twenty meters, at least since the year 2000 when the U.S. government stopped incorporating an error signal onto GPS transmissions for nonmilitary applications.

The three were now at maximal signal intensity, and were likely within a hundred meters of the source. Ayala paced back and forth over the forest and tried variable orientations until she had narrowed the signal to a few dozen candidate trees. The source was clearly in the canopy layer, and was invisible to them from the forest floor. As Ayala swung the antenna upward toward the trees overhead, she smiled wickedly and said, "There's your chimp. Now let's get him."

"How exactly do you plan that? Climb?" Susan asked, amused, as she looked at the large tree trunks rising up out of sight without any visible branches for climbing for fifty feet.

Carlos cocked one eyebrow, his face echoing Susan's question.

Ayala unshouldered her pack. "Not on your life," she said. "The tree trunks are full of snakes, toxic plants, and poisonous insects, half of which I wouldn't even recognize if I could see through their camouflage. Besides, most of the trees are so dense you can't pound a metal spike into them."

She pulled from her pack a crossbow, which she snapped into place. She then removed a cross tied to a long coil of tight, thin nylon rope. With a fluid movement, she shot the arrow straight up until it cleared the forest crown, and came crashing down, lodging out of sight into the canopy.

She put down her crossbow and pulled the slack out of the rope so it hung taut from the canopy. "First shot," she said with a wink. Reaching again into her pack, she pulled out a metal ascender connected to a pair of leather stirrups and clamped the ascender onto her boots with a snap. She donned some leather gloves, slung the antenna over her back, tucked a dart gun under her belt, locked the ascender on her feet around the rope, and hoisted herself up.

With athletic grace she pulled herself up with her hands in bounds, each time her feet locking into place as the ascenders gripped the rope to prevent her from sliding down. Her forearms scaled effortlessly up the rope until she was ninety feet above the ground. She stopped for a long moment, pulled out the antenna, and made an arc with the device. Replacing the antenna, she began to swing gently on the rope.

As she swung more vigorously, she flexed her hips and pushed to increase her speed. Soon she was flying back and forth on the rope. With one hand gripping the rope tightly, she reached down and pulled her feet from the stirrups, grasping the rope loosely between her feet. She flew back as the rope swung the other direction.

At the zenith of her arc, she flailed to grab an outlying branch and locked her arm around it. For a precarious moment, she hung motionless from the branch, her other arm grasping the rope. Then she swung her legs upward and locked one leg around the large branch. She hooked her other arm around, still holding the rope, and scrambled onto the large branch.

Ayala looked down at the small figures of Susan and

Carlos, just visible through the branches interposed. Ayala had entered a new world. Color blazed from the branches in the light percolating through the upper canopy. Exotic plants of every hue beckoned from each hanging vine and branch. Flowers grew on top of flowers, birdcalls rang through the trees, and the only thing missing was the giant at the top of the beanstalk.

Ayala was on the middle of the three canopies in the rain forest. The lower canopy, with the bulk of the trees ranging from 50 to 80 feet high, was visible below. The main canopy was the bulkiest, with trees from 90 to 130 feet high projecting densely interconnected branches. Above her was a layer of emergent trees too sparse to form a continuous layer, but overarching most of the forest with large elliptical branch formations. Ayala had ascended above most of the evergreens, and stood on a large, lower branch of the main canopy.

She fastened the rope around the branch and tugged at it to verify it was secure. Then she carefully walked down the moss-covered branch to where she could climb up to a higher branch and emerged into the heart of the canopy. Sturdy vines were abundant, and Ayala easily scrambled about the canopy through swarms of mosquitoes to find a good vantage point, on which she squatted down and waited. She scanned the horizon and watched.

A brilliantly colored bird fluttered down from above and perched a few feet over her head. It warbled its call with clarity and precision. A moment later, it flew off. Ayala crouched on her spot for several minutes until finally she was rewarded. A faint rustling sounded in the distance, followed by another, and then an unmistakable ape call. Ayala's body tensed as she struggled to locate the source. Silently, she pulled her dart gun from her belt, and raised it to her shoulder.

She quietly stood and began walking down a branch, steadying herself on vines every few steps. She climbed up a level, then down again until she was close to the source of the sound. She looked around. One tree over, about twenty meters away, Ayala saw the dark fur of a chimpanzee walking along a branch. A moment behind, another followed. This one was smaller, with an unmistakable blue collar catching a ray of sunlight as it walked into the open across from where Ayala hid.

Ayala looked down. It would take some time for the ketamine to take effect. The chimp would hopefully be in a stable position before losing maneuverability from the anesthesia. Nevertheless, the risk of a fall was a concern, as the chimp would likely not survive. She aimed her dart gun. "Just in reach," she thought. Her finger depressed on the pneumatic trigger.

The dart sailed over the chimp's head with a crash into the foliage above. Ayala quickly loaded another dart. Too slow. The sound of the dart had alerted the chimp to the intruder. He crouched down, and looked right into Ayala's dark brown eyes.

In a flurry of motion the chimp dived into the forest canopy, jumping from limb to limb, swinging deftly with one arm to locate the next branch. Within seconds he was completely out of sight, and Ayala heard the sound of his progress in the distance. She could not hope to follow at anywhere near that pace.

She wound her way back to her entry point, loosed the rope from the branch, and put her feet back into the stirrups. A couple minutes later, her nervous companions sighed with relief as she came back into view.

"You're crazy!" shouted Susan, half furious and half awestruck at Ayala's feat.

Ayala was breathless when she hopped off the rope onto the ground. "Too difficult," she said. "They're so much faster than anything I've tracked before. We'll have to track him on the ground and wait for him to come down." She paused for a breath every few words. With that, she picked up her pack, replaced the missing items, less the rope, and started off in the direction of the chimp's departure.

TWENTY-FIVE

JAMIE unfolded the antenna on the ringing satellite phone to hear Paolo's voice on the other end. "Paolo, I'm here."

"Jamie?"

"Yes, do you have a signal?"

"No. We're breaking for the night. Nothing on your end?"

Jamie sighed. "Nothing but static."

Paolo answered back calmly, "We'll have something by tomorrow. Talk to you in the morning . . . Jamie?"

"Yes?"

"You never really told me about your intentions, about what you want to do with this chimp."

Jamie felt her stomach tighten. She knew Paolo was a believer. But so was she, on some level, at least until now. The chimp had changed everything. *What would Paolo think about her plans?*

"Roger and Jeremy told you about my theory?"

"You can't disprove God in a laboratory, Jamie. Whatever you find. It's something you feel, Jamie. That you're not alone. That He's real."

"Are you angry?"

"No. But you promise no more secrets?"

"I promise."

"And be careful. Call if you have questions. About anything."

She clicked off the receiver, and sighed to herself. *What did he think of her now?* She turned to her two exhausted companions.

"We break here for the night. Jeremy, you have a springbar tent in your pack. Figure out how to set it up. David, clear an area for a fire. We could use some real food. I'm going to scout the area and make sure it's safe."

The other two were too tired to complain when she walked out of sight into the forest, and slumped against their packs.

Jamie retrieved her sat phone and snapped out the folded antenna used for transmission. She punched a few buttons on the display and soon heard the voice of Diego Garcia on the receiver.

"Hi Diego, this is Jamie. You all set up?"

"Sim, Jamie. We are about three hundred meters from the river, and have made camp. Anything we can be doing to help?"

"Not right now. We'll let you know if anything comes up. Just keep your phone handy. Both groups have stopped for the night."

"OK, Jamie."

"And keep an eye out for natives. We aren't sure exactly who the locals are here. We haven't seen any yet, but there are probably some settlements not too far from here. Much of the riverbank is populated, and some don't like outsiders."

She clicked off the receiver and reattached it to her belt. *Probably for very good reason,* she thought to herself. Like indigenous people in most of the Americas, the local Indians had been culturally ravaged, their settlements overtrodden by foreigners or capitalists, and their populations beset by foreign diseases until a small fraction of the original inhabitants remained.

More numerous than the Indians were Brazilians who had abandoned poverty and hunger in the cities to form frontier settlements in the forest. Some sought wealth by pillaging the abundant resources of the forest with cottage industries, and others simply sought to survive. From either group, outright conflicts were rare, and most of the Indian tribes either kept to themselves or embraced Western culture. Nevertheless, Jamie didn't know who the neighbors were, and she was wise enough to be cautious.

DIEGO and Juan Miguel reclined against large buttresses of a tree next to their makeshift camp. Both of them Brazilian nationals who had worked for years at Brain-Stem, they often slipped into a combination of English and Portuguese when they talked among themselves.

Outside of a silver springbar tent a short distance away were several crates of supplies: food, medicines, first aid supplies, tools, weapons, and an extra raft. On top of one of the crates were two tin trays and the scattered remains of their dinner. Diego had tossed a compact shovel against a tree after digging a small moat around the tent.

Diego had grown up in the state of Amazonas, born and raised in Manaus. His father was a merchant, and Diego had ample opportunity when he wasn't working in the store to take short weekend trips into the forest. Juan Miguel was a stranger to the forest. Having grown up in a suburb of Brasilia, he knew as little about the forest as he did about the Himalayas. This pleased Diego immeasurably, and he could not hope for a better combination of gullibility and excitability in a companion.

For years Diego had told stories of the dangers and mystery of the Amazon to Juan Miguel, who readily believed most of the exploits his friend described. To Juan Miguel, Diego was snake charmer, Indian trader, and herbal shaman par excellence.

Over dinner, Diego had told Juan Miguel a story from his youth when he and two friends had seen a jaguar. He described the beast's teeth, its claws, and the matted blood on its mouth from a fresh kill. After a long, terrifying stare, the animal had turned its tail in one motion and lazily sauntered away from the intrepid explorers. Of course, no such encounter actually took place, nor would Diego have remained continent had it occurred, let alone had the fortitude to unsheathe his hunting knife as he had also claimed.

Following the story they had traded attempts at impersonating the inimitable Skip Jordan. Juan Miguel had thrust out his pitifully undersized belly and proffered, "Jorge, you latrine skipper, put down your mop and come listen to what really goes on in the projects in South Cheecago."

Diego laughed heartily at the likeness, however poor it was. They both had a soft spot for Jordan, and were perfectly content working under his loose leadership. If nothing else, it made coming to work entertaining.

Juan Miguel stretched his arms over his head and asked, "Diego, you think they find that monkey?"

Diego shook his head in confidence. "No way, brother. The monkeys are too fast. They say this one is pretty smart, too."

"Jamie é inteligente."

"Sim, Juan, but to survive in the jungle you have to be smart and fast."

"But Jamie is smart. And good-looking, não?"

"Sem dúvida. But she is too smart and too fast for you, Juan Miguel."

"But not for the monkey?"

"The monkey will win; looks get you nowhere in the jungle." Diego winked and grinned broadly at Juan Miguel.

Juan replied, "Sim, I'd much rather look at her than the monkey."

The conversation led into a summary of Juan Miguel's dating prospects and a review of the women at the complex. Diego and Juan Miguel played a few hands of poker, but neither was enough of a gambler to make two-player poker worth their time in the dim light. After a phone call from Jamie, Diego rested the phone on one of the crates, and walked into the forest carrying a roll of toilet paper.

The forest did not get cold at night, not at this low altitude, and neither Diego nor Juan Miguel wanted anything more than the thin mat that each of them rolled out in the tent for sleeping. They removed their shoes, put extra

DEET on their exposed feet to ward off mosquitoes, and fell quickly asleep.

A moment later, Juan Miguel awoke with a start. His groggy mind searched to identify a sound he heard outside. As he rubbed the sleep out of his eyes, he dimly recognized that the sound came from all over, rain pelting his tent. He muttered a curse. The good weather yesterday had lulled him into thinking this was going to be an easy job. Tomorrow would be a long day. He put his head back down and closed his eyes.

Just before falling asleep again, or perhaps just after, he heard another sound. Not just rain.

Something scraping.

He crawled to his knees. Diego was still asleep. He opened the flaps of the tent door and looked out into the rain. The sound came again. He struggled to localize it, the dizziness quickly fading from his consciousness. He stepped out of the tent, covering his head with one hand from the drizzle falling through the trees.

He nearly tripped over a crate, strewn open in front of his feet. The contents had been scattered along the ground. The sound came again. It had moved.

Now broken branches, nearer.

How many footsteps? Two, four? Juan Miguel peered through the rain at the campsite, but it was too dark to see anything.

He took a few steps away from the tent.

Footsteps again, louder.

"Who is there?" he called. His muscles began to

tighten. He was soaked from head to foot. He wiped the water out of his eyes, and reached for his knife at his side.

Behind him. Moving quickly.

He whirled around to face the intruders, his knife poised. He let out a cry as he saw the outline of a figure, very close. His cry was caught in his throat as pain shot across his head. The darkness around him became blackness, and he crumpled to the ground.

PART III
CURSE OF THE FIRSTBORN

But we were born of risen apes, not fallen angels, and the apes were armed killers besides. And so what shall we wonder at? Our murders and massacres and missiles, and our irreconcilable regiments? Or our treaties whatever they may be worth; our symphonies however seldom they may be played; our peaceful acres, however frequently they may be converted into battlefields; our dreams however rarely they may be accomplished. The miracle of man is not how far he has sunk but how magnificently he has risen.

—(Robert Ardrey, *African Genesis* [Toronto: Atheneum, 1961])

And the LORD God said, Behold, the man is become as one of us, to know good and evil.

—(Genesis 3:22 [King James Bible])

TWENTY-SIX

RAIN pounded through the morning mist onto the forest soil. The customary cacophony of sound was even more feverish than usual, but damped by the omnipresent sound of rainfall on the trees above. Like the sound of a million soft drumbeats, the rain instilled the forest life with a primitive sense of urgency. The downpour came straight from the saturated trees, as though they manufactured water in their leaves and branches.

From inside the silver tent nestled amidst flanking tree trunks, the rain was a warning not to get out of bed. To David Mercer, the warning was especially poignant, although not because he was a habitual late riser. He most certainly was not. On this morning, the rain was a dull ache adding to the throbbing pain behind his eyes.

In a state somewhere between sleep and drowsiness, David's pain consumed his feeble efforts to wake up. He struggled to determine where the pain was coming from. It was most intense in his head, right behind his eyes, he thought to himself. But when he moved his arms to rub his temples, he realized that his head was only the most obvious source of pain. He ached from head to foot. It seemed every muscle in his body was on fire, and suddenly the rain seemed like a welcome salve.

He had not felt this way last night, had he? His confused mind fought to remember. He had actually slept quite soundly, which was unusual for him. He opened his eyes. *Big mistake.* The light was a dagger in each eye, fanning the searing pain behind them until he thought they would explode. Where was he?

David.

He heard a voice. No, he heard a voice *again.* Who was there? He opened his eyes again despite the pain of the light.

"David. Are you still sleeping?" The voice was soft, gentle, without reprimand. It was an elven, female voice. He looked toward the sound.

The blurry, hooded head protruded from the tent door. "David, are you all right? You look awful." The head was soaked, dripping from a green rain hood, but no more soaked than he. His head was damp, his hair drenched, along with the rest of his body. Was it raining in here? He tried to remember.

Jamie's face was more visible after Mercer wiped the sweat out of his eyes, wincing with pain. *What time was it?* They needed to get on their way. He must have overslept. *Why was he so wet?* He crawled to his knees, his body throbbing with pain after each movement. "I'll be right out," his raspy voice managed to say. The head disappeared. He heard two voices outside.

"I thought he just needed more sleep, but he looks pretty bad," said the female voice.

The other voice was harsher. "It's after ten. We should get going. Is he sick?"

"I don't know. He said he's coming out."

Mercer stooped under the tent's low ceiling. The tent began to spin, and he collapsed to the ground. A moment later his vision steadied, and he tried again. He managed to stumble out of the tent into a blaze of painful light. The light was quite dim, actually, but a few rays of sunlight managed to maneuver between the dark clouds and the sparse branches above in the small clearing of trees they were in. He looked over to Jamie and Jeremy, each clad in a dull green raincoat.

"David, you'll get soaked. Where's your coat?" Jamie asked.

He didn't know. All he knew was it hurt. "I'm sorry," he said weakly. "I'm not well." Jamie came over and took his arm. Immediately afterward, she put a hand to his forehead.

"You're burning up," she said calmly. "Let's get you back inside." She ushered him back into the tent, and then climbed inside herself. Jeremy stuck his head inside as well.

"How long have you been feeling ill?" Jamie asked.

"I don't know. Just now I think."

"What are you feeling?"

"Pain. Mostly behind my eyes but everywhere. And I'm tired. I feel drained."

Jeremy and Jamie exchanged glances.

Jeremy began asking questions. "Have you been outside of the complex before yesterday?"

"I went to scout the area four days ago when the chimps escaped. Made sure the homing beacon was working on the ferry." He was starting to think more clearly.

"Did you eat anything, put anything in your mouth since you've been here?"

"No."

"Do you remember any bites, like from mosquitoes or bugs?" Jeremy pressed harder.

"When have I not had bites since I came here?"

Jamie asked, "Have you been taking the mefloquine?" Most of the malaria in Amazonas was resistant to primaquine, but was still sensitive to mefloquine, and they all took it prophylactically.

"Yes."

"Anything like this before?"

"I had a case of dengue, about three years ago, that was similar but not so intense." Mercer remembered the episode like a dream.

Jamie put her head in her hands and rubbed her eyes. She turned to Jeremy. "I don't know. It could be malaria, but then it could be anything. I'm not a doctor, and all I have here are just a few medications. We could give him some doxycycline and Tylenol, but we should probably get him back to the compound where someone can take a look at him." She turned to Mercer. "Can you walk?"

"Yes, I'll be all right. I'm feeling better. Let's go. I want that chimp."

"Not a chance. You need to get back. Someone will have to go with you. I'll call our base camp." Jamie stepped outside the tent and rummaged through her pack until she found a small Ziploc bag. She removed a few pills and reentered the tent.

"Here, take these." She opened Mercer's hand and thrust inside two pills. He slowly swallowed the pills, one at a time.

JAMIE stepped out of the tent again, leaned over to keep out the rain, and punched some buttons on her sat phone and waited. She dialed again. This time she spoke briefly, and put the phone away in a waterproof pouch on her jacket.

She returned to Jeremy's side. "I can't understand it. Diego doesn't answer. They must not be listening to the phone."

She shook her head. "I gave the other group our coordinates. I think we can still continue, but someone has to go back with David and we shouldn't travel alone. Paolo, Roger, and Sameer will come here and then we'll have to split up two and two. We might lose a day's progress, but we can keep the trail fresh. We need Sameer to help with the chimp; either you or Roger should go back with David."

Jeremy looked up into the rain. "I'll go. I probably know the way back better."

Jamie nodded, and moved under a large tree to shield her from the rain. She slumped down and held her face in her hands, settling in for a long wait.

AROUND early evening, the day's boredom changed abruptly when Jamie heard voices again. Rather, she heard a voice. As best as she could make out, it was Stiles's voice suggesting they just leave some flares and some water and move on. She called Jeremy and walked toward the voice to meet the others.

The rain had slowed to a light sprinkle, and wasn't noticeably different from the humid air that hung over the forest when it wasn't raining.

Soon, they all arrived back at the tent. Paolo asked, "You two been busy?"

Jamie raised one eyebrow and gave a tired look back. "I've been looking at maps, but I honestly can't remember when I've been so bored."

"How is David?" asked Sameer.

"About the same. He's slept most of the day, and he's still got a nasty fever. The Tylenol didn't seem to touch it. You made good time."

"We wanted to get here by nightfall, and I think we were pretty slow today. I've been trying to get Diego all day. You haven't had any luck either?"

Jamie shook her head.

"I've got news." Paolo winked at Sameer and Stiles, and pulled out his antenna. "Listen to this." He unfolded the antenna, and fussed with the direction until a faint clicking marched through the static every second.

Jamie's eyes opened wide, and she gave Paolo a wild, excited look. "We have him! They must be doubling back."

Jeremy went inside the tent and woke Mercer. He looked a little better, and they both reemerged.

Stiles was the first to greet Mercer. "Say, Dave. I wasn't exactly expecting a good hair day, but you need some work, pal."

"We have a signal, David," Jamie said happily.

"That is excellent. You go on. I will wait here. I am feeling much better," Mercer offered.

"Not a chance," Paolo decided. "Jeremy will take you back to Diego and Juan Miguel. They should be able to ferry you back to the compound where you can get some real medical attention. How many phones do we have between us?"

Jamie answered, "Three. I still don't know what happened to the third antenna, but all of our phones are here. I have one, David has one, and Stiles has one."

Paolo continued, "Then Jeremy will take David's phone and start back tonight with him. We will track as long as we can tonight, and hopefully have contact by tomorrow."

Jamie set out to sort through Jeremy's pack and exchange items with her own and Mercer's until she was satisfied. Jeremy worked quickly to disassemble the tent, and review the path they had taken on his map.

When Jeremy was ready, he and Mercer started off, leaving Mercer's mostly empty pack behind. They had no sooner left than Sameer raised his antenna and the four remaining companions walked briskly in nearly the opposite direction. The faint signal they heard on the antenna was barely audible, a rhythmic heartbeat of their quarry.

TWENTY-SEVEN

SUSAN wasn't a bit tired. After a good night's sleep, she was ready to tackle the whole Amazon single-handedly, despite the rain that drenched the forest. In fact, it was a dream come true to have a real mission, with real consequences and real danger. After feeling panicked for most of the day yesterday, she had adapted to the chase, and felt that she belonged in the search party now.

They had been walking for nearly three hours this morning. They had made the decision to break for the night instead of tracking, since the chimp was likely to remain in the canopy overnight anyway. When morning came, they found the signal had become more distant, and they had traveled nearly two miles back toward the river before the signal started getting stronger again.

Ayala led the group with dogged persistence. She walked through the forest easily and silently, with Carlos and Susan following a few steps behind. Periodically, she would reorient herself with a compass or with a reading from the antenna, but mostly seemed to know exactly where she was going.

Carlos had turned out to be a particularly good companion. For everything from starting a fire to constructing a shelter, he seemed to have a natural instinct. The trees had been too dense last night to allow setting up a tent, and he had artfully lashed the tent canvas to adjacent trees to form a makeshift roof, and dug a gully that had kept them dry all night despite the thunderstorm.

He was thoughtful, too, and would steady fallen logs or branching roots for Susan as she walked. She enjoyed the attention, and as much as she appreciated her husband, fifteen years of marriage and two stressful jobs had resulted in a fair amount of attrition on the thoughtful gestures so frequent earlier in their marriage.

The rainstorm made visibility difficult, and Susan was grateful for the raincoats they had brought with wide hoods for better shielding. The coats were breathable, and made the rain a refreshing change to the heat they had experienced yesterday.

After rechecking a compass bearing, Ayala turned to Susan and said, "You've never told me why this chimp is so valuable. Why are you so anxious to find it? I thought you were a reporter." She raised her voice to be heard over the rain.

Susan answered, "I am. This chimp is the key evidence I need for a big story. We've discovered a company that's grown human fetuses for research in order to make intelligent chimpanzees. Without the chimp, we don't have enough proof to sell the story. It's all about visuals! If people see that chimp doing algebra, I could write anything I want and still win a Pulitzer for it. Without the chimp, the story just sounds like tabloid material."

"Why not just shoot a few pictures instead of going to all the trouble of capturing it?"

"It's not the same. I want a live demonstration, with witnesses. It has to be so convincing that no one will doubt that it's not some kind of parlor trick."

"Why are you so sure the chimp is as smart as you say?"

"I have records. They just weren't obtained legally!" Susan shouted with a grin at Carlos.

"I hope you don't mind cleaning his cage, because it's not in my contract! Once he's back in Manaus, he's your baby!"

"If he's all I think he is, he can clean his own cage!"

The conversation halted as the ground sloped sharply upward, and the route above was blocked by what looked like a large mudslide. Ayala surveyed the climb and began walking parallel to the slope. The slope was all but impassable for several hundred meters. She stopped and opened her pack.

"I think we can cross here, but we'll need to use the trees." She withdrew a coil of rope and her crossbow. With her hands dripping from the rain, she notched a cross and took aim at the top of the steep slope ahead. A twang sounded and the rope shot out from its coil until the cross burrowed into a tree trunk at the top of the ravine thirty meters up. Ayala tugged at the rope and started pulling herself up through the waist-high mud. "Follow once I secure the rope up top," she ordered Carlos and Susan.

Her progress was slow, and once she lost hold of the slippery rope and fell back, tumbling over until she was covered with mud. She braced herself against a tree trunk angling out of the slope and managed to slide horizontally until she could grab the rope again, now buried in the mud. She continued pulling herself up until she reached the tree near the top into which she had shot the rope. She grabbed the rope, pulled a few lengths of it around the tree, then cut one end and tied a bowline to secure the line. She waved to the others to follow.

Susan and Carlos in turn managed to scale up the slope hand over hand until all three rested behind the tree at the top. They were all caked in mud, especially Ayala, but able to scramble up to the top of the ridge where they continued walking. Through the rain they could see a patch of light ahead. Ayala pointed to the light and walked toward it.

As they got closer they saw a very large clearing, perhaps fifty feet across, into which sunlight streamed down, and the rain became even more intense. Carlos stood on the edge of the clearing, looking across the patch of short ferns and grasses. In the center he pointed to a pile of logs. "That looks artificial," he shouted. "Someone has been here."

The three walked toward the logs, when Susan screamed. Carlos and Ayala rushed to her side. She had turned her head and looked sick, and it took some time before she could turn her head back and point to the ground. There, in a patch of cleared soil, was a huge rat filleted open. The four limbs of the rat were staked into the ground with sharpened sticks, belly up. In a straight line down the rat's abdomen, the skin had been cut open and folded back, with the chest wall staked down on either side exposing the rat's organs like a frog in a biology class.

The rain had matted the bloody carcass of the rat, but the body was still relatively fresh and had not decomposed. Susan regained her breath and she and Carlos resumed walking toward the logs in the center of the clearing. Ayala began walking around the perimeter of the clearing, stopping periodically to look at the ground.

Carlos reached the logs first to find that they were arrayed even more intricately than he had thought. They were arranged in a pentagram, stacked four high on each of the five edges. Across the top of the base were laid flat logs with the bark completely scraped smooth. The entire structure was about three meters in diameter and about a meter high.

Susan walked around the strange altar, pausing when she reached the far side. On top of the stand, something caught her eye. She waved Carlos over.

Someone had not only scratched off the bark on all of the logs lying across the pentagram, but there were diagrams etched into the wood of one of the logs. The diagrams showed three images. In the first drawing, several humanoid figures were clustered close together, standing on what looked like a boat.

As Susan studied the diagram more closely, she realized that the figures weren't humanoid after all, but apelike, each hunched over with large front arms. The drawing was primitive, but not of bad construction.

Next to that image was another drawing of similar apelike creatures, but this time shown walking. There were perhaps six or seven figures in all, some more visible than others. The figure leading them was small, and walked upright.

In the third picture, a single apelike creature was

hunched over a small animal. The ape was holding a short, pointed stick. Under the pictures was an inscription:

I AM

Carlos was the first to comment. "I AM? What does that mean?"

Susan shrugged. "Looks like someone was trying to write something, and then quit. At least it proves it was written by people. Maybe someone saw the chimps and drew a picture. They might be able to help us find them."

Carlos studied the structure. "There's no moss on the logs. This probably has been etched within the last week or so."

At that point Ayala joined them at the structure. Carlos showed her the etchings and she examined them carefully for several minutes.

Ayala turned to Susan and asked, "Is there a note in any of your illegal records that your chimp is a homicidal maniac?"

"What?" asked Susan.

"The animal you stumbled across isn't the only one. There are three others, each set at opposite ends of the clearing: due east, west, north, and south of this platform. You saw how the one had been filleted open. Maybe what you didn't notice is that the animals had also been tortured."

"Tortured? What do you mean?" asked Carlos nervously.

"It's easier to see on some of the other animals, but there are burn marks on the skin, and signs of mutilation on the paws and eyes. There are some burnt sticks and signs of a fire near one of the animals. I know signs of torture when I see it; please don't ask me how." Ayala shuddered visibly.

She continued, "I'd say the animals have been staked

down within the last couple days—they've barely started to decompose. These drawings are pretty good evidence to me that whoever wrote this was talking about your chimps."

Carlos looked again at the drawings. "Maybe the animals were some kind of a sacrifice, a way to ward off the chimps or bad luck or something. Probably the work of a local tribe."

Susan had now withdrawn her camera from her backpack, and she photographed the altar from each side. Each picture was more chilling, and she felt like a homicide investigator at the scene of a particularly bloody crime.

Ayala stretched and raised one eyebrow to Susan. She said comfortingly, "Don't worry. I've dealt with worse."

"I'm not sure," Carlos said. "We know almost nothing about this chimp. I suspect he's much more dangerous than we've given him credit for. This altar confirms that somebody didn't like what they saw in the chimps. I suggest we all keep that in mind."

They left the altar and continued walking into the forest in the direction of the signal.

TWENTY-EIGHT

MERCER and Jeremy had made excellent progress after Mercer had rested most of the day. Freed from the weight of his pack, Mercer had been able to keep a reasonable pace, and by nightfall the two had covered several miles of the return trip. It had helped that the rain had all but stopped by early evening. Jeremy had tried to reach Diego a couple times without success, but decided there was little they could do anyway until he and Mercer had returned to base camp. Hopefully by tomorrow afternoon they could be on their way back to the compound.

This was none too soon for Jeremy. Although he was not lacking a sense of adventure, he found he was enjoying the expedition less and less: he was covered with mosquito bites; he was starved for a real meal; and he was too out of shape to enjoy the incessant hiking.

He had decided not to push Mercer too hard, lest he not be prepared to make the journey back by tomorrow, and stopped to set up camp late in the evening. After a brief meal, he set up the small springbar tent and they both crashed, Mercer admittedly more quickly than he.

Mercer slept restlessly. Although Jeremy was generally a heavy sleeper, Mercer's throes of delirium kept Jeremy up most of the night listening to his companion wake with a start, moan, or thrash in his sleep every short while. When the night's darkness turned to the dim light of morning, Jeremy was hammered. Eventually his bladder forced his hand, and he got out of bed.

A few minutes later he returned to the tent to check on Mercer. From outside of the tent, he heard Mercer's coarse, raspy breathing. He grabbed his pocket flashlight and reentered the tent. His flashlight lit up the dark interior, and his eyes adjusted to the light.

On Mercer's ashen face was smeared blood covering the right side of his cheek. A stream of dried blood tracked from his nostril to a pool of sticky red paste on his mat to the side of his head. His lips were slightly blue, and his hair was a tangle of sweat and blood.

Jeremy shook his companion. Mercer would not rouse. Then Jeremy grabbed his hand and felt for a pulse. He was finally rewarded with a rapid, faint pulse. Jeremy shook him again, this time shouting at him "Wake up, David! Wake up!"

With no response, he clamped his fingers on the nailbed of one of Mercer's fingernails. Mercer's arm weakly withdrew, but no other response could be elicited. Jeremy grabbed his flashlight, pried open Mercer's eyelid and shined the light in his eye. Mercer's pupil sluggishly constricted. Then Jeremy saw the arm.

Up and down his arm was a rash consisting of small,

scattered, red-purple splotches. There were perhaps two dozen on his arm in all, each a few millimeters in diameter. Jeremy swore and started thinking more quickly than his tired brain was prepared for. He darted outside and picked up his sat phone, dialing twice because his fingers were too clumsy.

No answer. He swore again.

He considered his options. There was no way he could carry Mercer by himself the many miles back to Diego and Juan Miguel. He needed help. He quickly foraged through his pack and removed a canteen and some dried beef. He checked the GPS coordinates on the sat phone, repeating the coordinates in his mind over and over to commit them to memory.

Then he placed the phone on the ground by Mercer's sleeping body. Setting his pack inside the tent, he zipped the tent flap shut. After checking his compass, he started off at a jog toward the base camp.

SAMEER was the first to awaken. Sweat trickled down his forehead, as the nightmare's effect slowly dissipated.

He had been running, slowly, tripping over roots and branches. Pursuing him relentlessly had been a pack of chimpanzees. Some were above in the canopy, throwing rocks. Others chased him on the ground with knives. In the lead was the small, vicious, alpha male—the one with the blue collar. In his dream the other chimpanzees were chanting and grunting to a cadence led by their leader as the cult closed in on its last victim.

Wiping the sweat from his eyes, Sameer crawled out of the tent wherein the other three slept in close quarters.

He stretched in the early morning light, filtered through the sky of green. On the ground was something completely unexpected. Their packs, which the scientists had set outside the tent because of cramped quarters, had been ransacked.

The contents of three of the four packs had been littered across the soil outside the tent. Only one pack remained undisturbed against the tree. Sameer began collecting the items together in piles. As he checked the items against a mental inventory, he began to see a pattern in the rummage. Most of the items were intact, except for a scarcity of food that they carried with them. One of the canteens was missing as well. Fortunately, all of the other essential items were picked over and left.

As he began repacking the equipment, Jamie stretched as she exited from the tent. Her expression was shocked. "What happened?" she asked wearily.

"When I came out, these three packs had been ransacked. Whoever did it took only food, as far as I can tell, and one pistol," Sameer added.

"Do you think?"

Sameer nodded. "It could very well have been chimps. Perhaps some of the nontagged ones, even. Looks like their handiwork. The pistol would certainly be an interesting novelty."

A flash of an idea crossed Sameer's face. He reached down to the ground and picked up an antenna. Opening it, he pointed it in the direction of last night's signal and slowly moved it back and forth. Static sounded from the speaker. He made a careful sweep, to no avail.

Sameer frowned. "Well, they've been on the move all right, but it doesn't look like our little friend was the one who helped himself to our food. We better get moving before the trail is cold."

Jamie nodded. They woke the others, and after dividing the food from Stiles's untouched pack among the others, they all moved quickly to strike camp. After a hurried breakfast, Paolo laid out the plan.

"Jamie and Sameer are the most experienced trackers, and we have two antennas. We should split up and flank the signal direction from last night. If we make good time, one of us should pick up the signal before long. Jamie and I will head in this direction. Sameer and Roger, you go that way." He pointed in two directions forming a V-shape from their present location. "Don't worry too much about exact direction, approximate directions will be fine if we hurry. We'll make phone contact as soon as we have a signal."

Sameer sensed that Paolo's real intent was to ditch Sameer and Stiles for a while, who admittedly were slower than Jamie and Paolo. Jamie didn't seem at all displeased with the change, either. Honestly, neither was Sameer. Losing their long-legged guide might be a welcome change of pace. Stiles would be more accommodating in that regard.

TWENTY-NINE

BY mid-afternoon, Stiles barely noticed the lush greenery they were marching through. He certainly didn't notice the change in humidity or the slight darkening of the skies that a native would have picked up without even realizing it. His indifference to what was going on around him was not because of a lack of vigilance. Ironically, it was because he was concentrating too hard on what was not right around him.

"I can't shake it, Sameer. Something's not right," he finally voiced.

"What do you mean?"

"That's the trouble. I'm not sure. It's just an instinct," Stiles said as he swatted a mosquito on his arm.

"Did I just hear the great Roger Stiles say he is concerned about something his gut is telling him, about which he has no other clue? I thought you were the one person in the world immune to superstition."

Sameer's answer did not help Stiles's irritation. "Not superstition. It's subconscious angst. And it is something worth listening to. You remember seeing the first experiment we ran?"

"Of course."

"With an experiment like that, what do you think can go wrong?"

"I suppose a great deal. I don't know really."

"You'll have to take my word for it that there are at least a thousand different snags that can completely ruin the experiment. The chimp could have a reaction to the anesthesia; I could perforate an artery when placing a line; any of seven different software packages could become unstable or not record data; we could get line noise that drowns our data; the magnet can malfunction; there could be a power outage at the wrong moment; our temperature probe could stop working. I could go on forever. There are hundreds of pieces of equipment needed for such an experiment, and any one of them can malfunction in multiple different ways."

"OK, I believe you," Sameer said.

"The point is," Stiles said didactically, "that suppose each problem you face in such an experiment has only a one in one thousand chance of going wrong. Well, to get through an experiment, you would expect at least one or two of these very unlikely problems to be encountered almost every time. It's trained me to be vigilant, because one slipup and a very costly experiment is ruined. So in every experiment I panic from the moment I start until the moment I finish, and the only thing that keeps me sane is a bloody sense of humor."

"Thank goodness for that," said Sameer.

"There is no way to anticipate every problem, but I've found that more often than not you get a warning of some sort, if you don't blow it off. Maybe a noise is just a bit different than it was last week, or there is a smell you don't recognize. I get a warning like that, and I've learned not to ignore it. Most often, I can't even tell you what the warning is. I just feel something is wrong, maybe only subconsciously, and the hair on the back of my neck stands up until something blows up in my face or I find it first. That's what I'm feeling."

"And is there something in particular that is warning you now?"

"Nothing," Stiles admitted. "It may be that I'm a paranoid shell of a man who's out of his element."

"Now that you mention it, I have been worried about Mercer all morning, and have been thinking about calling Jeremy. Maybe you have a similar thought?" asked Sameer.

"No," said Stiles, and made a gesture to Sameer to stop walking and be still.

"You mean you don't think it's a good idea to call, or . . ."

Stiles cut him off. In a whisper, he continued, "No. I just figured out what's bothering me." He pointed ahead through the trees. "Them."

Both Stiles and Sameer listened intently in the direction he pointed. They were quickly rewarded with the sound of footsteps and voices. They were too far away to see clearly, and the voices could not be distinguished, but they could see three distinct individuals intersecting their path at a thirty-degree angle about hundred meters ahead.

"Jamie?" mouthed Sameer.

Stiles shook his head. He held up three fingers to indicate that there were three of them. He then pulled out of his pack a compact pair of field glasses they had brought to look up into the canopy. He studied the visitors until they had passed out of sight.

Stiles motioned noiselessly to Sameer to pull out his antenna.

Sameer dutifully extracted the device, opened it and began sweeping the horizon in front of them. Midway through his arc, he heard the telltale clicking of their target's signal. The direction of the signal was almost precisely the direction into which the intruders had gone.

"We should tell Jamie and Paolo," Sameer said, still in a soft voice.

"Tell them what, Watson?" Stiles asked.

"We have the signal, of course."

"Maybe that's not all. Doesn't it strike you as odd that someone besides us would be in this precise part of the jungle on an expedition?" Stiles spoke cautiously, reasoning through the situation as he spoke.

"The jungle is full of people. Some live here; some are tourists; some are adventurers; some are filmmakers. There is no shortage of possibilities. We are fairly close to a major city. This forest has probably been crisscrossed thoroughly by visitors."

Stiles was already shaking his head. "That's what I mean by not ignoring a warning. It seems odd to me that they would be here at precisely the same time and going in the same direction as our signal."

Sameer shrugged as though waiting for something more substantive.

"I had a good look at them in the field glasses. There

are three: two women and a man, all in good physical shape by the look of things. They carried packs. At least one was carrying a gun." Sameer looked unimpressed. "And the one in the lead was carrying a Yagi."

"An antenna? What would they be doing with an antenna?"

"Obviously the same thing as you. There's another group tracking the chimp, Sameer. And it's pretty clear to me who it is."

Stiles hesitated, as though Sameer should read his mind. The expectant look on Sameer's face told Stiles to continue. "Probably some sort of guides, poachers, zoologists. I don't know, but I think I know who put them up to it: Mercer. He set us up."

"What?!" asked Sameer.

"Isn't it strange that he happened to get sick in time to get out of the area before we met up with these guys? It's a good bet that they know exactly where we are. Which is more likely, that the chimps went through our packs last night, who as best we can tell are a good five miles away, or these neighbors who happen to be a stone's throw away? Where else would they get that antenna? You didn't give it to them. And that might be our gun I saw with them. Who else but Mercer? He's hired another group to get his chimp, and maybe knock us off as well where nobody could possibly suspect foul play. Think about it. Hell, it's dangerous enough out here: anything could happen. We know too much, and he's up to something. I've never trusted the guy." Stiles gritted his teeth.

"I don't know, Roger, David looked pretty sick."

"How hard is that to fake? He looked well enough when we saw him. It's the only explanation. There's someone out there with one of our Yagis closing in on our chimp. No wonder Jamie was so confused when the antenna turned up missing. It may be the only reason we're still alive is that they're waiting to see who comes up with the chimp first and make sure he's safe. Then all bets are off what's going to happen," Stiles concluded.

"So did he kill Nakamura too?"

"You ever see the body?"

"Well, no, but . . ."

"How do you know old Ken isn't alive and well, using this as a ruse to rub us off? He's held back what he's really up to every step of the way with me. Like he didn't want me to know any more than necessary to do my job. And it's been real clear to me that he's got something going on he's not going to tell me."

"I'm starting to think you might be right. Nakamura's never been totally open with me either, and I've been working for him for over five years. We should run it by Jamie and Paolo."

Stiles was already fumbling through his pack for the phone. "Sure enough, but not until I warn Jeremy. He's the one in danger right now, alone with Mercer."

Stiles rifled through his pack again. "It's gone. Someone took our phone."

"Are you sure?" Sameer was worried.

Stiles looked through his pack again. "Positive. It was right in here yesterday."

"But your pack was the one that wasn't touched last night."

"At least that's what someone wanted us to think. I don't know. I'm not thinking straight." Stiles closed his eyes.

"So what now?" Sameer asked.

"Jeremy's a smart kid. Don't count him out. We'll never find him without a phone. We need to find Jamie and Paolo."

"And how do we do that?"

"We find that chimp, and we find it first. Everything depends on it." Stiles's jaw was set, his anger turned to resolve.

"We'll be hard-pressed to find him before Jamie and Paolo, if I know them," Sameer said.

"Let's hope for their sake that we do." Stiles looked heavenward. "And I just figured out something else that's been bugging me." He blinked as a drop of water fell into his eye. He pointed to the sky and frowned.

Sameer needed no help with this one, and fished out his raincoat as the cloudburst signaled its presence with a loud thunderclap.

IT was evening when Jamie smiled at Paolo as her antenna sounded through the heavy rain with the rhythmic pulse of the chimp's radio collar. "We're back in business," she called.

"Which direction?" asked Paolo.

"There." She pointed wide to their left.

Paolo stopped and frowned. "Something's wrong, Jamie. I know it."

"I thought you'd be excited."

"If the chimp's over there, then Roger and Sameer should have picked it up hours ago. That makes no sense unless they're not checking their readings, which also makes no sense. Why haven't they called?"

"Well, let's let them know." Jamie picked up her phone and began dialing. Nobody answered.

She tried again. "They're not answering."

Paolo looked deep in thought at the possibilities. "Call Jeremy. See if they've heard from Roger and Sameer."

Jamie dialed again. No answer.

"He's not answering either. This is bizarre. It must be that our phone is malfunctioning. Maybe it's a solar flare or something. The batteries look OK."

"I hope you're right," said Paolo. "Let's assume it's our phone, and Stiles is already tracking the chimp." He didn't seem any less worried. "Let's go."

They continued walking in silence, when Paolo asked, "Jamie, why do you think this chimp has a soul?"

"I don't. But I think that nothing that defines us as spiritual beings is different from what he experiences. Why should we have souls if he doesn't?"

"What about charity, hope, self-sacrifice?"

Jamie thought for a moment. "That's why I need him back. I believe he's capable of feeling emotions as poignantly as we do. I just need to find a way to prove it."

"A dog feels poignant emotion."

"Then what makes us so special?"

"It's not how much emotion you feel. It's what type of emotion. Some are higher than others. Having a soul isn't about feeling pain or desire, it's what makes us bigger than any of that."

"So I'll show he can feel love."

"Why don't you show he can feel God?"

"Maybe he's smarter than that. I used to think I knew—absolutely knew that God was real. That he loved me. My whole life, Paolo, it's always been about God.

Finding him, running away from him, fighting him." Her eyes teared as she spoke the words.

"Stop fighting."

"I can't. Not until I find something I know is true—absolutely, scientifically true. When God can show me that, I'll believe."

"What if the chimp does have a soul, Jamie?"

"Are you saying old Kenji is God?"

"Or inspired by God."

"What do you mean by that?"

"Years ago, before college, I lived in the jungle, but for a different reason. I was running too."

"Running from what?"

"Life. I couldn't stand the cruelty on the streets, the savagery in just finding food and shelter. So I left. I made a home for myself in the forest. I didn't need anyone. Do you know how lonely it can be when you don't talk to anyone, anyone at all, for months, for years?"

He took her hand and led her to a tree stump, where he sat down. She sat beside him, but didn't let go of his hand. The touch overwhelmed all other sensations. She closed her eyes and felt the strength and warmth of his hand covering hers.

"I can't imagine."

"You can't escape it. Even when you're totally alone, maybe especially then, that there's someone there with you. I thought I was going crazy. I got so bored, I started reading a copy of the New Testament. Not even sure why I packed it along, sort of a family heirloom I didn't want to leave. Something of a good luck charm, I guess."

"What happened?"

"It changed me. I can't explain it. One day I was reading

and just felt such a powerful feeling come over me that I started to cry and couldn't stop. That was the day I learned how to pray. I prayed most of the day, felt like I was forced to kneel, and I talked to God."

"He spoke to you?"

"He spoke in me. He spoke in the wind, in the grass, in the trees. He was everywhere. I knew it, like I'd known nothing else before. And I felt such a feeling of gratitude I couldn't stop praising Him, thanking Him, just for being with me, for watching over me."

"That sounds very powerful."

"When you feel that, you can't say we don't have a soul. You just know it."

"But if you can create a soul like that in the laboratory? Not even knowing what you're doing?"

"What begins in biology can end in transcendence. Don't underestimate God's creation."

Jamie's phone rang. She paused as Paolo's words sunk in. The phone rang again, drawing her back to the world, and she pulled it out. "See, someone probably just couldn't get to their phone for a minute." She looked at the digital display on the phone. "Hold on; it's Diego! About time they showed up." She answered the phone. "Diego?"

On the other end of the receiver was the feeble voice of Jeremy Evans. "No, it's Jeremy."

"Jeremy, thank goodness. You made it back. How's David doing?"

"Listen, I've got a real problem here, Jamie."

THIRTY

THEIR prey had been moving quickly. After their experience with the altar in the clearing, Susan, Ayala, and Carlos had followed the chimp on the ground the rest of the day. By nightfall, they were still some distance from the chimp, and had broken pursuit to make camp. Ayala considered it too dangerous to continue traveling at night, especially if the chase might last several more days. They would need their strength.

The following morning, they had set off early in pursuit of the chimp. The dryer weather was a boon and they were making good progress. As the day wore on, however, they were disappointed to find that they seemed to be losing ground rather than gaining. By midday, the signal was considerably weaker than in the morning. Carlos seemed to be losing patience. "We have to move faster," he said.

Ayala reprimanded him gently. "A little distance isn't unhealthy. We've already found we can't match the chimps' speed. Fortunately, the chimp isn't going to go forever in a straight line. We'll catch up. It is patience that wins the hunt."

Susan was proud of herself for maintaining her pace. She really wasn't in as bad shape as she feared. The hiking in many respects had been therapeutic. The scenery was beautiful, the air intoxicating, and the exercise regenerating. There was a smell in the rain forest, a dank, animate smell that had first been repulsing, but now was a welcome invitation into the sanctum of the forest.

Her thoughts had been wandering. Inattentive to the occasional exchange between Carlos and Ayala, she reflected on her husband. Likely, he barely remembered she had left. She traveled not infrequently, often for several days or a week at a stretch. Although he cared for her a great deal, the traveling gave him opportunity to bury himself in the management of his company. His one vice was an insufferable competition that would not let him sleep, rest, or love if a looming obstacle threatened the success of his business.

This trip had been on short notice, and when she told him she would be going to Manaus for a week or two for some investigation, he seemed to be relieved. "Truth is," he had said, "it's probably a good time for it. Until our acquisition clears the FTC next week, I'm going to be hovering over the office. I'd probably be a bear to live with, too."

She had not mentioned that she would be racing through the rain forest after a new species of homicidal chimpanzee. Of course, neither had she anticipated it. The development was certainly best left uncommunicated, she decided. Her husband was liable to make some testosterone-fueled effort to come save her, which would spoil everything, and which she would never live down.

She fantasized about what this story would do for her if they succeeded. She had craved wealth as a young woman growing up in Indianapolis in a family of modest means. When her marriage to a young business student unexpectedly provided her with exactly that, she found that she never really wanted wealth at all. She wanted power. Her career was a start, but she was too timid, too security-seeking to ever achieve her goals. Now her window had come, and she was going to change that. It was time to risk everything, until her husband was the one who was the chaperone at charity balls.

She planned again the details of her story. It would be a piece for network television, or maybe a documentary, a stand-alone piece. She would tell the story of human ambition run amok. After public opinion had circled for years above the moral complexities of human cloning, she would draw the line in the sand. She would tell the story that would galvanize the public into making a stand between what would be permitted and what would not. She would . . .

At that moment she slipped on an unstable patch of ground.

No, not unstable, *moving.*

She lost her footing and tumbled backward, landing on her left thigh. Well before her brain had processed what was happening, her attention was riveted to movement. A swirling, dancing serpentine movement consumed her view and she instinctively threw her arms out in front of her.

As the gray, winding form took shape in front of her she felt something cold brush against her hand. Reflexively, she grabbed onto the branch with a vise grip, hoping to break her fall. As she clamped down, the branch in her hand began to pull against her grasp, and her eyes recognized the form only inches from her face.

As her body lurched against the ground she had fallen on, she saw the writhing object in her hand was connected to the open jaws of a spear-headed snake, its tongue flailing toward her neck. At the same instant she realized what was happening, her scream pierced the forest din like the screech of a howler monkey.

The snake was easily six feet long, four inches in diameter, and strong. The tail writhed back and forth in her grip, swinging her body in similar motion as she sought control. Her other hand snapped into place on the snake's neck, and she wrestled with the powerful, winding viper. The snake was gray from head to tail, with a black, diamond-laced pattern that covered its scaly hide.

Its eyes were looking right at her.

Susan could only watch the menacing head of the viper, as the seconds ticked away. *Black eyes!*

Time passed in slow motion as it stared at her. The eyes were monolithic voids without a trace of emotion or fear. She held the snake until her hands throbbed under the pressure. Then she heard a voice. "Susan!"

She looked up and saw Ayala kneeling by her side, machete in hand. Then she saw the snake. About a foot below her grip, the snake had been cleanly severed in two, dripping digestive juices from Susan's half. She felt her grip loosen, the writhing terminated. Emotion flooded back into her mind as she hurled the snake's head twenty feet against a tree and began panting.

"Get it off me!" Susan thrashed hysterically, screaming in terror.

Carlos kicked the lower end of the snake with his boot, sending the creature several feet away where it stopped twisting and lay motionless.

Ayala stooped up and offered Susan a hand. "Good catch, girl." Susan eventually saw her hand and took it.

"What happened?" Susan asked, dazed.

"You stepped on the poor thing. What was it supposed to do?" Ayala seemed indifferent.

"What was it?" Susan asked.

"Pit viper. They call it fer-de-lance. Irritating little beasts. They tend to always be underfoot during the day all coiled up. Pretty good camouflage. And not that big for around here, actually. Anacondas can be seven times as long."

"Poisonous?"

"Quite. Not always fatal, but often is without treatment. It's a good idea to keep an eye under your feet in the jungle," Ayala said. "Your little friend almost ended our quest."

Susan did exactly as instructed as she slowly regained her wits. For the next hour she watched the ground meticulously, finding that she was much more comfortable before she knew what types of creatures lived on the forest floor.

As Susan began to focus less on the ground ahead, her attention was jerked back to the ground when Ayala held up a hand for Susan and Carlos to stop.

Susan saw nothing.

Ayala's attention was apparently focused on a distant sound, and she was listening carefully. She had been checking their course with the antenna, and had put the antenna down. After a short pause, she continued walking, more briskly.

"What's the matter?" asked Susan.

"We have company. Must be your scientist friends."

"Why do you keep referring to everyone as my friends?"

Ayala shrugged.

"Where are they?"

"Behind us, over there." She pointed. "Maybe a couple hundred meters."

"Do you think they know we're here?" Carlos asked softly.

"Can't tell. Let's get a move on it. I'm sure we can get a good lead on them."

The travelers picked up their pace and hurried off in the direction of the chimp under a darkening sky.

THIRTY-ONE

JEREMY panted as he ran, his eyes stinging with sweat. A few paces later his legs rebelled and he slowed once again to a brisk walk. His mind was dazed, bewitched by the miles of interminable forest, rendered incapable of clear thought. He had run faster and farther than he ever wanted to again. *What was happening to him?* Jumping from thought to thought, his mind was desperate to avoid the one thought that loomed always in the periphery: the pain in his right heel. He had stopped to reposition his boots against the raw flesh on his heel three times during the day, and was now heavily favoring his left foot as he walked.

To keep himself from thinking of the pain, he tried once again to sort through what had happened to Mercer. The image of Mercer's bloody face was chilling, but it was the raspy breathing that kept sounding in Jeremy's ears like a psychotic voice. The sound of the breathing and the memory of the motionless, unresponsive body he had discovered that morning pushed him harder to reach help. What was going on? Was Mercer dying? *Was his disease contagious?* Did Jeremy already have it, festering and swelling inside of him?

Either way, he had to find Diego. He needed someone to help him get Mercer back, and . . . *what were the coordinates again?* He cursed, unable to remember the position at which he had left Mercer. He stopped and rubbed the rain out of his eyes. Finally, he took a few deep breaths, and tried to remember the digital readout. The numbers came back to him, and he started jogging again, repeating the numbers in his head.

He had to be close; the forest was becoming dense and difficult to navigate. He slowed to a walk again. *Where was Diego?* He slogged through the jungle, crawling under branches and climbing over interwoven tree roots until he heard something different. It was water.

Of course it was water! He was drenched from head to foot, not having his pack or his raincoat. No, this sounded like waves—the sound of surf beneath the patter of the rain. He walked faster. A few minutes later he could see through the trees and rain out into the coursing waters of the Amazon.

He emerged from the trees onto the riverbank. The boat was nowhere in sight. Jeremy panicked. It had to be here. He pulled out his GPS link to find it soaked through and nonfunctional. He began to hyperventilate. He fell to his knees and shielded himself from the pelting rain, the protective canopy no longer shielding him from the full force of the storm.

He had to find them. Rising again to his feet and wincing with the pain in his heel, he started walking

along the riverbank. A half hour later, he was about to
turn around and try the other direction when he saw the
boat. Tossing back and forth in the river, the moored
boat sent courage surging through his feet, and he ran
until he reached the ship. He started inland again, barely
recognizing their departure point several days earlier in
the rainstorm.

How far did Jamie say Diego had set up camp? Three
hundred meters? He tracked inland, shouting for Diego
and Juan Miguel. No answer. He hacked through the undergrowth with his arms, ignoring the stinging of the
branches and vines against his hands. Ahead he saw light
streaming through the trees, and caught a glint of metal.

He had found them! He shouted again. No response.

Jeremy ran through the ferns, vines, and trees toward
the camp. When he reached it, he shouted again.

"Diego, Juan Miguel! It's Jeremy! Where are you?!"

He started walking toward the tent. They must be in
there. He stopped.

Why is the tent frame so bent?

The tent was half folded over on itself with one side
limply draped over a crooked frame. He walked faster.
On the ground he could see broken crates with their contents scattered on the ground and covered with dirt. What
had happened here?

He reached the tent and walked around to the opening.
The flap was unzipped, quivering in the rain. He looked
inside. Half buried in a blanket was Diego's dead body,
lying in a pool of purple blood. His throat had been cut
open and a dinner knife protruded from his chest. His
eyes were wide open, a terrified look immortalized on his
face.

Jeremy felt sick.

He thrust his head out of the tent and looked through the campsite. As he wandered through the wreckage, he almost tripped over Juan Miguel's body. It was lying face down in the mud. The back of Juan Miguel's head was oddly shaped, with a noticeable dent on the left side of his skull. A few feet from the body lay a shovel, half covered by the mud. Jeremy had only to turn Juan Miguel over with his boot to verify he was dead. Bruises on his neck and arms showed that his head was not the only place that had been hit.

The rain washed out the tears in Jeremy's eyes faster than they could form. He sat down and buried his head in his knees and cried. What was he doing here? What were any of them doing in this death trap? After a long pause, he slowly got to his feet and began looking through the debris. Where was the phone? He eventually found it sitting next to an overturned crate a few meters from the tent.

He took a deep breath and started punching buttons, raising the phone to his rain-soaked head. An answer came. "Diego?" Jamie asked urgently.

"No, it's Jeremy." He responded flatly.

"Jeremy, thank goodness. You made it back. How's David doing?"

"Listen, I've got a real problem here, Jamie. Diego's dead. Juan Miguel is dead. Mercer's not far behind. I don't know what to do." Emotion flooded back into Jeremy's voice as he spoke.

Jamie sounded horrified. "Jeremy, what are you talking about?"

"They're dead, Jamie! Dead!"

Jeremy recounted what he had found at the campsite, the condition of the bodies, and the state of their supplies.

"Where is David?"

"I had to leave him back in the tent this morning. When I woke up, he was breathing heavily. He was bleeding from his nose and who knows where else. His skin is covered with a rash. His fever is worse, and he won't respond to me at all. I ran back for help."

A long pause at the other end. "Jeremy, we're two days away at least. There's nothing we can do. You have to call someone back at the compound and get help. Do you remember where David is?"

Jeremy recited the coordinates in his mind. "I have the coordinates."

"Call and tell them to get there now. They should be able to send someone that could reach him by morning, if he's still alive. How are you?"

"I don't know, Jamie. Not good." His voice trailed off.

"You have to get away from the campsite. It's too dangerous. I don't know who killed Diego and Juan Miguel."

"Do you think the chimp did it?" At the thought, Jeremy felt his shoulder sting where the chimp had assaulted him.

"I don't see how. All of our tracking data suggest he hasn't been within miles of the base camp. There's no shortage of pirates, thieves, and criminals in the forest. Whoever did it may well come back. Is the boat still there?"

"So far."

"Do you have any food?"

"I don't know. I'll have to look around and see what's left."

"Please be careful, Jeremy. There's something else you should know. Sameer and Roger aren't answering their phone. I don't know why."

Jeremy's bitter voice spoke into the receiver. "Like you said, there's no shortage of possibilities."

He switched off the phone and put it in his pocket. Who should he call? Did he know a single phone number in Brazil?

The boat. There had to be some document on the boat with a phone number. He tightened his jacket around him and combed through the wreckage for the keys. He found them inside the broken tent after a short search and started back toward the river.

He stopped suddenly. Something was moving in the trees. He listened to the rustle. It was off to one side, coming closer. He ran, branches whipping his face and arms as he stumbled through the jungle. The sound was louder.

Then he heard another one, close behind and above him. Something was following him. Pain surged upward from his foot as he increased his pace, blinded by the undergrowth.

A call sounded from above him. The sound was militant, shrill. Jeremy understood perfectly what it meant. The sound was repeated from the side, then above again.

There it is!

He saw the metallic form of the boat, fifty yards ahead. *Faster!* He had to go faster.

A thud sounded behind him, and he whipped his head back as he ran. A black chimpanzee was now immediately behind him, brandishing a large, sharpened stick.

Jeremy fought to press forward through the dense ferns as he heard the sound of another figure to his right, invisible but drawing closer.

He ducked his head under a final low-lying branch and sprinted across the beach toward the boat. The chimp behind him dove at his feet, lunging toward him with the stick, and Jeremy sailed forward in a faceplant on the sand. He spat out the sand and crawled to his feet, watching from the corner of his eye the second chimpanzee now scooting toward him on all fours from across the beach. The chimp behind him had also regained its footing, and jumped toward him.

Jeremy spun to the side, grabbed a handful of sand and threw it in the face of the ape.

He sprinted the last few strides to the boat and heaved against the side of the bow, pushing it into the waters of the Amazon. He reached up to grab hold of the bow railing and struggled to pull himself inside the boat. A stick sailed next to him, striking the bow like a spear and falling harmlessly into the water.

Within a few seconds he had loosed the rope anchoring the ship, and looked back to see three chimpanzees now on the beach watching him as the boat drifted slowly away from shore.

The boat was heading toward an outcropping a short distance down the beach, the eddy current moving him to an inevitable landing. The chimps realized this as well, and began scooting toward the shore where the boat was approaching.

Jeremy reached into his pocket to pull out the key and thrust it into the ignition. Nothing happened. He tried it again, pumping the gas. The boat continued to drift toward the waiting chimps.

Jeremy ran to the back of the boat, splashing through the six inches of water covering the floor. *No time for the bilge pumps.* He yanked open the covering to the engine and grabbed a toolbox from inside. *Where was the fuel intake valve?*

He jammed the screwdriver to loosen the valve and ran back to the ignition. He turned it again. The engine sputtered, then roared to life as Jeremy threw the throttle into gear and turned the wheel frantically, now just meters from the shore. The boat responded and began to float away from the howling cries of the chimps.

JAMIE looked up at Paolo's hooded face, and saw in his concerned eyes that he understood what had happened. She summarized the conversation with Jeremy.

"Paolo, this trip was a very bad idea." Jamie began to cry, an inconsolable guilt gnawing at her conscience.

He nodded silently as he reached for her hand and held it in his own wet hands. Jamie dived into his arms as he held her and her pack in an awkward embrace. He stroked her wet hair with his fingers until she stopped crying.

"It's getting late. We should get something to eat and stop for the night. We can start fresh in the morning." Paolo's voice was calm and reassuring. Jamie nodded.

With the rain still too heavy for a cooking fire, they sat against a large tree for shelter and ate some dried meat and fruit. Jamie hadn't realized how hungry she was. She ate in silence, sitting close enough to Paolo that she could feel each movement he made. *What was he thinking?*

"Should we give it up?" Jamie finally asked.

Paolo shook his head. "If their phone is not working, our best hope for finding Roger and Sameer is to find that chimp. Hopefully, we'll meet them there."

Jamie thought for a moment and agreed that he was right. She looked up at Paolo and said with all the sincerity she felt, "I'm so glad you're here, Paolo."

Paolo responded by reaching out one finger and stroking her cheek softly in the light rain. He reached with his other hand, removed her hood and held her head in his hands. He kissed her forehead lightly as she slid his hood off his head.

An instant later they slipped into each other's arms as their lips met. The pain and fear they both felt melted away with each kiss until they had forgotten everything else but the warmth and comfort of their bodies. Their unhurried, grateful embrace shielded them from the violent, primal noises of the forest.

Jamie rose to her knees facing Paolo. He slid his hands on her waist, under her shirt. He slowly moved his hands higher, then stopped. She wrapped her own hands around his and slid them around onto her chest, tossing her head back at the sensation.

She lifted her shirt, pulling his head tightly against her breast, wrapping her arms around it, and kissing the top of his head affectionately. He closed his arms around her waist. She slid down until their lips met again, then opened her eyes and smiled gratefully at him. "Hold me, Paolo," she whispered.

He unzipped his raincoat and wrapped his arms around her tightly, pressing her to the ground beneath him as he kissed her neck and face.

THIRTY-TWO

AS night fell over the forest, Carlos, Ayala, and Susan were reluctant to break pursuit. "I know we're getting close," Ayala said to the others as she listened to the strong signal from the Yagi.

Susan shrugged. "Should we keep going? I'm feeling OK, and the rain has stopped."

Carlos said, "The chimp probably won't come down for the night. They sleep in the canopy. Is it worth trying an ambush?"

Ayala fidgeted at the thought. "It's quite dangerous to try and move around the canopy at night. I think we should give it one more day."

Carlos nodded. "Then why don't we make a fire and have a real meal? I've got some yams and could cook up some biscuits and beans as well. What do you say?"

Susan smiled gratefully and Carlos went about gathering some wood for a fire. Soon, a healthy fire was crackling under Carlos's makeshift campstove. Susan and Ayala wandered a short distance away and began to talk.

Susan had been engaging Ayala more during the day, and had learned much of her past. It amazed Susan that her companion was not much older than herself, but had led such a different life with so much more intensity. Most of all, Ayala's independence intrigued Susan. What would it be like to live a life for yourself, to face risks and dangers more real than an editor's tongue, to shun the comforts of society and tame a new world?

Susan sat on a broken stump by Ayala and asked, "Do you think you'll stay here forever?"

Ayala shook her head. "This was a retreat for me. I still have the nightmares and flashbacks, but I've mostly conquered my demons. Someday, maybe soon, I'll be ready to try again. I don't know where yet, or what I'll do."

Susan cocked her head, "I'd bet you could pretty well do anything you want. Would you go back to Israel?"

"I'm not sure I'm ready for that yet. What about you? Has this story changed your priorities?"

"I don't know. I hope this story will be a breakthrough for me, but I'm still just a Midwestern girl who values security, and I don't think my husband will be too keen on my becoming a high-risk investigative journalist. I'm not sure where this all will lead."

"Have you thought about a family?" Ayala's tone of voice betrayed curiosity, and Susan wondered if this was something Ayala had wondered about more than once.

"Tried for a while. Maybe someday." Susan was about to tell Ayala about how her run-in with the quintuplets the week before had cured her for awhile of any motherly aspirations, when the calm of the night was shattered by an explosion. Susan looked around in confusion, searching for an explanation.

Ayala was already on her feet. "Get down!" she shouted to Susan as she scrambled to her pack and retrieved her pistol.

Simultaneously, Susan and Ayala looked over at the campsite to see Carlos sprinting off into the darkness. Another gunshot rang out through the trees, then there was silence. Ayala crept through the trees, circling to where Carlos had gone. She met him behind a large tree covered by ferns.

"Gunshots?" she confirmed with Carlos.

He nodded, neither of them a stranger to the sound.

"We need our packs," she said.

"I'll get Susan's," he offered.

Carlos held up a finger, then two, then three, and the two figures burst from behind the tree in a blind run toward the fire. They each scooped up their packs, and Carlos managed to drag Susan's as well, and bolted off away from the small clearing. As they ran away, the silence was broken again by another gunshot, striking the fire and scattering charred wood around the clearing.

Susan watched in horror as the two ran through the open and the sound came again. Who could be shooting? She had never heard the sound of gunfire, and was terrified as she hid behind her tree stump. A moment later she jumped as she felt something touch her back. It was Carlos.

"Here's your pack." He handed it to her. With a rifle in one hand, he pointed in a direction away from the fire. They both walked quietly away from the stump. A minute later, they met Ayala, her pistol poised and her body tense and alert.

They took cover between the buttresses of a large tree.

Susan whispered first, "Who's doing this?"

Ayala shrugged and whispered back. "Must be those scientists. They play hardball. I can't tell where it's coming from. Too many echoes."

"What do we do now?" asked Susan frantically.

"We don't get shot," Ayala answered.

She communicated with Carlos with a glance and a nod of her head. He agreed, and the two started out at a brisk walk, weapons at ready, with Susan following closely behind.

They walked silently, listening carefully as they went, for about a half hour. Eventually Ayala raised a hand to stop them.

"We should be clear now," she said softly. "From now on, we keep a twenty-four-hour watch. I don't know what that chimp can do that is so valuable, but someone else wants him pretty bad. I'll take first watch."

Susan was still too frightened to sleep, but Carlos nodded and dutifully stretched out on the ground, his head on his pack. Susan decided it would be a very bad idea to lose her opportunity for rest and she followed his example. The ground was soft, and after a long, restless interval, her weariness overtook her and she started drifting asleep.

After what seemed like five minutes, Carlos awoke her and asked softly, "You up for a watch?"

Susan rubbed her eyes. She nodded blankly. "What do I do?"

"Everything has been quiet so far. If you hear a peep out of place, wake me up." He handed her his rifle, and lay back down.

Susan took the weapon cautiously, having never held one before in her life. She put it across her lap and reclined against the tree, her nerves instantly jolted into full alertness. She was surprised they trusted her to hold a watch. Maybe the sleep was too valuable to lose in their situation.

She could already see a few rays of sunlight through the trees. Probably only a couple hours until they would be ready to move again. Maybe they hadn't trusted her quite as much as she thought.

In any case, she was correct in assuming that her anxiety would be more than adequate to keep her alert the rest of her watch.

THIRTY-THREE

JAMIE rubbed her eyes as the humid morning air percolated through her senses. She looked over to see Paolo's sleeping figure stretched out on the ground next to her. She sat up. Slowly, the events of the last three days returned to her memory, and she began sorting through the emotions and problems that faced her. She felt partially responsible for the misfortune of the expedition, as she had technically arranged the trip. Such thoughts were not helpful, however, and she forced them out of her mind.

She allowed herself to reflect on her encounter with Paolo last night, remembering how their kissing had calmed her, cleansed her, and allowed her to rest. She enjoyed lingering on the thought.

But it was time to focus, and she started by resting her hand on Paolo's leg and pressing gently. He awoke. After a moment's confusion, his mind came into focus as well.

He kissed her once, then said, "We need to plan. The

most important thing we can do is find Sameer and Roger. I don't know how else to do that but to keep moving toward the chimp at a good pace," Paolo began.

"We should try to call them again." The thought no sooner crossed her mind than she had begun looking for her phone. She had it with her last night, she remembered. But where was it?

She searched her pockets without finding it, stood up, and brushed off her clothes. Her eyes found the object a few feet away and she rushed to pick it up. It was nearly submersed in a puddle of dark water just behind where she had been laying. As she pulled the phone out, it was dripping water onto the ground.

She opened the sat phone and turned it on. There was no sign of life. She shook it, pushing buttons with more and more force. The phone was dead. She looked up, embarrassed, at Paolo and communicated the obvious.

"Maybe it will start working again when it dries out," he said generously.

"Well, let's go." Jamie retrieved the antenna from her pack, flipped it open, and performed a sweep in the direction they had been traveling. She was pleased to find a clear pulsing signal of good amplitude in the same direction it had been last night. She smiled thankfully. Paolo held out his hand, and she responded by backing him into a tree and wrapping her arms around him. She reached up and kissed him slowly, affectionately, and told him, "Stay close, eh?"

He nodded happily and took her hand.

They tracked the chimp for most of the morning, and did not stop until after midday for a brief meal. Their rations were running low, since their packs had been raided. Both recognized it, but neither chose to comment on it.

They had probably one more day, at best, before they would have to start supplementing with food from the jungle. They sat close together on a fallen tree trunk, each quietly thinking about the expedition.

Paolo turned to Jamie after a moment, reading her thoughts, and commented, "Jeremy knows what he's doing. He'll get help to David."

"It's not so much that I'm worried about as what happened to Diego. It just seems awfully brutal for a robbery. What would they gain from attacking?"

"Safer, I suppose. This way there's no chance of their being pursued. Diego and Juan Miguel could be a threat. Who knows, maybe Diego confronted them, attacked them?"

Jamie wasn't listening to his answer. She was concentrating on something else. "What's that sound?" she asked hurriedly to Paolo. They both listened.

The sound of something walking came again, out of sight through the trees. It must have been a large animal, from the sound of the footsteps. Both Jamie and Paolo knew that large animals were rarely encountered in the forest, and that when they were, it was not generally a good thing.

"Jaguar?" whispered Jamie.

"Don't know." Paolo retrieved his pistol by quietly unzipping the side pocket of his pack and pulling it out. They held very still, lest their movement alert the intruder. They knew where it was, and that was an advantage they couldn't afford to lose.

The footsteps stopped. Jamie's breathing was shallow, her legs tensed. If it were a jaguar, there was nowhere to run. They climbed trees expertly, they could run many times faster than she, and they loved a chase. She would have to be deliberate, not panicked. The footsteps started again, coming closer. They could almost see the animal through the trees, judging by the sound.

Then another sound came from the animal. "Bloody mosquitoes!" Stiles's voice was faint but distinct. Jamie and Paolo relaxed, grinning at each other. They stood up. "Bite them back!" Paolo called out a suggestion.

The footsteps stopped.

Sameer's voice called out through the trees. "Paolo, Jamie?!"

In a moment the companions were reunited. Paolo greeted Stiles and Sameer warmly, saying, "We've been waiting here for hours. What kept you?"

"It takes some time to make a proper cup of tea in the morning here," Stiles answered.

"Thank goodness you are safe. We were afraid they would get you before we did," Sameer said enigmatically.

"What are you talking about?" asked Jamie.

Stiles answered her, his tone at once more serious. "After we split up, we found that whoever took our gun and food also got into my pack as well and took my phone."

Recognition spread across Jamie's face. "So that's what happened."

Stiles continued, "Yesterday, I think we saw who did it. We almost ran into another group of people. I don't think they saw us. There were three of them, and I got a good look at them with my binoculars. There were two women and one man, visibly armed, and carrying a Yagi antenna."

Jamie gasped. "Our missing Yagi? It must be. Who else could be out here? Where did they come from?"

Stiles nearly spat out the answer, "Mercer. He set us

up. He hired someone else to get the chimp, and probably rub us out as well. It's the only thing that makes sense. He's up to something."

Paolo shook his head. "I don't know. He's pretty sick. Jeremy had to leave him that first night and go for help. He's barely alive."

Stiles's eyebrows narrowed. "That may go for us as well. You're sure Jeremy's safe?"

"No," Jamie admitted. "When he got back to the camp yesterday, he found Diego and Juan Miguel had been murdered and the camp ransacked. He was going to call back to the compound for help." Jamie looked pained to go further, but did. "I lost my phone in some water last night, and we don't have a working phone either. I haven't heard from him since last night."

Stiles cursed. "That's exactly the wrong thing for him to do. If Mercer isn't responsible for that group, someone back at the compound is. They may just send someone to finish off Jeremy."

Jamie hesitated. "How are you so sure the company's behind it?"

"Nakamura's been so secretive about all this from the beginning, even from us. I don't think he wants us to know all that we do. What it boils down to, though, is there's no alternative. Who else could have given our Yagi to an outside party?"

"Where are the people you saw?" asked Paolo insistently.

"Ahead of us a bit, I think. We haven't seen them today. They're definitely tracking the chimp, though," Stiles finished.

"I don't want to take chances. I'm the only one left

with a weapon, except for the darts. I don't want to be taken by surprise," Paolo said grimly as he slipped the pistol into his pocket.

"I say we get them first, permanently. I have no doubt they mean the same for us."

"Time to move. We're very close to the chimp now. From now on, no talking unless necessary," said Paolo.

THIRTY-FOUR

MERCER'S eyes opened.

Where am I? How long have I been sleeping?

His head was throbbing. *How long have I had this headache?*

He didn't know. In his dim awareness of his surroundings, there was a vague uneasiness with his situation, but he was too confused at first to articulate exactly what was wrong.

Then he heard the ringing in his ear. What was that awful ringing? He fumbled around with his hand at the sound and gripped a metal object. He brought it to his face and studied it for a long time. *Why was it ringing like that?* He pulled at it with his fingers and the ringing stopped.

"Hello . . . hello . . . David?" A man's voice sounded.

"David? It's Jeremy! How are you?" The voice was pleading, insistent.

Mercer spoke. "Hello?" His voice was raspy, flat.

"Good, you're there. You sound terrible. Do you know where you are?" Jeremy asked.

Mercer put the phone down, confused at what it wanted. He focused his mind to isolate what was bothering him. *What's wrong here?*

He didn't recognize that he was in the jungle; he didn't understand he was alone; he certainly didn't know that in capillaries throughout his entire body, blood was oozing out of his largely depleted bloodstream and that his kidneys and liver were failing. About the only thing he did understand was that he was dying of thirst. His tongue felt dry and cracked, and the pounding behind his eyes was a fire that had to be put out with water. He ignored the ringing in his ears, all his efforts aimed at finding a drink.

Water.

His delirious mind summoned his legs to move. Eventually, he rolled to one side, and found that his whole body ached. He tried to sit up, and started to feel blackness closing in on him. After a brief rest, he tried again, more slowly, and supported his body with one arm. Sliding around to his knees, he was able to look up at the canvas enclosing him. He was trapped.

Who made this house so small?

Finally, a glimmer of faint light shone through one of the walls, and he crawled out slowly and painfully.

Water.

Mercer felt the damp earth under his hands. He brought his hands to his mouth and licked off the moist earth from his fingers. Then he spat in revulsion, coughing at the gritty taste of dirt and dried blood.

Water.

He slowly rose to his feet, swaying with unsteadiness as his legs fought the urge to collapse. One shaky step after another, he stumbled into the dim morning light. He had to find water.

For another dozen steps he staggered ahead, until his foot caught on a root and twisted as he fell forward. He forgot the pain in his head and his intractable thirst as he felt something give in his knee, causing an explosion of pain. He drifted off into sleep.

He awoke sometime later with the curious sensation of tingling on his legs. He shifted his head around to see dozens, perhaps hundreds of ants crawling over his legs. He felt their small bodies crawling under his pant legs, up and down across his legs.

Why are they crawling on me? The question was too hard for his feeble mind.

He heard a noise. It sounded like footsteps. Then the pain shot through his head again. No, not his head. His face. He felt it again, a pelting that left his jaw stinging. He looked up.

In front of him, he made out the shape of four chimpanzees, standing around a perimeter a few feet from him. He watched one of them pick up a rock from the ground and whirl it in his direction. It caught him on the chest, taking the wind out of him. Another chimp picked up another rock, and then all of them stooped to pick up larger and larger stones, when a crash to his head sent him back into sleep.

LATE morning found Jeremy exhausted. He had been walking most of the night after the Manaus search and rescue team had arrived. He had spent nearly an hour on the phone trying to find someone to mount a rescue operation. He had finally found a number for the BrainStem compound on his third attempt to find an English speaker at directory assistance and managed to get Skip Jordan on the line.

Jordan, who was devastated by the news of Diego's and Juan Miguel's deaths, passed him on to the Manaus police, who ultimately were able to get Jeremy in touch with an emergency management division.

After feeling like hours had passed before anyone arrived, now Jeremy could barely keep up. Fortunately, he had been able to bandage his foot with the supplies he found on the boat. He had agreed to help with the tracking, as he was most familiar with the route, but the four officers that accompanied him were in much better shape and seemed far more capable at maneuvering through the forest. The officers, who were actually Brazilian soldiers, were armed to the teeth. One of them spoke reasonably good English, and Jeremy had been able to quickly update them on Mercer's condition and whereabouts.

Now, about eight hours after the team had arrived, they had returned to the coordinates he had memorized the day before. There was nothing at the site. Had he forgotten the coordinates? He looked uneasily at the members of the search team, indicating that they had arrived at the spot. The team leader nodded, and instructed the rest of the team to fan out in a spiral in two groups, looking for the silver tent that Jeremy had left Mercer in.

After about ten minutes of searching, Jeremy spotted

something familiar and quickly located the tent. The other group was still in audible range, and they quickly joined Jeremy's group at the scene. Before Jeremy could reach the tent, one of the others was already peering into the tent flaps. The look on his face told Jeremy that whatever he saw couldn't be good.

"He is gone," the man said in halting English. Jeremy looked in to find a small trail of blood such as he had seen the day before, but no Mercer.

"We should search the area," Jeremy instructed, not sure what else to do.

His command was superfluous, as the others were already combing the surrounding area for clues to which direction Mercer had gone. The search didn't take long. About three minutes later, Jeremy heard some shouting. He ran to observe.

Face down, with his arms spread wide apart, was the body of David Mercer. Jeremy quickly verified that he was not breathing, nor was there any remaining pulse.

Jeremy winced in distress, and buried his face in his hands. He felt the weight of Mercer's life on his shoulders, and was too tired, too overwhelmed, and too emotional to try to reason with himself. After fighting down the guilt he felt over Mercer's death, he finally asked the others, "Can we carry him back?"

They nodded, and the five started the long journey home. No matter how tired he was, Jeremy decided he didn't want any part of another night in the rain forest. He refused to even acknowledge the fear that reigned in his subconscious, that Stiles may already have met the same fate.

THIRTY-FIVE

PAOLO, Jamie, Stiles, and Sameer all felt invigorated after their meeting, and the renewed sense of purpose showed in their energy, motivation, and pace. Their lunch break was brief, all of them eager to locate the chimp. The radio signal was strengthening; they were getting very close.

Paolo sat over lunch studying the topo map. After relocating their coordinates on the map, he traced the terrain and began reorienting himself to the features. Jamie came to sit next to him.

Without her asking, Paolo began explaining his thoughts, pointing on the map. "If I've oriented correctly, we should be right here, tracking in this direction." His finger ran across the relatively sparse isoelevation lines into a large blue chasm on the map.

"You mean we're heading right for a river?" Jamie asked, surprised.

Paolo nodded. "Exactly. It's difficult to know how

accurate these maps are. The water levels fluctuate so much with the season that tributaries may vary dramatically in size or even disappear some times during the year. This one looks a pretty good size, and we're likely to see a sizeable river. I'm doubting the chimps can cross."

"So that's why we've gained so much ground lately. The chimps have hit the water and aren't moving much." Jamie's musing was overheard by Sameer and Stiles, who wandered over.

Sameer asked, "So the chimps have stopped by a river?"

"That's the way it seems," Paolo answered.

Sameer's expression became animated. "That is perfect. There is an excellent chance we'll catch them on the ground. They're almost certain to come down to drink with so much available water."

Stiles grinned wryly. "It appears your luck has run out, Kenneth."

Sameer spoke again. "It will be very important to approach carefully; we don't want to alert them if they are on the ground."

Stiles's expression became more serious. "I'm actually more concerned about alerting Soliton's thugs. I'd be inclined to have that thing ready." He motioned to Paolo's pistol. "There's a pretty good chance they'll be in spitting distance before this thing's through."

Paolo nodded, and the four shouldered their packs and resumed the chase.

AYALA held the antenna casually, and rechecked her quarry's signal. She was listening frequently now, the antenna never leaving her hand. The hunt was on, and all three of them knew they could spot their target any minute.

"What's that sound?" Carlos asked suddenly.

Ayala and Susan stopped to listen.

Ayala caught his expression and frowned back. "River. You're right. Let's hope it will be harder for the apes to cross than us. If the canopy overlaps, they may have a natural bridge."

In another fifteen minutes, they had reached the water's edge. Ayala was relieved to see the river was a good fifty meters across. On each shore, trees grew up out of the river, their trunks submerged in the water. In the center, however, the river made a clean separation through the forest, with an impassable watery barrier segregating the two edges of the forest. Carlos grinned broadly while Ayala rechecked their bearings.

The signal was weaker. She raised the antenna slowly overhead, concentrating on the audible pulsing. A clearly identifiable maximum emanated from the antenna as it pointed up at an angle into the canopy.

"How do we get to them?" Susan asked, her heart pounding at being so close to their goal.

Ayala whispered back, "We don't. We wait for them to come to us." She led them through the trees a bit farther inland to a good vantage point behind a mound of earth. Settling onto the ground, the three organized their ambush.

"I hear water," Jamie announced softly as she walked. The others, listening more carefully, picked up the sound as well. Sameer rechecked their bearing with the antenna, and they began walking single file through the denser forest. Slipping through low palm fronds and ferns, the group trekked toward the river.

A few minutes later, they could see past the trees into the large body of water. Light streamed through the opening in the canopy over the river, and the humidity increased noticeably. Each of the four travelers was sweating heavily.

"Let's get a bearing on him. We should be able to narrow it down to a few trees." Paolo's voice was calm, efficient, and intense.

Sameer raised his antenna to isolate the signal, while Stiles squinted through his field glasses into the canopy, following Sameer's position. Slowly, after three or four passes, Sameer identified the target direction, and raised his hand to beckon the others to follow.

After a few steps Jamie whispered harshly, "Stop!" The others obeyed, and turned to face her.

"There," she said more quietly. "I see someone through the trees, beyond that small hill. Maybe a hundred meters."

"Good eyes, kid," Stiles complimented, raising his binoculars. After a brief look, he announced, "It's the same crew all right. We might have run right into them."

Jamie gave a questioning look to Paolo. "Do you think we could capture them, take them by surprise?"

Paolo raised his revolver, keeping it trained on the source, and was about to speak when a loud voice echoed through the trees from behind them.

"Freeze! You're surrounded."

Sameer jumped at the sound. All four of them slowly turned around to the direction of the voice. A short distance away, in plain sight, was a single figure, her pistol pointed directly into Paolo's chest. She was roughly dressed, with her hair short and her cold, efficient eyes penetrating her quarry.

"Drop it." Ayala motioned to Paolo. He obeyed. "You too." She indicated the dart gun Sameer was holding. Sameer tossed the gun a few feet away.

"Step back a few paces."

She gathered the dart gun and the revolver, clipping them to her belt, and motioned the four to walk toward her two companions.

Glumly, the four began walking toward Carlos and Susan, each aware that their next few steps might be their last.

THIRTY-SIX

CARLOS and Susan rose to their feet when they heard voices and saw Ayala leading the scientists toward them. Ayala had slipped away secretively only a few minutes before, refusing to tell them anything except to "watch out." Now they understood what she had heard. Carlos quietly disciplined himself for not paying more attention to the possibility of the scientists approaching them from behind. He should have expected it.

When Ayala and her four captives arrived at Carlos and Susan, Ayala unclipped the revolver from her belt and tossed it to Susan, who tried to hold it as if she had the slightest idea what to do with it.

Paolo was the first to speak. "Who are you?"

Ayala sauntered around to join Carlos and Susan. "Interesting question for someone who's been trying to kill us," she responded.

"What?!" said Jamie.

Paolo motioned for the others to let him speak. "I can assure you we haven't done any such thing. We don't have any idea who you are or where you came from, and we haven't made any hostile actions. The only hostile act so far was your raiding our supplies."

Ayala looked unimpressed. "Then who was shooting at us last night? The chimps?"

"How do you know about the chimps?" Paolo pressed further.

Susan motioned to Ayala to put her gun down. She stepped forward, taking control. "Listen, I have no intention of taking the chimp at gunpoint. No one is going to be hurt. Maybe we can help you, but I really would like some honest information. We were shot at last night, and we haven't touched any of your supplies."

"I tell you none of us has fired a shot since we arrived in the jungle," Paolo insisted.

Susan raised an eyebrow. "Are you willing to tell me about the chimp? The whole story?"

Stiles couldn't resist any longer. "Hasn't Nakamura told you anything? He's using you." His voice was taunting.

Susan looked at Stiles. "None of us has ever spoken with Nakamura, and he's certainly not using us. We thought he was dead. Are you telling me you're not working for him either?"

Stiles looked embarrassed. "Soliton didn't hire you?"

"No," Susan answered.

Paolo was beginning to understand when gunfire exploded through the trees, ricocheting off a rock in front of the group. All seven of them dived down behind the hill, looking frantically for a source.

"Tell your people to stand down! What do you want from us?" Paolo hissed.

"It's not us!" Ayala replied, searching the horizon fervently. "There's only the three of us."

Another shot exploded from above.

"Hold off, now!" Paolo said.

"Look at us! We're being fired on too!" Susan shouted back.

A screech sounded from the trees.

"It's that monster! He's got a gun!"

Carlos pointed his rifle at the canopy, searching through his sight for a target. He fired.

The hunters held their breath, waiting for another shot. Carlos continued searching the trees. A flock of birds flapped out from below the sound of snapping branches in the tree.

Carlos whirled his rifle to the sound. It was a crashing, hurtling, reckless sound. An instant later the seven travelers saw movement in the trees and a large dark animal came crashing through the canopy onto the ground.

"You got him, Carlos!" Ayala said.

Carlos nodded. "Wasn't sure for a minute." He trained his rifle toward the trees from where the animal had come. He could see nothing. Ayala whispered to Susan and Carlos, "Cover me." She began inching forward through the trees to inspect the fallen animal.

Susan promptly turned to Paolo and handed him the revolver. "I don't need this thing," she commented, to Ayala's apparent displeasure. Paolo held the weapon loosely. Everyone watched uneasily while Ayala moved toward the animal. She stooped over where it had fallen, and became invisible for a short time. A moment later they saw her look up, then look down and stoop over again.

A couple minutes later, still without any further sound of gunfire, she casually walked back to the group. In her hands was a blue collar.

"Looks like your friend wasn't so careful after all. Any of you recognize this?" She held out the collar.

Sameer examined it. "That's him all right. Dead?"

"That's an understatement. Blew his head off," Ayala answered. "Nice shot," she added to Carlos.

Sameer asked uneasily, "You see the pistol?"

Ayala shook her head. "But next time you lose a homicidal chimp, keep an eye on your stuff. We almost took a few of those bullets last night."

Stiles walked toward the dead chimp, turning its remains over with his boot. "Not much left of his brain, I'm afraid," he called out glumly.

The others joined him. "Seems a bit anticlimactic," Stiles said sarcastically.

"In a way I'll miss him," Sameer said sadly as he stared at the body. His expression changed. "Get back! All of you!"

"What!" Jamie shouted, as the entire group ran for cover behind neighboring trees. A gunshot exploded from the tree above, narrowly missing Sameer.

Sameer shouted out to the group, "He switched the collar! That's a mature female. Plain old chimp. Let's get out of here!"

From the trees, Jamie froze as a sound started to grow from all around her, descending from the trees like a husky Gregorian chant.

Carlos yelled out, "I know that sound!" In unison, gutteral mutterings coursed back and forth among the trees.

"What are you talking about? When could you have heard it before?" Jamie asked back.

"Shit! Why didn't I realize . . ." Carlos called out softly and urgently, "There's more than one! Lots more!"

"What are you talking about!"

"The chimps I saw. Dozens of them. They were making this sound. Nakamura made more than one, and they all escaped."

Jamie's throat tightened. Another gunshot sounded from above, and the entire group of humans broke into a chaotic race away from the chimps.

PART IV
THE SEED OF ABRAHAM

Chimera:

- *Biol.* An organism in which tissues of genetically different constitution coexist as a result of grafting, mutation, or some other process.
- A fabled fire-breathing monster of Greek mythology, with a lion's head, a goat's body, and a serpent's tail.
- An unreal creature of the imagination, a mere wild fancy; an unfounded conception.

—(Oxford English Dictionary, 2nd Ed., 1989)

Homo sapiens, the first truly free species, is about to decommission natural selection, the force that made us . . . . Soon we must look deep within ourselves and decide what we wish to become.

—(Edward O. Wilson, Consilience, The Unity of Knowledge)

And it repented the LORD that he had made man on the earth, and it grieved him at his heart.

And the LORD said, I will destroy man whom I have created from the face of the earth; both man, and beast, and the creeping thing, and the fowls of the air; for it repenteth me that I have made them.

—(Genesis 6:6–7 [King James Bible])

THIRTY-SEVEN

AT the sound of the explosion Jamie took off at a sprint. Wild, unmitigated terror drove her muscles as adrenaline spilled into her veins. Her stridorous breathing was panicked, frenzied, as she choked down air with each step. She could only look forward, certain that behind her the barrel of a revolver was pointed at her head. Another gunshot fired.

Jamie winced, waiting for the bullet to hit, then forced herself to run faster. *Can't panic!* She focused on her breathing, slowing to a rhythmic pattern every other step. She could never keep this up. Her pack was oppressive; the temptation to drop it and run was overwhelming.

Paolo. Where was he? She threw her head over her shoulder, nearly smacking her face against a low-lying branch. She saw a rustle behind her in the ferns, but couldn't make out who it was. She knew someone was ahead and to the left as well. *Where were the chimps?*

Stay with the group; keep everyone together. The thought oriented her as she nearly burst into Ayala, who had slowed to catch her breath with her arms clasped on top of her head as she stumbled forward.

Jamie whispered to her, gesturing with her arms. "We have to regroup. Can't split up."

Ayala nodded, and the two made a beeline toward the forest interior where the secondary forest faded into more regular, open terrain with larger trees and less undergrowth. "Everyone this way!" she shouted in a hoarse voice.

Jamie slowed their pace to a brisk walk, scanning the forest for the others. Paolo dove out of a cluster of ferns and took a deep breath when he saw Jamie. He held out his hand for them to stop and wait. Silently, he disappeared back into the forest.

Jamie and Ayala walked around a tree, both of them panting. Jamie's eyes were drawn upward, as she scanned the canopy for signs of life.

A minute later, they heard a rustle in the trees just out of sight. Instinctively, Jamie and Ayala crouched behind trees, peering out at the noise. Jamie saw the shape of a man. *Was it a chimp?*

"Hey! Over here!" Ayala hissed. Carlos stepped into the dim light, waving his arm behind him. A second later, Susan followed him out, and they both crept toward Jamie and Ayala.

"We're waiting for the others," Ayala whispered as they drew near.

Susan was white. She looked completely out of breath, faint.

Just then, Paolo scrambled into view followed by Stiles

and Sameer, neither one of whom was carrying their pack. Breathing heavily, Paolo glanced up at the trees above and led the group to the far side of a huge fallen tree trunk.

"Carlos," he said, verifying that he had remembered his name. "What did you mean about other chimps?"

Carlos looked over his shoulder. He spoke softly, urgently. "I've been in Nakamura's lab. The secret one behind his office. There were rows of cages. Chimps."

Sameer shook his head. "Some of the females, perhaps a dozen or two; he kept them for other experiments. They're just regular chimps. I know about them."

Carlos said, "Fifty of them?"

Sameer's eyes grew wide.

"Most of them young. I saw the females too. They were all pregnant. The ones I'm talking about were males and females. Dozens of them. And that sound. I'd remember it anywhere. It's like they're chanting, singing. It's got to be them."

Nobody spoke for a moment; the implications were sinking in for Jamie. *A whole colony, possibly as intelligent as her chimp.*

Paolo's eyes scanned the group. "All right. At this point, we get out of here alive. That's it. Everyone follows orders and nobody goes anywhere alone."

Ayala looked furious. "I don't take orders from anyone. We do this together."

Paolo ignored her comment. "What do we have for ammunition? I have a pistol, a little ammo."

Carlos patted his rifle. Ayala brought out her pistol.

"So we've got enough to cover us if we're smart about this. We don't take them for granted. I don't know what they want from us at this point, but we treat them as a mortal threat until we're back to the river."

Nobody argued.

"We're safest if we keep together. More eyes to watch and a harder target to attack."

"All the easier to peg us all at once," Ayala said angrily. She retracted her statement immediately. "No, I agree. We stay together. For now."

Paolo pulled out his compass. After a quick check, he pointed. "We head straight back for the ferry. I figure two and a half days at a brisk pace and we'll be there. We have to pace ourselves."

Susan bit her lip. "Let's go straight through. I won't sleep with them out there."

Jamie shook her head. "Paolo's right. We won't make it unless we keep our strength. They can move in the canopy faster than we can on the ground. Our only chance is to take control of the pace."

Paolo looked at Stiles and Sameer. "We keep as quiet as we can. No talking until we break for the night unless absolutely necessary."

Stiles nodded.

"How much food do we have?"

Stiles and Sameer looked embarrassed as the only two without packs.

"The two of us have a couple meals worth," Paolo said, looking at Jamie.

"We should have enough to get us back," Carlos offered.

Paolo nodded to Stiles, then to Susan, and Stiles held out his hands to carry Susan's pack, which she gratefully handed over.

"Then let's go." Paolo looked around, then stepped out from their huddle into the forest toward the Amazon.

The group followed single file, Paolo in the lead with Jamie. Carlos walked last behind Ayala.

AFTER two hours of walking Jamie was spooked. Every bird call, every rustle of the wind in the canopy sent the entire group searching above in the trees. The forced silence was maddening, isolating, especially when she was dying to find out who these people were, how they ended up here.

She turned her attention to the trip home. It was early evening, as far as the sparse glimpses of the sky allowed her to tell. The ever-present dim light changed little until dusk, when the forest faded to near blackness.

Something was wrong. Were the chimps not following them? Surely they would be easy to track from the forest canopy. The chimps could move at three times their speed. *What were they waiting for?*

Maybe they had what they wanted. The hunt was over. They won. Now that we're leaving, maybe that will be enough.

She heard the snap of a branch from above, and spun her head upward. She saw nothing. Following her lead, several of the others looked up, then resumed walking after another false alarm.

It was Susan that interested her most. *Who was she? Clearly not at home in the jungle.* Spoke an American dialect, but not native. Yet she had the look of someone thoughtful, someone *interesting.* The sort of person she might want as a friend . . .

Another snap from above. Before Jamie could even localize the sound, she saw two dark figures jumping out of the sky. Carlos shouted. It was a startled, ineffectual cry. The chimps moved instantaneously, landing literally on top of Carlos.

How many? She ducked and put her hands over her head reflexively.

She heard the sickening sound of Carlos hitting the ground, then a loud bellow as the chimps screeched a demoniacal war cry. She searched for the chimps, but they were already moving, dragging Carlos between them toward a clump of trees.

"Get them!" she shouted.

Before she could shout again, she heard a gunshot, and Ayala stood with her pistol outstretched. One of the chimps toppled from behind the tree onto the ground, writhing in pain.

Before she could fire again, another chimp jumped out of the sky between her and the injured chimp. It looked back at the wounded animal, and loped over to it, standing in front of it. It raised its arms in a menacing gesture as the other chimp scurried away, standing its ground resolutely as its comrade escaped.

Ayala fired again, and the new chimp toppled to the ground. Ayala raced around the tree to get in range of the other, but it was already out of sight.

Jamie stared in amazement. *Had the chimp understood what it was doing? Did it sacrifice itself so the other could escape?* She heard a grotesque crunch of ligaments and bones stretching from where the chimp had dragged Carlos. Then from behind the tree, she watched, paralyzed, as the chimp raced across the forest on three legs, carrying a long, shiny object in his fourth. *He had Carlos's gun!*

Ayala was already at Carlos's side. Paolo was right behind her after firing wide of the escaping chimp. Jamie ran to join them.

Carlos was lying limp, his head rotated unnaturally to one side. He was wheezing through each agonal breath, his eyes desperate.

"He took the rifle," Ayala warned Paolo as she reached for Carlos's head.

Jamie's eyes widened as she looked directly from across the clearing at a third chimp, holding a pistol with outstretched hands. "Over there! He's got a gun!"

Susan screamed at the same time.

The shouts spurred Paolo into action, his reflexes already keyed. Two explosions sounded simultaneously, and Jamie saw a spattering of blood from the chimp's arm. The chimp's shot ricocheted off a tree behind Ayala.

The chimp bellowed viciously, then retreated into the forest at full speed.

Ayala and Paolo stood back to back, slowly circling until they could see nothing more in the canopy or on the ground.

Jamie looked back at Carlos, then jumped to his side as she reached to his neck to find what she already knew. He had no pulse. His chest heaved one final time and his snapped neck stopped quivering.

Jamie dropped her head over Carlos's body and wept.

Ayala pointed her rifle at the chimp on the ground,

which was still suffering from a wound that opened his belly.

"Save your bullet," Paolo shouted.

Ayala ignored the command and fired, twice, silencing the chimp before walking toward it and kicking it savagely.

THIRTY-EIGHT

IT didn't feel right leaving Carlos exposed. Everyone sensed it, and Paolo spoke it. Ayala agreed, and Paolo set to digging a shallow grave for their fallen comrade.

While Paolo worked, Stiles went to the body of the chimp. He stood over it briefly, then removed some supplies from his pack. He found a pickaxe in Carlos's pack, and used it to crack the animal's skull, letting the herniating brain ooze out. He worked quickly and efficiently, as Jamie watched in amazement.

"What are you doing?"

"I'd be the bloody fool if I let him rot out here with his brain practically in my hands."

He continued working, taking a delicate knife and slicing through the brain, excising a chunk of tissue and placing it in a small vial of liquid from his pack. He next used the knife to pare off the surface of the brain, peeling the top layer as though it were a mushy apple. He placed this thin film on a few microscope slides, then sprayed them with a tiny bottle of fixative, replacing all of the specimens in a Ziploc bag in the side pocket of his pack.

Jamie shook her head, not knowing whether to be disgusted or impressed at Stiles's audacity.

Paolo and the others finished piling leaves and stones on top of the grave, and Ayala acknowledged that they needed shelter before nightfall. Sameer shouldered Carlos's pack, and the group set off again.

Nobody seemed in the mood to walk again, least of all Jamie. She wondered where the chimps were. Certainly not far. And she no longer suffered any illusion about their intentions.

They walked for an hour in silence, Paolo leading and Ayala bringing up the rear with her pistol in hand.

Susan was not doing well. She had been wandering around Carlos's body in a daze, the fear never quite leaving her eyes long enough for anyone to see what else was playing across her mind. She walked in the middle of the group, and had not spoken since the attack.

Paolo stopped. He pointed to a hill on the horizon, where a small amount of waning light came through a large opening in the trees. They reached it a few minutes later, and Paolo dropped his pack.

"We stop here."

Nobody was in the mood to argue.

"Roger, Sameer. Start a fire. Ayala, let's look at what we have here for defenses." Ayala nodded.

Jamie motioned to a rock for Susan to sit down. While Susan rested, Jamie gathered some fern leaves and smoothed the ground to make four beds, figuring two should stand watch at all times. Rain or no rain, nobody was going to want to sleep like a sitting duck in a tent to-night. She wondered if she would be able to sleep at all.

She sat on the ground by Susan, a good distance away from the roaring fire that Sameer and Stiles had built. The temperature had dropped some with sunset, but not much, and the stifling humidity made the fire an unwelcome necessity.

Paolo and Ayala had returned from their survey, and Paolo sat by Jamie on the ground. Ayala faced the opposite direction, lazily waving her pistol as she looked at the trees. Sameer collapsed on the ground by the others, guzzling from his canteen.

Stiles sat a few feet closer to the fire, elbows on the ground behind him as he watched the flames and the trees beyond. He held a makeshift torch between his knees.

"Pity we didn't make hot dogs out of the bastard."

"That's not helping, Roger, and we all need to eat," Jamie chided. She opened her pack as well as Paolo's, and began passing out dried meat and bread. She turned to Susan. "I'd say we have a little catching up to do."

Susan said nothing.

"I'm Jamie." She raised her eyebrows expectantly.

Susan slowly turned her head. "It's my fault he died." Her voice sounded weak, flat.

"The hell it was, kid. But that kind of attitude's going to get the rest of us killed," Ayala interjected over her shoulder.

Susan continued. "I brought him here. It was my idea."

"What was your idea?" Jamie asked softly.

"The chimp. Carlos discovered the chimp. I found out about it. I wanted it."

"How did he know about all this?"

Susan turned her head toward Jamie angrily. "All right. I'll tell you. He's a corporate spy. His employer leaked the story to me. I'm a reporter. I just didn't like the idea of growing human babies in chimps to slice open for research. Thought I could prove it if I had the chimp."

Stiles turned around suddenly. "What did you say?"

"Yeah, I know all about your experiments."

"Then you'd better tell us, because I don't have any idea what you're talking about."

Susan looked confused. "Carlos was in Nakamura's lab. He saw inside the freezers."

Stiles came closer and sat on the ground by Susan and Jamie, holding his torch away from the group. "Then I guess everyone who's looked in those freezers is dead."

Sameer and Paolo turned around also, listening intently. "He did what?" Sameer asked.

"Don't tell me you all don't know anything about this."

Jamie put her hand on Susan's arm. "Nakamura hired us just in the last couple weeks to study this chimpanzee. We have no idea what you're talking about."

Sameer's eyes were wide open. "I've worked at the lab for over five years, and never has anyone mentioned anything about what you have said. Are you sure Carlos was telling the truth?"

Susan nodded feebly.

"Then we'll help you with your story," Jamie said. "Let's just get out of here alive."

As Jamie spoke, Ayala whirled around shouting, "Get down!"

Jamie saw a flash of movement as a chimp streaked through their campsite toward the fire, dragging a flaming log as he scampered out the other side. Ayala's pistol echoed from the trees behind as the chimp dodged out of sight, the flame disappearing in the forest.

Paolo had already moved to a flanking position behind Ayala, his gun held at arm's length pointing into the trees. The others crouched down in between.

The hum of the insects was deafening. The air was still, and Jamie strained to hear the rustle from the trees that would mean the chimps were there.

Watching her.

"What are they waiting for? Why haven't they killed us already?" Susan asked, her eyes showing she bordered on losing control.

"They led us in here," Stiles answered. "They're studying us, the pompous beasts."

"We can't just sit here and wait to be killed." Susan was shaking her head. She paced toward the fire, grabbing a long branch and holding the end in the flames.

Jamie followed Susan to the fire. "Oh, yes we can. We're not going anywhere until we can see as well as they can. And we get some sleep."

"Yeah, right."

Jamie followed Susan's example, and made her own torch. She nodded to Sameer to make one as well.

"What are they going to do tonight?" Sameer asked.

No one answered.

"What's that?" Susan asked suddenly.

Jamie listened. From the trees all around emanated a low-pitched rhythmic sound. Softly at first, the inhuman call increased in cadence and volume until the grunting resonated with each repeated syllable, the rhythm growing more complex and syncopated with each added voice.

Then she saw the lights—distant, flickering, like fireflies in the forest night. She turned around in a full circle slowly. On every side, barely visible in the trees, was the faint glow of two dozen torch lights encircling them as the sound of the primal chanting pounded with urgent malevolence.

THIRTY-NINE

JAMIE tensed under the sound of the chimp's battle song; her breaths came forcefully, as though her throat were closing up from inside.

"We go, now!" Ayala commanded, raising her gun in an arc, searching for a target.

She fired into the trees, the shot echoing near one of the closer torchlights. The chanting continued unabated.

Paolo grabbed her arm as she headed toward the edge of the clearing. "Ayala, stop! It's suicide." He held his weapon poised as they spoke.

"Look, General Custer. Let me tell you what suicide is. This is suicide." She gestured her arms around the group. "Sitting here waiting for one of those bastards to come make a soup bowl out of my skull."

Jamie glanced at Susan, who watched transfixed as the chimps melded in and out of view through the trees. She was all but oblivious to the conversation between Ayala and Paolo, consumed by terror.

"They're faster. They're stronger. They're smart. This is their home. They'll pick you off the minute you step outside, just like they did Carlos. We have to stay together. You'll never make it just charging out there." Paolo shifted his aim to one side, focusing on a new target.

"The hell I won't. I've seen worse. These aren't soldiers; they're a bunch of damn monkeys. We'll see how they do once they get a taste of blood and guts. Seems like a fair enough fight to me." She shook off Paolo's hand and took another step toward the trees, straining her eyes as though choosing her path.

"You don't have enough ammo for half of them, even at one shot apiece. Neither of us do."

"So tell me. How the hell do we get out of here? Cause if you don't come up with something in the next five minutes, it's not going to matter one way or the other."

Paolo shook his head vigorously. "We're tired. It's a day and a half back. If we leave now, it's over."

Jamie's mind drifted off. There had to be some weakness, some advantage they could find. But it was true. The chimps were better adapted in every way. They could travel faster, stay out of sight, attack swiftly. They could . . .

"They can't swim," Jamie said, an epiphany forming.

"Oh, that's brilliant. Chalk one up for humans. Too bad it does us no good in the middle of the bleeding forest."

"She's right," Paolo agreed, looking at Jamie gratefully. "They can't cross the river. We can. We're not far from the tributary we saw earlier. We've been moving almost parallel;

it's probably only a mile or two." He dropped his pack, one hand on his gun and the other unzipping the flap.

"I'm listening," Ayala said.

"Do you have any rope?" He rifled through the pack, stuffing his pockets with food. "Everyone, take what food you can carry. The packs stay here."

Ayala nodded. "Enough. I think I see what you mean." She threw down her pack and slung a coil of rope around one arm while her other hand gripped her gun and followed the chimps around the perimeter.

Jamie had her compass already in hand. She retraced the contours on the map by memory and looked in the direction of the river. Her eyes moved up from the compass needle to see three torches flickered close together beyond a row of trees.

Jamie moved to put her shoulder around Susan. "Can you make it?"

Susan nodded.

Stiles dropped his pack and placed the small flask in his pocket. He filled his other pockets with some dried meat. Sameer reached down to refasten his shoelaces.

Paolo stood close to Jamie as the others readied themselves. She put her arm around his waist, and kissed him once.

He motioned the group together. "We go this direction. Stay close together, because if someone gets lost there's no going back. Is that understood? I'll clear the way. Ayala will be the rearguard. The rest of you, just remember what's behind you and keep running."

As he spoke, Ayala whirled around as one of the chimps began streaking toward the group. Jamie turned a moment later to see the chimp brandishing a long sharpened stick. Ayala's gunshot rang in Jamie's ears as the chimp crumpled in midstride.

"Let's go!" Paolo shouted.

Jamie sprinted behind him as he ran toward the trees, his pistol held at arm's length.

He fired twice in rapid succession at two dark figures ahead of them. Jamie saw a flurry of motion and continued running.

Paolo turned to the side and fired again. A chimp screamed in pain.

Jamie heard Susan's footsteps right behind, her breathing already rapid and loud. The sound of the other footfalls was harder to make out.

She cut sharply to the right around a looming evergreen, stepping over a large root, when her eyes darted to the movement of an animal jumping from above, landing a few feet in front of them.

"Paolo!"

Paolo whirled around, the trigger pulled before she had finished screaming.

Then there was only the hum of insects around them in the jungle, their rapid retreat the loudest sound, now that the chanting of the chimps had faded in the blackness of the forest night.

Jamie ran until her thighs burned, sweat stinging her eyes. She focused on her footsteps, each one ticking off the passage of time; each one coming with greater difficulty.

Branches whipped Jamie in the chest as the forest slowly transitioned from the sparse trees of the inner forest to the gnarled undergrowth that signaled the forest edge. The group continued their pace, and fanned out in the thickening forest beyond visual contact.

How far had they come? How long had it been—ten minutes?

She strained to hear the sound of the rushing water. At first, questionable, now definite. They were going to make it.

With every step, she had to part the dense ferns with her hands to move forward. The footing grew softer and more uneven. She planted her feet firmly, pushing off with each step to maintain her speed.

Her foot caught on a rocky crack, stuck, and then twisted as her body crumpled straight down face first into the tall grasses. She yanked her leg out of its grip. Pain screamed back. She lay for a moment, panting, trying to catch her breath to signal the others. Her voice was weak, hoarse. "Paolo!" "Susan!" There was silence.

She tried again, this time pulling her foot free but almost blacking out from the pain. She scrambled to one knee, then the other, and tried to stand. Her foot gave out on her, and she tumbled back to the ground. More slowly, she stood and limped forward, barely tapping the injured foot on the ground between footsteps, steadying herself by gripping the meshwork of lianas threading through the trees and ferns.

FORTY

SAMEER ducked under one final low-lying branch and stepped onto the narrow beach. He searched in panic up-river, seeing nothing, then ran toward the shore, looking the other way. He saw movement in the trees and ran toward the waving arm, exhaling in relief. Most of the others were already there.

"Where's Jamie?" Paolo demanded.

"Didn't—see—her," Sameer panted.

"That's it. I'm going back. Leave us if you have to." Paolo grabbed a loose segment of rope and disappeared into the trees.

"Wait!" Ayala hissed, too late.

Sameer watched as Ayala's fingers tied knots around two large pieces of driftwood she had begun lashing together. Several rope handholds were already stretched across the logs.

Stiles had his hands on his knees, bent over and

breathing heavily. Susan knelt in the sand under a tree, also gasping for air.

"What are you doing?" Sameer asked Ayala.

"Current's too strong. We have a better chance together."

Sameer looked out at the river. It was huge, the other side at least fifty meters away, and the current was a raging torrent of bubbling foam. Sharp rocks jutted up from the middle of the river in several locations. His stomach sank.

"We're crossing that?! I thought the chimps were bad."

Ayala didn't look up from her work. "Then stay here." With a throw of her arms she tightened one final knot, and cut the rope with the hunting knife at her side. "Come on, help me carry this to the river."

Sameer, Stiles, and Susan each grabbed ahold of the log, and heaved. It didn't budge. "One, two, three . . . ," Ayala counted. On the final count, Sameer dug his feet into the sand and pulled on the rope. It slid reluctantly across the sand.

Slowly, they heaved the log to the water's edge, where Susan collapsed on top of the log, catching her breath. Ayala tossed the rest of the rope onto the beach and sat on top of the log.

"What's keeping her?" Susan said. "The chimps will be here any minute."

"Correction. They're here. Come on. Let's go." Ayala stood up and pushed on the log.

"We can't leave Jamie and Paolo!" Sameer said. He scanned the beach and saw a chimpanzee emerge from the undergrowth only a hundred meters upriver.

"Sorry, no choice here." Ayala raised her pistol and fired at the chimp. Within moments, three more jumped out of the undergrowth and ran toward the beach.

"This boat's leaving!" Ayala said. "Who's coming?" She tucked her pistol into her belt. With one heave, she pushed the log farther into the water, grasping hold of the rope handle.

Sameer splashed into the water, Susan and Stiles behind him, each grabbing a rope handle as the current soon swept them in, legs dangling from the driftwood.

The chimps raced to the water's edge, one still carrying a torch. Another chimp picked up a large rock and hurled it just short of the receding driftwood.

"Look out!"

"PAOLO?" Jamie limped through the undergrowth, her progress painfully slow. *How far behind was she?*

She heard a rustle from behind her. She crept into the grass, her head covered by foliage and looked up.

It must be one of the group.

She was about to call out when her eyes warned her just in time. A bulky black figure scooted through the ferns just a few feet to one side. She held her breath.

The chimp stopped, sniffing the air. Jamie could smell the musty odor of the beast. *Could it smell her?* It pawed at the branches, looking in the ferns to the far side.

Please. God . . .

A crunch sounded in the brush ahead of her, and the chimp jumped forward to the sound, out of sight. Jamie waited a full two minutes before moving. Slowly, she knelt in the grass and listened. Hearing nothing, she struggled forward another few steps. If anything, the pause had made her foot more painful.

Another sound came from ahead. She sank again to her belly, listening closely. Regularly spaced footsteps; no sound of dragging arms.

Should she risk calling out? She waited another few seconds.

"Jamie?" a voice whispered.

"Paolo! Over here!" She stood up, and listened again.

Suddenly, the sound of gunfire came from the beach. Seizing the opportunity, she called out again. "Paolo!"

He stepped into view and ran to embrace her.

"What happened!"

"I'm sorry . . . I . . ."

He motioned to cut her off, and she pointed to her foot.

"Can you walk?" he whispered more softly.

She nodded.

Jamie threw one arm around his shoulder, and he supported her as they walked toward the beach. She heard a rustle overhead, and stopped. She gestured, and he nodded.

They listened as Paolo raised his revolver. The sound came again, moving above them, growing more distant.

Paolo pulled her forward, and she limped on. The sound of water grew louder. Then Paolo stopped. Jamie could just make out the outline of the river through the remaining trees.

Paolo knelt down, inching forward for a better look. "There's half a dozen of them on the beach. It'll be close. There'll be more if we wait." He pulled out a small length of rope and wound it around his wrist, giving the other end to her. She tied the other end to her arm.

Paolo helped her to a crouching position, and they both watched as the chimps scooted back and forth across the sand. Paolo picked up a stone, and lobbed it to the far side of the beach.

The chimps turned at the sound, their backs to the trees.

Paolo nodded, and they ran the final twenty meters to the water's edge. Halfway through the run, several of the chimps whirled around and ran to intercept.

A few feet from the shore, one of the chimps bowled into them, knocking Jamie into the water. She kicked to disentangle herself. Her foot stung with pain.

The chimp gripped her boot, its other black, hairy arm pawing at her leg. Jamie felt her skin peel away under the grip.

The chimp bellowed, its teeth bared as it tugged in the water to pull Jamie to shore. She kicked harder, freeing her foot from the boot, and stroked her arms overhead into the current, swallowing big gulps of water as she fought for air.

The rope tugged on her arm as Paolo towed her into the water. The chimp screeched, carried away by the current as it thrashed to keep its head above water.

Her legs spun around helplessly in the strong current, the rope chafing her wrist as it pulled taut. She raised her head again above the water and looked ahead. Paolo's arms swung toward an eddy current on the far side. She took a deep breath and paddled blindly in the same direction.

Just short of the slow waters, she watched Paolo get sucked into a tight whirlpool. She took another deep breath and felt her arm pulled unnaturally by the rope into the circling current.

Her head flew underwater, lungs bursting from the strain as she kicked to reach the surface. She felt herself losing strength, the urge to open her mouth irresistible when her arm tugged again and she rocketed out of the water into the slower current on the far side of the whirlpool. She blinked twice, then saw Paolo a few feet away and swam to his side.

He pointed to the far shore, now only twenty meters away. They swam furiously against the current until Jamie felt slack on the rope and reached down to find a foothold on the bottom. She clambered out of the water and lay prostate on the beach.

She coughed up a mouthful of water and crawled to her knees, moving forward until she climbed on top of Paolo, laughing and coughing, throwing her arms around him while the sound of the water churned behind them.

FORTY-ONE

JEREMY Evans had plenty of time to think. After he and the search team had returned to their takeoff point, he needed to sleep. He had notified Skip Jordan at the compound as soon as they found Mercer's body, and Jordan offered to talk with Mercer's family and help make funeral arrangements.

By the time Jeremy had made it back to the riverbank, a second call found that the compound was already humming with activity. Soliton president Tyler Drake was on his way to oversee damage control. Jordan was "restructuring" company security, which really meant he was two crates of Ding Dongs into what would happen to him when Drake arrived. Remaining scientists were meeting fervently, discussing exactly who was in charge and who was to answer to Drake for what had happened.

All of this left Jeremy with the most unpleasant job of

all: waiting. He sat on the ferry with a rifle across his chest hoping for the return of his four companions, anchored off shore away from the looming chimpanzees. After losing phone contact not only with Stiles and Sameer, but also with Jamie and Paolo, Jeremy felt like a complete failure. Much more poignantly, he felt the loss of his close friend Roger, as well as of the other colleagues he had grown to trust and respect.

The wait was interminable, punctuated only by two brief reports from the BrainStem compound. One report was following Mercer's autopsy. The medical examiner called on Jeremy's request. Mercer had died of Dengue Shock Syndrome, she announced.

It had likely been contracted by mosquito bite on his early survey of the chimp's escape, incubated for four days, and quickly consumed him. Her opinion, she said, was that "Mercer bled from his capillaries, suffered disseminated intravascular coagulation, and then experienced multiple organ system failure. If he had obtained earlier medical treatment, it is possible he would have survived." Jeremy showed his appreciation for this last, unintentionally guilt-provoking statement by hanging up on the examiner.

The second report came from Jordan, who said that someone by the name of Sally Heathrow, whom he did not know, wished to speak with a member of the expedition as soon as possible and was a close friend of Kenji's. Jeremy didn't even write down her number. He didn't want to talk to anyone.

Except for Stiles, of course, and he was determined to wait for the opportunity. With nothing of note left for him to do, he was prepared to wait for two weeks—as long as he had food—before leaving his phone and a note at the base camp and heading back across the river.

So he waited. After two more nights, he had all but lost hope, and was suffering from a dangerous combination of guilt and boredom. He had toyed many times with the idea of going to look for the others, be they dead or alive, and each time rejected the idea as ludicrous. It would be impossible to find them, but if he did, he would likely be of little help, and would probably run into the chimps again.

Such were his thoughts, when to his great surprise he heard shouting. It was not just any shouting but with a distinctly familiar voice. "Jeremy, you bum! If I find you out surfing, I'll cancel your bloody grant!"

Jeremy grinned and shouted back, "Do it and you'll never collect enough data to publish again!" He turned to see the outlines of his companions walking downriver toward him in the distance. He noticed two new figures among the group, and guessed the explanation was going to be good. He turned the key and the engine roared to life.

THE following day, Jamie was cleaning out her office at the BrainStem compound. Paolo had gone to tie up some loose ends at the research station because they had arranged to take an extended vacation away from the jungle. She had thought of little else all day.

Her sprain had improved with some rest and a pair of crutches, but was a vivid reminder of the events of the last few days. She had taken it on herself to notify Tyler

Drake about what she had learned of the contents of the freezer behind Nakamura's office.

He had vehemently denied any knowledge of the experiments, but seemed somehow not particularly surprised, as if the information made sense in a way he cared not to explain. When speaking with Drake, she had agreed to help him with one last request. "This Heathrow woman is driving me nuts with her questions," he said. "Will you please get her off my back?"

Jamie agreed to call. For the rest of the morning, she had reflected on the assignment, wondering who this woman was. An instinct flashed through her mind, and she placed a call to Skip Jordan. He answered.

"Skip, it's Jamie. Do we have any resources to track down a phone number, see who it belongs to?"

"Sure, Jamie. I still have some connections on the force that could do that," Jordan said, lying. The fact was, it was not that difficult even without connections to trace a number that someone wasn't trying too hard to conceal. Jordan was eager to redeem himself from his recent slipups, and he was trying to show his best face while Drake was in town.

Jamie gave him the phone number and hung up.

Later that evening he called back. "Jamie?"

"Yes?"

"I have the information on that number you gave me."

"Great! Who is it?"

"It's a cell phone number, with the name of Kathryn Batori listed as the owner."

"Thanks, Skip. Good work."

"It was nothing, to be honest."

Jamie hung up and dialed the number. A female voice answered.

"Hello, this is Jamie Kendrick. I'm trying to return a call to Sally Heathrow," she said in a businesslike tone.

"Oh yes, thank you for calling back. You see, I'm a friend of Kenji Nakamura's, and was horrified to hear of his passing. I was just hoping you could tell me a bit surrounding the circumstances of his death."

"Just a freak accident, it seems."

"At one point, Kenji told me he was doing some work on a chimpanzee."

"That's right."

"Any idea how that worked out?" Her voice was tense, and Jamie sensed that the woman cared very much about the answer to this particular question. "Just for closure, you know. His last project and all."

"I suppose it was that last project that did him in. His heart couldn't take it," Jamie answered.

"I see," said the woman. "Well, thank you for returning my call. It helps me very much to deal with Kenji's passing to know more about how he died."

Jamie gave a final greeting and hung up.

She immediately dialed Susan's hotel room in Manaus.

"Hi, Susan, it's Jamie."

Susan extended a warm greeting.

"You know, I wonder if your story might not be finished after all. I have a hunch."

"Go on."

"Why don't you check out a person by the name of Kathryn Batori in San Francisco? It may be nothing, but she seemed to be awfully interested in what happened to that chimp, and she lied to me about her name."

"You don't say," Susan remarked. "I remember something about a phone call Carlos recorded between Nakamura and someone named Kate . . ."

FORTY-TWO

KATHRYN Batori hung up the phone, barely able to keep her hand from trembling as she replaced the receiver. She was breathing heavily, the anxiety that had consumed her for days now felt suffocating. Kenji dead. Michaels and Simons dead. She was alone, and that Jamie woman knew more than she had let on.

Her worst fears had been realized. She cursed Naka-mura. *How could he have been so stupid?* Chances were she had only months before her name would turn up in an investigation. *Sloppy.*

Mental arithmetic sprang from her mind. Three weeks since the first implantation. She had performed how many, three implantations a day with the altered em-bryos? At least fifteen women had been implanted with embryos containing the new gene. Surely one would take. But she needed thousands in order to get a solid gene pool for the modified gene to thrive, assuming the children even lived to birth. She would have to work fast. Her own implantations wouldn't be enough. She would have to spike the sperm donor pool with the altered gene. *Risky, but doable.*

Her mind replayed the earlier telephone conversation with Skip Jordan as she assimilated the information he had unwittingly given her.

Clearly not a simple enhancement. Probably dramatic behavioral changes. Perhaps a new human subspecies. Maybe two new subspecies, if homozygous offspring were ever born.

She sat at her computer and pulled up her electronic medical record software. Her unsteady fingers began typing in the search fields. One couple at a time. T-A-T-E, H-I-R . . . she punched in the name, and a record popped up. Her heart beating faster than she had ever remembered, she moved her mouse to open the demographics tab. A page of phone numbers, addresses, and insurance information filled the screen.

She had to see where she stood. *What time was it?* She glanced at her watch. She picked up the phone and dialed a telephone number. There was no answer. *Damn.* She dialed another number, also without response.

She slumped back in her chair. She massaged her temples, deciding where to start, and listened to her phone messages. She punched a button on the phone.

"You have one new message. <BEEP> Hi, Dr. Batori, this is Richard Tate. I just couldn't wait to call and give you the good news. Hiroko's pregnant! We are so grateful for all that you've done. We can hardly believe it's true! Anyway, we won't be able to keep our next appointment. I booked a trip to Europe. We're going to take a month off and celebrate. We'll contact you when we get back. Thanks again! <BEEP>"

Kate Batori closed her eyes and bit her lip. *Success!*

She called her secretary. "Hi, it's Kate. Can you please cancel all nonimplantation appointments this afternoon. Something's come up."

She clicked back into her patient records module and found the first name. She dialed the number.

"Hello, Mrs. Allen? It's Dr. Batori. Good. You know, I've just had an opening come up sooner than we thought in my schedule, and if you're ready, I think we could go ahead and start your first IVF cycle this week. Wonderful!"

FORTY-THREE

JAMIE sat huddled next to Paolo on the floor of his hut. She massaged his head in her fingers. It felt intoxicating.

"So Roger is going to try to go back?" Paolo asked.

"That's what he says. 'Take in a bloody commando team and get one of them.'" She imitated his voice. "He can't leave it alone."

"What did he see in the tissue sample he took?"

"It looked like normal brain. Nothing out of the ordinary."

"Are you going with him?"

Jamie stroked his forehead. "I don't think so. Maybe I'll change my mind. It's all so confusing to me still."

He smiled. "And I feel the opposite. I can't remember when I've felt life was so clear, so wonderful." He lay down with his head in her lap, kissing her thigh, and then looking up at her. "What are you going to do with your data?"

"You mean with the chimp?" She paused. "I guess I'll have to see how this plays out. It's not much good without one of the chimps for show and tell. Sounds kind of unbelievable, don't you think? I mean, the altar, the chimp throwing himself in front of a bullet for his comrade, the chanting, the torches . . ."

"God's ways are higher than man's."

"Or chimp's?"

Paolo put his arm around her waist.

She looked into his eyes. Their intensity drew her in, made her want to believe him.

"What do you think I should do?"

He sat up and took her hands in his.

"Marry me."

Jamie's eyes went wide. She threw her arms around him and pushed him to the ground, sealing her lips to his.

"I love you," she whispered.

"We'll find it, Jamie."

"Find what?"

"Truth, enlightenment. Together, we'll find it."

"I know."

Bibliography and Further Readings

Bernhard, Brendan. *Pizarro, Orellana, and the Exploration of the Amazon.* New York: Chelsea House Publishers, 1991.

Caufield, Catherine. *In the Rainforest.* New York: Alfred Knopf, 1985.

Chenn, Anjen, and Christopher A. Walsh. "Regulation of Cerebral Cortical Size by Control of Cell Cycle Exit in Neural Precursors." *Science* 297 (2002): 365–69.

Churchland, Patricia. "What Can We Expect from a Theory of Consciousness?" Vol. 77, *Advances in Neurology,* edited by H. Jasper, L. Descarries, V. Castellucci, S. Rossignol (Philadelphia: Lippincott-Raven, 1998).

Crick, Francis. *The Astonishing Hypothesis.* New York: Touchstone, 1994.

Dale, Anders M., Arthur K. Liu, Bruce R. Fischl, Randy L. Buckner, John W. Belliveau, Jeffrey D. Lewine, and Eric Halgren. "Dynamic Statistical Parametric Mapping: Combining fMRI and MEG for High-Resolution Imaging of Cortical Activity." *Neuron* 26 (2000): 55–67.

DeLucchi, M. R., B. J. Dennis, and W. R. Adey. *A Stereotaxic Atlas of the Chimpanzee Brain.* Berkeley: University of California Press, 1965.

Despres, Leo A. *Manaus: Social Life and Work in Brazil's Free Trade Zone.* Albany, NY: SUNY Press, 1991.

Dubowitz, David J., Kyle A. Bernheim, Dar-Yeong Chen, William G. Bradley Jr., and Richard A. Andersen. "Enhancing fMRI Contrast in Awake-Behaving Primates Using Intravascular Magnetite Dextran Nanoparticles." *Neuroreport* 12 (2001): 2335–40.

Dubowitz, David J., Dar-Yeong Chen, Dennis J. Atkinson, Miriam Scadeng, Antigona Martinez, Michael B. Andersen, Richard A. Andersen, and William G. Bradley, Jr. "Direct Comparison of Visual Cortex Activation in Human and Non-Human Primates Using Functional Magnetic Resonance Imaging." *Journal of Neuroscience Methods* 107 (2001): 71–80.

Dunbar, Robin. *Primate Social Systems.* Ithaca, NY: Comstock, 1988.

Fukuyama, Francis. *Our Posthuman Future: Consequences of the Biotechnology Revolution.* New York: Farrar, Straus, and Giroux, 2002.

Gazzaniga, M. S. "Brain and Conscious Experience." *Advanced Neurolology* 77 (1998): 181–93.

Goodall, Jane. *Chimpanzees of Gombe.* Cambridge, MA: Harvard University Press, 1986.

———. *In the Shadow of Man.* Revised Edition. Boston: Houghton Mifflin, 1988.

Gubler, D. J., and G. Kuno. *Dengue and Dengue Hemorrhagic Fever.* Cambridge CAB International, 1997.

Guerrant, Richard L., David H. Walker, and Peter F. Weller., eds. *Tropical Infectious Diseases.* Second Edition. Philadelphia: Churchill Livingstone, 2006.

Hauser, Marc. *Wild Minds: What Animals Really Think.* New York: Henry Holt, 2000.

Hofstadter, Douglas. *The Mind's I.* Toronto: Bantam, 1981.

Jacobs, Marius. *The Tropical Rain Forest.* Berlin: Springer-Verlag, 1988.

Karten, H., ed. *Evolutionary Developmental Biology of the Cerebral Cortex.* Novartis Foundation Symposium. Chichester: John Wiley & Sons, 2000.

Kenward, Robert E. *A Manual for Wildlife Radio Tagging.* San Diego, CA: Academic Press, 2001.

Mabberley, D. J. *Tropical Rain Forest Ecology.* Glasgow: Blackie and Son, 1992.

Marino, Lori, James K. Rilling, Shinko K. Lin, and Sam H. Ridgway. "Relative Volume of the Cerebellum in Dolphins and Comparison with Anthropoid Primates." *Brain Behavior and Evolution* 56 (2000): 204–11.

May, Robert. "Unanswered Questions in Ecology." *Philosophical Transactions of the Royal Society of London* 354 (1999): 1952.

May, Robert M., and Michael P. H. Stumpf. "Species-Area Relations in Tropical Forests. *Science* 290 (2000): 2084–86.

Nature Neuroscience. Editorial: "Does Neuroscience Threaten Human Values?" November 1, 1998, 535–36.

Newman, Arnold. *Tropical Rainforest.* New York: Facts on File, 1990.

Newson, Ainsley, and Robert Williamson. "Should We Undertake Genetic Research on Intelligence?" *Bioethics* 13, nos. 3–4 (1999): 326–42.

Nichol, John. *The Mighty Rainforest.* London: David & Charles, 1990.

Nowak, Martin, and Karl Sigmund. "A Strategy of Win-Stay, Lose-Shift That Outperforms Tit-for-Tat in the Prisoner's Dilemma Game." *Nature,* July 1, 1993, 56–58.

Penn, Anna A. "Early Brain Wiring: Activity-Dependent Processes." *Schizophrenia Bulletin* 27, no. 3 (2001): 337–47.

Philadelphia Newspapers, Inc. v. Hepps, 475 U.S. 767 (1986).

Plotkin, Joshua B., Matthew D. Potts, Douglas W. Yu, Sarayudh Bunyavejchewin, Richard Condit, Robin Foster, Stephen Hubbell, James La Frankie, N. Manokaran, Lee Hua Seng, Raman Sukumar, Martin A. Nowak, and Peter S. Ashton. "Predicting Species Diversity in Tropical Forests." *PNAS* 97, no. 20 (2000): 10850–54.

Roemer, G. W., C. J. Donlon, and F. Courchamp. "Golden Eagles, Feral Pigs, and Insular Carnivores: How Exotic Species Turn Native Predators into Prey." *Proceedings of the National Academy of Science* USA 99, no. 2 (2002): 791–96.

Russon, Anne E., Kim A. Bard, and Sue Taylor Parker, eds. *Reaching into Thought: The Minds of the Great Apes.* Cambridge: Cambridge University Press, 1996.

Savage-Rumbaugh, Sue, Jeannine Murphy, Rose A. Secvik, Karen E. Brakke, Shelly L. Williams, and Duane Rumbaugh. *Language Comprehension in Ape and Child.* Monographs of the Society for Research in Child Development, ser. 233, vol. 58. Oxford: Oxford University Press, 1993.

Savulescu, J. "Procreative Beneficience: Why We Should Select the Best Children." *Bioethics* 15, nos. 5–6 (2001): 413–26.

Tomasello, Michael, and Josep Call. *Primate Cognition.* New York: Oxford University Press, 1997.

U.S. Dept of Health and Human Services. *Report of the Ad Hoc Task Force to Develop a National Chimpanzee Breeding Program of the Interagency Primate Steering Committee.* Tanglewood, North Carolina, June 2–3, 1980. Bethesda: National Institutes of Health, 1982.

Whitmore, T. C. *An Introduction to Tropical Rain Forests.* Clarendon Press: Oxford, 1990.

Wiederholt, J. L., and Forest J. Rees. "A Description of the Comprehensive Test of Nonverbal Intelligence." *Journal of Child Neurology* 13, no. 5 (1998): 224–28.

Penguin Group (USA) Inc.
is proud to present

GREAT READS—GUARANTEEI

**We are so confident you will love
this book that we are offering a
100% money-back guarantee!**

If you are not 100% satisfied with
this publication, Penguin Group (USA) Inc.
will refund your money!
Simply return the book before
October 1, 2006 for a full refund.

**With a guarantee like this one,
you have nothing to lose!**